The Shattered Mosaic

A father's search for proof in a world of faith

AW Schade

AW Schade

Dedication

"*If you've ever held someone you love as they died, if you've ever whispered promises in hospital rooms that you didn't know how to keep, if you've ever stared at an empty bedroom and wondered whether death is the end of everything or just the beginning of something....*"

~AWS

"*I* *have been a seeker and I still am, but I stopped asking the books
and the stars. I started listening to the teaching of my soul.*"
~Rumi

Contents

Chapter One

PROMISES

Today sunshine. Tomorrow, death. Then the search for why God is silent

The call came at 4:23 p.m. Jacob Hinsen sat stalled in traffic near Lincoln Elementary, debating fish tacos versus beef for Jessica's dinner, when his phone rang.

Unknown number. "Jacob Hinsen."

"Mr. Hinsen, this is Mercy General Hospital. You need to come now." A lifetime of silence. "Your daughter's been in an accident

Jacob's hands tightened on the steering wheel. Behind him, someone honked. The light   had turned green.

"Is she hurt?" The question came out steady, lawyerly, as if controlling his voice could control reality. "How bad?"

"Please come to the hospital. Dr. Patterson will explain when you arrive."

Twenty-three years of cross-examinations had trained him to recognize evasion. The non-answer told him everything.

"Is she alive?" He screamed.

A pause that lasted forever. "Please come quickly, Mr. Hinsen. The doctors are with her now."

The line went dead.

Jacob drove without remembering the turns, his knuckles bloodless on the steering wheel. Traffic lights pulsed red, green, yellow signals for a world still operating on schedule, unaware it had already ended.

At stoplights, memory invaded.

That morning. Breakfast. Jessica at the kitchen table in her over-sized blue sweater, sleeves rolled twice so her hands could function. She'd climbed into her chair with ceremony, legs swinging as she arranged her place setting with surgical precision.

"Look at that, round at last," he'd said, sliding two perfect pancakes onto her plate.

"They've always been round, Daddy. Otherwise, they'd just be cake in a pan." She'd grinned, revealing the gap where her front tooth used to be. "The shape is essential to their pancake-ness."

He'd laughed. God, he'd laughed.

Mid-bite, she'd set down her fork, fixing him with the serious expression that meant a Big Question was coming.

"Daddy, Sister Ellen says during First Communion we get to eat Jesus but not really eat him. What does that mean?"

How do you explain transubstantiation to a child who still left cookies for Santa?

"It's sacred," he'd said carefully. "Something that helps us feel close to Jesus and remember his love."

She'd gestured thoughtfully, processing. "So, Jesus is like Grandma's cookies for your soul? That tracks."

Then: "I just hope he tastes better than Sister Ellen's sample wafers. They were like eating cardboard someone forgot to flavor."

He'd nearly choked on his coffee.

That was six hours ago. Six hours ago, she was alive, comparing Communion wafers to cardboard, making him laugh.

His phone buzzed on the passenger seat. Jessica's text from lunch still glowed on the screen:

Daddy, I made you something amazing in art class. Can't wait to show you. You'll love it!

The last words she'd ever sent him.

By the time he reached Mercy General, sweat had soaked through his shirt collar. He parked crookedly across two lines and abandoned the car.

The sliding doors opened with a mechanical sigh. Antiseptic smell. Fluorescent lights humming. His left eye twitched violently, a consequence of combat in a war decades before.

"Mr. Hinsen?"

A nurse hurried toward him, her badge crooked, ponytail frayed. Her face carried a practiced calm, someone who'd walked this walk too many times.

"Jessica. My daughter."

"Please follow me. Dr. Patterson is waiting."

The hallway stretched impossibly long. Jacob passed rooms containing other people's emergencies, the beeping and humming of machines that measured the boundaries between life and death.

Where was the hospital chaplain? Where were the priests who were supposed to appear when children were dying? Where was God in this fluorescent corridor?

Room 7's door stood ajar.

Dr. Patricia Patterson was younger than expected, early thirties, with the composed demeanor of someone who'd delivered world-ending news countless times. Her scrubs were too clean, either a good sign or evidence she'd changed after working on Jessica.

"Mr. Hinsen. Please, sit down."

The request confirmed his worst fears. Good news could be delivered standing.

"Where is she? Can I see her?"

"Mr. Hinsen." Dr. Patterson's voice carried infinite, terrible patience. "I'm very sorry. Jessica died from her injuries. There was nothing we could do."

The words hit like fists. Died. Nothing. Could do.

"No." Jacob shot to his feet, the chair scraping against tile. "She was waiting for me at school. Same spot, every day. She always waits,"

His knees buckled. He grabbed for the chair, but it slid away. The floor rose up. A sound tore from his throat, animal, inhuman, something broken beyond language.

When he could breathe again, Dr. Patterson was kneeling beside him, not touching but present.

"What happened?" His voice came out shredded.

"A seventeen-year-old driver struck Jessica on Oak Street near the school." Clinical precision like shards of glass. "The driver was texting and didn't brake in time. Witnesses say Jessica ran into the street suddenly, trying to retrieve papers that had blown from her backpack."

"Papers?" The word came out strangled.

"Art projects. Schoolwork. They scattered in the wind."

Can't wait to show you. You'll love it.

The solar system project. She'd been working on it for weeks. She died chasing schoolwork.

Nine years of life erased because papers blew away and a teenager couldn't stop texting.

Where was God when Jessica ran into the street? Where was He when the car struck her? Where was He when she lay dying on the pavement?

"I need to see her," Jacob said.

Dr. Patterson led him down another corridor, through doors that whispered open and closed. She stopped outside a different Room 7. Where bodies lingered for review.

"Take as much time as you need.

Jacob pushed open the door.

Jessica lay on a table covered by a white sheet pulled to her shoulders. Someone had closed her eyes and arranged her hands across her chest in unnatural serenity. She looked smaller than she had that morning, as if death had diminished her.

Her hair, autumn-colored, impossible to tame, still held the shape of the pigtails she'd wrestled into submission. Perseverance and Victory, she'd named them. The left one never gives up even when it's having a good hair day. The right one always looks perfect in the end.

She'd had a theory about everything. Days of the week. Digestive acid. Why Thursday was the best day because it was almost-there excitement.

This morning she'd asked about Communion. About eating Jesus. About sacred things that helped people feel close to God.

Now she would never taste Communion wafers. Would never have theories about Fridays. Would never ask another question about God or the universe or anything.

Jacob moved toward her on legs that belonged to someone else. His hand reached out, then stopped. Permission felt necessary.

He touched her hand.

Cold.

The wrongness of it detonated something inside him. Jessica's hands were never cold. They were warm, sticky with syrup, always reaching for his.

"I'm sorry sweetheart." His voice cracked. "Jess, I'm so sorry."

Two months ago. Bedtime. Jessica's voice small in the darkness.

"You'll always protect me, right Daddy?"

"Always," he'd said. "We'll always be together."

"Promise?"

"Promise."

She'd believed him completely. Children believed their parents could hold back death itself with promises and good intentions.

He had lied to her. The promise was broken.

But where was God's promise? Every Sunday in church, priests promised God was watching, God was protecting, God loved children above all else.

Where was God this afternoon at 4:23 when Jessica needed Him?

Time passed. Jacob held her hand until a nurse appeared, murmuring about forms.

He grudgingly followed her to an office where a woman with kind eyes asked questions that reduced Jessica to data points. Name. Date of birth. His relationship to her.

"We'll need you to identify some personal effects." Linda Chen gestured toward a plastic bag on the desk.

Inside: Jessica's backpack. The blue sweater with sleeves rolled twice. One sneaker with the perpetually short lace. And scattered across the bottom, crumpled pages covered in crayon drawings of planets.

The solar system project.

Jacob picked up one page with shaking hands. Earth, rendered in blue and green crayon, surrounded by puffy white clouds. In Jessica's careful handwriting: *The only planet with life. The only home we know.*

These papers had killed her.

"Mr. Hinsen?" Linda Chen's voice came from far away. "Is there someone we can call? Family?"

"Margaret," he heard himself say. "Margaret Mitchell. Jessica's grandmother."

Linda Chen made the call while Jacob sat holding the crumpled drawing of Earth, the only planet with life, now one person emptier.

Where was God when Jessica bent down to pick up these papers? Where was He when the car came too fast? Where was He now?

Margaret arrived within the hour, her face pale, eyes red-rimmed. She saw Jacob first, collapsed in a waiting room chair, suit jacket twisted, tie pulled loose, eyes staring at nothing, and something in her expression crumbled.

"Where is she?" Her voice came out strangled. "Jacob, where's Jessica?"

He couldn't answer. Could only gesture vaguely toward the corridor.

Margaret turned toward Linda Chen. "I'm Jessica's grandmother. Can I see her?"

"Of course. Room 7. Take as much time as you need."

Jacob stood. "I'm coming."

They walked together down that terrible corridor. At the door to Room 7, they both paused. Neither wanted to go in.

Jacob pushed open the door first.

Jessica lay exactly as he'd left her, white sheet, folded hands, pigtails carefully fixed.

Margaret made a sound, something between a gasp and a sob, and her legs buckled.

Jacob caught her, his arm around her waist, holding her upright even as his own body threatened collapse.

"No," Margaret whispered. "No no no."

They moved toward the table together, two people leaning on each other because standing alone was impossible.

Margaret reached out first, her hand trembling as it touched Jessica's cheek. Then she jerked back as if burned.

"She's so cold." The words came out broken, shocked. "Jacob, she's so cold."

Her trembling hand returned to Jessica's face, this time staying there, fingers gentle against skin that would never flush with warmth again.

"Baby," Margaret whispered. "Oh, baby girl. Grandma's here."

Her voice cracked. She bent over Jessica's body, her forehead nearly touching her granddaughter's, and the sobs came, wrenching, animal sounds torn from somewhere deeper than her lungs.

Jacob stood beside her, his hand on Jessica's shoulder, and felt his composure shatter again.

"I'm sorry," Margaret kept saying between sobs. "I'm so sorry, sweetheart. I'm so sorry."

Where was God? Where was He when Margaret needed to say goodbye like this? Where was He when grandmothers had to touch cold skin and whisper apologies?

Margaret straightened slowly, wiping her tears with trembling hands. She touched Jessica's hair, smoothing the pigtails with careful attention.

"I fixed these this morning," Margaret said, her voice distant. "She called me before school. Said her pigtails were having a rebellion. I talked her through fixing them over the phone. She was laughing."

She picked up Jessica's hand, holding it between both of hers as if she could warm it back to life.

"She has dirt under her fingernails," Margaret observed, her voice taking on a strange detachment. "From recess probably. She was always digging in that sandbox, making archaeological discoveries."

The mundane details, dirt under fingernails, pigtails needing adjustment, felt more devastating than grand statements about loss.

"She was going to show me her art project tonight," Jacob said, his voice barely audible. "The solar system. She texted me during lunch."

Margaret looked up at him, her face destroyed. "She showed it to me yesterday. Pluto was her favorite. She said Pluto got a bad deal, being demoted. She was going to write NASA about it."

A horrible laugh escaped Jacob's throat, half sob, half hysteria. "She was going to lobby NASA."

"She believed she could change their minds." Margaret's face crumpled again. "She believed if she just explained it right, she could make them fix their mistake. She thought the universe was fair like that. That reason and justice mattered."

But the universe wasn't fair. God wasn't fair. Where was the justice in a nine-year-old dying while chasing schoolwork?

Margaret released Jessica's hand and moved around the table to Jacob. She took his face between her hands, hands that had held Jessica's face the same way a thousand times and forced him to look at her.

"You loved her," Margaret said fiercely. "You were the best father she could have had. She died knowing she was loved completely."

"Where was God?" Jacob's voice came out raw, anguished. "Where was He, Margaret? You pray every Sunday. You light candles. You believe He's watching over us. Where was He when Jessica ran into that street?"

Margaret had no answer. Tears streamed down her face.

"Everyone says God loves children," Jacob continued, his voice rising. "That He protects them. That He has a plan. What plan involves a nine-year-old dying for art homework?"

"Jacob,"

"Where is He?" Jacob pulled away from her hands. "If God exists, where is He? In this room? In this hospital? Where?"

Margaret pulled him into an embrace, and they stood there with Jessica between them, two people trying to hold each other together in a room where God was nowhere to be found.

When they finally separated, Margaret returned to Jessica's side. She bent down and kissed her granddaughter's forehead, a goodnight kiss delivered too late, to skin too cold.

"I love you, baby girl," Margaret whispered against Jessica's hair. "Grandma loves you so much."

She straightened, wiping her eyes. "We should go."

They walked to the door together. At the threshold, Margaret turned back.

"Goodnight, my love," she said softly. "Sweet dreams, baby."

The words she'd said a thousand times at bedtime, automatic, loving, now unbearably cruel.

Jacob couldn't look back. If he looked back, he'd never leave.

They walked out together. The door whispered shut.

In the waiting room, Margaret collapsed into a chair. Jacob sat beside her. For a long moment neither spoke.

Finally, Margaret pulled out her phone, hands still trembling. "I need to call people. Brenda needs to know. Your parents. The school." Her voice gained fragile competence. "Someone has to handle things. Arrangements. The funeral."

She stood, steadying herself. "I'll call Brenda first. Even if she hasn't been a mother to Jessica in seven years."

The bitterness in Margaret's voice was new.

She walked toward the hospital entrance; phone pressed to her ear. Through glass doors, Jacob watched her pace, saw her free hand gesturing, probably to Brenda's voicemail.

She returned fifteen minutes later, her face somehow both harder and more fragile.

"Voicemail," she confirmed. "I told her Jessica died. I told her there would be a funeral. I told her she should come home for once in her goddamn life."

Jacob had never heard Margaret curse before.

She made more calls. Her sister in Phoenix. Jacob's parents in Vermont. Each conversation was similar: news delivered in careful, measured words that barely contained the screaming underneath.

Between calls, she sat with Jacob in that horrible waiting room.

"I was supposed to pick her up tonight," Margaret said suddenly. "You had that late deposition. I was going to take her for ice cream. Work on her math homework." She stopped. "She called me this morning. Asked if I'd help her with fractions tonight. Said 'Thanks, Grandma. You're the best.' Those were her last words to me."

Margaret's face crumpled. "And I didn't even pay attention. I just said love you and hung up because I was balancing the firm's accounts. I didn't know those were the last words I'd ever hear her say."

"You couldn't have known," Jacob said softly.

"But I should have paid attention!" Margaret's voice rose. "Every word, every conversation, I should have treated them like they mattered. Like they were precious." She turned to face him. "We don't have time, Jacob. None of us do. We just pretend we do. Jessica proved that. Nine years. That's all she got."

She stood again, needing motion. "I need to call the funeral home. Make arrangements. Choose a..." Her voice caught. "Choose a casket for a nine-year-old."

"Margaret, sit down. You don't have to do this right now."

"Then when?" She whirled on him, anger flashing. "Tomorrow? Next week? When exactly is the right time to plan your granddaughter's funeral?"

Jacob had no answer.

Margaret's anger deflated. She sank back into the chair. "I'm sorry. I don't know how to do this. I don't know how to exist in a world where Jessica doesn't."

"Neither do I," Jacob said, holding his arms tightly against his chest. Crying.

Margaret made the call to the funeral home, voice steady, professional. When she hung up, she looked at Jacob with eyes that had aged a decade.

"They'll pick her up tomorrow. We can see her again before the funeral if we want."

The clinical language made Jessica sound like a package.

"I need to write an obituary," Margaret continued, voice distant. "How do you summarize a nine-year-old's life? 'Jessica Hinsen, aged nine, died Thursday. She is survived by her father and grandmother.' That's it?"

"That's not all her life amounts to," Jacob said.

"Then what?" Margaret's eyes blazed. "She was nine. She didn't have a career or accomplishments anyone will remember. She was just a little girl who loved pandas and wanted to be an astronaut. And in five years no one will remember she ever existed!"

Margaret covered her face, trying to mask her emotions. "I'm sorry. I didn't mean,"

"You're right," Jacob groaned. "In five years, no one will remember her. Except us."

"And when we're gone?"

The question hung in the air, the unbearable truth.

A police officer appeared. Young, uncomfortable. Officer Morrison.

"Mr. Hinsen, I know this is a terrible time. But I need to ask a few questions. For our report."

"Report," Jacob repeated numbly.

"The driver, Kayla Thompson, seventeen years old, says she didn't see Jessica until it was too late. Multiple witnesses confirm your daughter ran into the street suddenly, chasing papers. The driver will likely face charges for distracted driving, but..."

"But what! Accidents happen. But blame is complicated."

"She was getting her schoolwork," Jacob answered sharply. Each word felt like pulling glass from a wound. "She worked on that project for weeks."

Morrison nodded, making notes. "The driver is devastated. She's at the station now with her parents. She didn't mean,"

"Didn't mean to kill my daughter while texting?" Jacob's voice came out flat, dead. "No, that doesn't help."

Morrison flinched. "I'm sorry, Mr. Hinsen. For your loss."

After Morrison left, they handled the remaining paperwork in silence. When there was nothing left, Margaret touched Jacob's arm.

"Come home with me. You shouldn't be alone tonight."

But Jacob knew that whether he was in Margaret's house or his own, he would be alone.

"I'll drive you home," Margaret amended. "Make sure you get there safely."

They drove in her Camry, both silent. When they pulled into Jacob's driveway, Margaret turned off the engine but didn't move.

"Don't make any big decisions tonight," she said. "Just get through tonight. One hour at a time."

"And what about you Margaret?"

"I'll be okay. Just okay."

He nodded, he knew he wouldn't be able to ease her pain.

He walked to his door. Inside, the house waited, every surface bearing evidence of Jessica's life, every room echoing with her absence.

Her backpack hooks by the door, empty now. Her shoes lined up in the hallway. The drawing of Earth on the kitchen counter next to this morning's coffee cup, still half-full.

Jacob stood in the kitchen doorway, unable to move.

She'd sat right there this morning. That chair. Swinging her legs, arranging her place setting with precision.

"Can we feed the birds after school?" she'd asked. "The bossy cardinal needs boundaries."

The cardinal had been terrorizing other birds for weeks. Jessica had taken this as a personal affront, convinced that proper bird etiquette required sharing.

"We can set boundaries for the cardinal," he agreed. "Strong ones."

"Good. Someone needs to teach him about community cooperation."

Jacob had gazed at her and smiled. She'd been made of a thousand contradictory pieces that somehow fit together perfectly. Fierce enough to argue about cardinals, tender enough to worry about bird's feelings. Bold enough to challenge NASA about Pluto, shy enough to whisper bedtime questions in the dark. Questions sharper than glass, laughter that could light a room, and quiet moments when she'd stare out windows thinking thoughts she never shared.

A mosaic. That's what she'd been. Each piece is distinct, curiosity, compassion, defiance, gentleness, all held together by the fragile adhesive of being alive.

And this afternoon at 4:23, it all shattered.

Not disappeared. Not faded. Crushed.

The pieces remained, in the kitchen, in his memory, in Margaret's grief, in every person who'd ever loved her. But they no longer formed the whole. They lay scattered, sharp, cutting anyone who tried to gather them.

A shattered mosaic.

And Jacob didn't know if the pieces could ever be reassembled. Didn't know if God, if He existed at all, could put back together what a texting teenager and fleeting papers had broken.

Or if Jessica was simply gone. Irreversibly fragmented. Lost in pieces that would cut him for the rest of his life.

He was searching for God.

And he would demand answers.

***

Time drifted in dazed pieces. That was the only way Jacob could describe it. The neat, linear progression of minutes into hours, hours into days, the structure that had governed his entire life, shattered into jagged, unconnected moments.

There was the moment the phone rang at 4 a.m. and it was his brother, Michael, his voice thick with sleep and disbelief from Chicago. "It's not possible, Jake. Tell me it's not possible." Jacob had said nothing because the truth was a stone in his throat.

There was the time he walked into the kitchen and saw the paper sun still on the counter. *For Daddy. More sunshine.* He'd crumpled it in his fist, his hand shaking so violently he tore the paper, then stood there holding the ruined pieces of her final message, a sob tearing from his chest with such force he had to grip the counter to keep from collapsing. He only wanted to tear up the paper; not the memory.

Then came the phone call. A man's voice, practiced in the art of gentle intrusion. His name was Mr. Abernathy, from Murphy & Sons Funeral Home.

"Mr. Hinsen, my name is William Abernathy from Murphy & Sons Funeral Home. I know this is an impossibly difficult time, but there are some arrangements we need to discuss whenever you feel able."

Jacob gripped the phone, the words washing over him without meaning. Arrangements. As though Jessica's death was a social event requiring coordination rather than the end of everything that mattered in his life.

"We'll be there this afternoon," he heard himself say.

***

Murphy & Sons occupied a restored Gothic Revival mansion on Elm Street, its careful dignity designed to suggest that death was simply another life transition requiring professional guidance. Jacob had driven past the building thousands of times without considering that he might someday need its services. The brass nameplate beside the front door caught autumn sunlight, polished to a gleam that spoke of institutional permanence.

William Abernathy met them in the foyer, a man in his sixties with silver hair and the measured composure of someone who guided families through their worst moments. He wore a dark suit that managed to be expensive without being ostentatious, his manner calibrated to project both competence and compassion.

"Mr. Hinsen, Mrs. Mitchell, please accept my deepest condolences. I knew Jessica from the children's choir at St. Catherine's. She had such a beautiful voice."

The personal reference hit Jacob unexpectedly. He'd forgotten that in a town this size, death was always personal, that the people who handled final arrangements had likely known the deceased in life. Jessica's Wednesday evening choir practice, her off-key enthusiasm for hymns she didn't fully understand, the proud way she'd worn her white robe during Christmas services.

"Thank you," Jacob managed.

Abernathy led them into a consultation room furnished with comfortable chairs and soft lighting, designed to facilitate difficult conversations. A mahogany table held tasteful arrangements of fresh flowers and boxes of tissues positioned strategically within reach. On the walls, framed certificates spoke of professional training in grief counseling and mortuary science, credentials meant to inspire confidence in processes no one wanted to understand.

"I know this is overwhelming," Abernathy began, settling into his chair with practiced ease. "We'll take this step by step, and you can ask questions or take breaks whenever you need to."

He opened a leather portfolio filled with forms that reduced the complexity of death to checkbox decisions. Burial or cremation. Religious or secular service. Open or closed casket. Each choice carried implications Jacob wasn't prepared to consider, questions that demanded he think about Jessica's body in ways that violated every parental instinct.

"Most families find it helpful to start with the basic service structure," Abernathy continued. "Will this be a traditional Catholic funeral Mass, or would you prefer something less formal?"

Jacob looked to Margaret, who had attended every important event in Jessica's life but whose own faith had been shaken by her daughter Brenda's abandonment of both family and church. Her eyes were red with recent tears, her usual composure strained by grief and the impossibility of making appropriate decisions about her granddaughter's funeral.

"Jessica loved the church," Margaret said quietly. "She was preparing for First Communion. I think she'd want the full Mass."

"Very good. Father Morrison at St. Catherine's has already called to offer his services. He mentioned that Jessica was in his Communion preparation class."

The detail struck Jacob with fresh pain. Jessica's Wednesday classes, her earnest questions about transubstantiation and the meaning of sacrifice, her gap-toothed grin when she'd explained that Communion was "like Grandma's cookies for your soul." She would never receive First Communion now; would never experience the ritual she'd been preparing for with such earnest dedication.

Where was God during those Wednesday classes when Jessica asked her questions with such trust? Where was He when she believed the answers mattered?

"Now," Abernathy said gently, "we need to discuss the casket selection. I know this is difficult, but there are several options designed specifically for children."

The phrase hit Jacob like ice water. Options designed specifically for children. As though there was a market for such things, an entire industry built around the unthinkable reality that parents sometimes had to bury their children.

Abernathy led them down a carpeted hallway to a showroom that Jacob would remember for the rest of his life. Caskets in diverse sizes and materials lined the walls like some grotesque furniture store. Adult-sized models in mahogany and bronze dominated the space but tucked into an alcove were smaller versions that made Jacob's throat tighten.

"These are designed for children," Abernathy explained, his voice carefully neutral. "The craftsmanship is identical to our adult models, just appropriately sized."

Jacob stared at the display, his legal mind seeking some framework for processing what he was seeing. White caskets with angel motifs. Pink models with flower patterns. A small blue casket that looked like it belonged in a fairy tale rather than a cemetery.

"How often do you sell these?" Jacob asked, the question emerging from his need to understand the statistics of parental nightmares.

"More often than anyone would wish," Abernathy replied honestly. "Car accidents, childhood illnesses, tragic incidents. Every family hopes they'll never need these services, but when they do, we try to provide options that honor their child's memory."

Margaret approached one of the white caskets, running her hand along its polished surface. "She loved white," she said softly. "Her First Communion dress was going to be white. She said it would make her feel like an angel."

Jacob watched Margaret evaluate caskets for her granddaughter and felt something break inside his chest. This was wrong in every conceivable way. Jessica should be outgrowing clothes, not being fitted for a final resting place. She should be asking impossible questions about homework, not inspiring impossible choices about burial arrangements.

"This one," Jacob said, pointing to a simple white casket with silver handles. It looked appropriately dignified without being ostentatious, suitable for a nine-year-old who had preferred substance over style.

"An excellent choice," Abernathy said. "Now, regarding the burial site, do you have a family plot at a particular cemetery?"

Jacob hadn't thought that far ahead. Death had always been an abstract concept, something that happened to other people's families.

He'd never considered where he might want to be buried, much less where Jessica should rest.

"St. Mary's has a children's section," Margaret offered. "It's under the big oak tree where Jessica liked to look for squirrels during cemetery visits on All Souls' Day."

Of course. Jessica had always been fascinated by cemeteries, not from any morbid curiosity but from her endless questions about the people buried there. Who were they? Did they have children? What did they like to do? Were they happy? Her innocent curiosity about mortality now felt like terrible foreshadowing.

"I'll make the arrangements with St. Mary's," Abernathy said, making notes in his portfolio. "They're very accommodating for families in your situation."

"Our situation," Jacob repeated. "What do you call our situation?"

Abernathy looked up from his notes, recognizing the edge in Jacob's voice. "Parents who've lost a child. It's unfortunately more common than people realize, but it never becomes routine. Each family faces unique challenges in processing such a profound loss."

"And what advice do you give those families?"

"I tell them that grief has no timeline. That there's no right way to mourn. That healing doesn't mean forgetting." Abernathy's voice carried the weight of years spent helping families navigate unthinkable loss. "And I tell them that love doesn't end with death. Their child is at peace now, free from pain, in God's care."

Jacob's hands clenched. "How do you know that?"

Abernathy paused, clearly recognizing the lawyer's tone. "It's what we believe. What the church teaches. That God receives children with special tenderness."

"But how do you know?" Jacob pressed. "Has anyone verified this? Has anyone come back with evidence that God exists and receives dead children?"

"Mr. Hinsen, I understand you're angry—"

"I'm not angry. I'm asking for evidence. You're making a claim about where my daughter is. I want to know how you know that's true."

Margaret touched his arm. "Jacob—"

"No." He pulled away. "Everyone keeps saying the same thing. 'She's with God.' 'She's in heaven.' 'She's at peace.' But where is God? Where is this heaven? How does anyone know Jessica is there?"

Abernathy's expression was gentle, practiced. "That's a question of faith, Mr. Hinsen. We trust in God's promises even when we can't see the evidence."

"Trust." Jacob's voice went flat. "My daughter is dead. Everyone tells me God has her. But nobody can tell me where God is or provide any evidence, He exists at all. You're asking me to accept the most important claim of my life based on nothing but institutional tradition."

"Sometimes," Abernathy said quietly, "faith is all we have when reason fails us."

Jacob stood abruptly. "Then faith isn't enough."

The remainder of the consultation passed in tense silence. Decisions about flowers, music, and pallbearers. Details that would have seemed important in any other context, but which now felt like elaborate stage dressing for the worst performance of Jacob's life.

When they finally left Murphy & Sons, Jacob sat in his car for several minutes before starting the engine. Margaret waited beside him, saying nothing.

"I'm sorry," he finally said.

"Don't be." Margaret's voice was soft. "You're asking the questions I'm too afraid to ask."

"Are you?"

"Afraid? Yes. Of course." She turned to look at him. "But I still believe, Jacob. Even when I'm afraid. Even when I have no proof. Because the alternative is unbearable."

"What if the truth is unbearable?" Jacob asked. "What if there is no God, no heaven, no Jessica anywhere? What if she's just gone and all these promises are lies; we tell ourselves to make death tolerable?"

Margaret had no answer. They drove home in silence, both carrying questions too heavy for words.

***

The next few days blurred together. Forms signed without reading. Relatives, he didn't recognize filling the house with casseroles. Brenda called from whatever city she'd landed in, her voice breaking over the phone, but she didn't come home. Michael arrived from Boston, his presence solid and quiet, asking nothing, simply staying close.

The viewing at Murphy & Sons was filled with hushed voices and the heavy perfume of lilies. Jessica lay in the white casket, dressed in the blue dress from her last school picture, a stuffed elephant tucked under her arm. Someone had smoothed her curls into obedience, taming the wildness that had always framed her face. The orderliness felt wrong, as though death had imposed its own aesthetic on a child who had never belonged to neat lines.

People filed past, laying words at his feet like offerings meant to console.

"She's with God now."

"God needed another angel."

"She's in a better place."

Jacob nodded mechanically, his jaw tight. Inside, the words scraped him raw. Where was this God who supposedly needed angels? Why would He take a nine-year-old from her father? And if He existed, why wouldn't He show Himself to the man whose daughter He'd claimed?

A neighbor squeezed his shoulder. Jessica's teacher pressed a handmade memory book into his hands, pages filled with children's drawings and blunt, luminous truths: She shared her snacks. She helped me when I was sad. She said I was smart. Each line revealed pieces of his daughter he hadn't fully known, the quiet ways she had already shaped lives around her. The discovery cut as deep as the loss.

***

The morning of Jessica's funeral dawned gray and cold, October's bite sharp enough to cut through the heaviest coats. Jacob stood at his bedroom window watching neighbors emerge from houses to retrieve newspapers and start cars, their ordinary Friday routines a stark contrast to the day that would end with his daughter in the ground.

He'd slept perhaps two hours, his mind cycling through memories that felt both precious and unbearable. Jessica's laugh echoing through the house. Her off-key singing in the shower. The way she'd arranged her stuffed animals in careful hierarchies based on their "emotional needs." Every recollection was another weight added to his chest.

Margaret arrived at 8:30 with the black suit she'd pressed for him, her own grief hidden behind the practical necessity of getting through the day. Michael was already there, having spent the night on the couch, his quiet presence an anchor. They drove to St. Catherine's in silence, Jacob's hands steady on the wheel despite the tremor in his left eye that had started at the hospital and never stopped.

The church parking lot was already full. Cars lined the street for three blocks, license plates from neighboring towns and distant states as family members converged to say goodbye to a nine-year-old who should have had seventy more years ahead of her. Michael walked beside Jacob up the church steps, his hand briefly touching Jacob's shoulder—two men who shared blood but not always words.

Inside St. Catherine's, Jessica's white casket rested before the altar, surrounded by flowers that filled the sanctuary with the cloying sweetness of lilies and roses. The sight stopped Jacob in the doorway. During the viewing, the casket had been open, allowing him to maintain the fiction that Jessica was simply sleeping. Now it was closed, sealed, final.

Michael's hand steadied his back, and Jacob forced himself forward.

Father Morrison approached with the careful movements of someone who had presided over too many funerals for children. His face carried the wear of a man who regularly stood before families and attempted to make theological sense of senseless loss.

"Jacob, the turnout is remarkable. Jessica touched so many lives in her short time with us."

Jacob nodded, not trusting himself to speak. The sanctuary was indeed packed. Jessica's classmates sat with their parents, small faces struggling to understand why their friend would never return to school. Teachers from Lincoln Elementary occupied two full pews. Neighbors, soccer teammates, children from the church choir—all gathered to honor a life that had ended before it truly began.

The funeral Mass began with "Amazing Grace," Jessica's favorite hymn from choir practice. The congregation's voices rose in harmony, but Jacob heard only silence. The words that had once promised hope now felt like mockery. What grace was there in a child's death? What divine plan could possibly justify cutting short a life so full of curiosity and kindness?

Father Morrison's homily struggled to balance honesty with comfort. He spoke of Jessica's joy, her questions that had sometimes stumped Sunday school teachers, her insistence on sharing her snacks with classmates who had forgotten lunch money. But when he turned to God's plan and eternal rest, his words felt hollow.

"We cannot understand why God calls some home so early," Father Morrison said, his voice carrying across the packed sanctuary. "But we trust that Jessica is now in the presence of perfect love, free from pain, welcomed into heaven where she waits for those who loved her."

Jacob's hands clenched in his lap. Trust. Faith. Divine plan. Heaven. The same meaningless phrases he'd heard all week. What evidence supported such claims? Father Morrison spoke with absolute certainty about Jessica being in God's presence—but where was God? Where was this heaven? How did anyone know Jessica was there?

The priest continued: "Jesus said, 'Let the little children come to me.' We can take comfort knowing that Jessica is now in the arms of our Savior, safe and loved for all eternity."

Safe. Jacob's throat tightened. She wasn't safe. She was dead. If God existed and wanted to keep her safe, He could have stopped the car, could have prevented the wind from scattering her papers, could have done anything except let a nine-year-old die chasing schoolwork across a street.

After communion, which Jacob did not take, came the eulogies. Margaret spoke about Jessica's artistic talents, her elaborate drawings that covered their refrigerator. Mrs. Patterson shared stories of her student's intellectual curiosity and her kindness toward struggling classmates. Tom, his voice thick with emotion, recalled Jessica's theories about courthouse architecture.

Each speaker painted a portrait of a child who had been fully alive, completely engaged with the world. Jacob listened and felt the magnitude of what had been lost. Not just his daughter, but a future teacher, scientist, artist. A woman who might have changed the world in ways both large and small.

The final hymn was "On Eagle's Wings," chosen because Jessica had loved the image of soaring. But Jacob could only think of her broken body on hospital machines, of life that had simply ceased when her brain stopped functioning.

The procession from church to cemetery moved slowly through downtown streets where businesses had placed signs of condolence in their windows. "In memory of Jessica Hinsen." "Our prayers are with the Hinsen family." "Forever nine, forever remembered." The outpouring of community support should have been comforting, but Jacob felt disconnected from it all, watching the funeral of his own daughter as though observing someone else's tragedy.

At St. Mary's Cemetery, under the oak tree where Jessica had once delighted in watching squirrels, a grave waited. The earth was hidden beneath artificial turf, the harsh reality of burial softened by funeral home aesthetics. Chairs arranged in neat rows faced the small grave, the whole scene choreographed to minimize the visual impact of putting a child in the ground.

Father Morrison spoke the ancient words of committal—dust to dust and ashes to ashes—while Jacob stared at the casket suspended over the hole that would hold his daughter forever. The October wind carried the scent of dying leaves, autumn's reminder that all things must end.

"Into your hands, O merciful Savior, we commend your servant Jessica," Father Morrison intoned. "Acknowledge, we humbly beseech you, a sheep of your own fold, a lamb of your own flock."

Where were those hands? Jacob wanted to scream. Where was this merciful Savior when Jessica needed Him? Where was God now?

When it came time to throw dirt onto the casket, Jacob's hand trembled as he grasped the ceremonial handful of earth. The sound of dirt hitting the wooden lid was unbearable; a percussion of finality that echoed in his chest. Michael followed, his jaw clenched, his silence heavy but solid. He stayed close when Jacob felt like he might drift away.

Margaret leaned against him as the crowd began to disperse, her quiet sobs the only sound he could focus on. She had lost her granddaughter, the bright spirit who had filled the absence left by Brenda's abandonment. Now both were gone from their lives, one by choice and one by chance, leaving them to navigate grief without the family structure that was supposed to provide comfort.

As the cemetery workers waited respectfully at a distance, their shovels ready to complete the burial, Jacob remained beside the grave. The thought of leaving Jessica alone in the ground was unbearable, but staying would not change anything. The earth would cover her casket whether he witnessed it or not. She would remain dead whether he stood vigil or went home to an empty house.

Tom appeared at his shoulder. "Jake, we should go. Let them finish their work."

Jacob nodded but didn't move. Some part of him believed that walking away would make Jessica's death real in a way it hadn't been before. As long as he stayed beside her grave, some connection remained. Once he left, she would be truly gone, reduced to memory and a stone marker that would gradually fade with weather and time.

"I promised her we'd always be together," Jacob whispered.

Tom's hand found his shoulder. "You will be. Just not in the way you thought."

The words were meant as comfort, but they raised the question that would consume Jacob's life: How? If Jessica was truly with God, where was God? If she was in heaven, where was heaven? And how could Jacob be with her again if he couldn't find the God who supposedly had her?

As Jacob finally walked away from the graveside, he carried these questions like stones in his chest. The funeral was over, but his search for answers was about to begin.

Behind him, the cemetery workers began their quiet labor, covering Jessica's casket with earth. Father Morrison had promised she was with God. Margaret believed it through her tears. The entire congregation had sung hymns proclaiming divine love and eternal life.

But not one person could tell Jacob where God was.

And if he couldn't find God, how could he ever find Jessica?

***

A few weeks after the funeral, Jacob sat in Jessica's bedroom, surrounded by the artifacts of her interrupted life. Her art supplies lay scattered across the desk, colored pencils worn down to stubs, watercolor sets with dried paint, construction paper curled at the edges from countless projects.

Detective Martinez had returned Jessica's belongings from the accident scene in a manila envelope: her backpack, some scattered homework, and the hand-drawn card that had cost her life. Jacob held it now, purple crayon hearts surrounding "FOR MY DAD" in her careful cursive, with a drawing of the two of them holding hands under a yellow sun.

On the back, in smaller letters, she'd written: "I love you more than all the galaxies, Daddy. You're the best dad in the universe."

The universe. The same universe that had allowed wind to scatter her papers, allowed a teenager to prioritize a phone call about hair, allowed his daughter to die chasing a gift she'd made with love.

Jacob's phone buzzed. A text from Tom: Take all the time you need. The Henderson case can wait.

Everything could wait. Everything except the question that consumed him: Where was Jessica now?

The priest at her funeral had spoken about heaven, about God's plan, about Jessica being "in a better place." Empty platitudes. If God existed and had a plan, that plan included nine-year-olds dying for trivial reasons. If God didn't exist, Jessica was simply gone, her laughter, her creativity, her boundless love reduced to nothing more than fading memories.

Jacob looked around her room. The bookshelf lined with stories about brave princesses and talking animals. The bulletin board covered with ribbons from school art contests. The window where she'd pressed her nose against the glass every morning, watching for birds.

Did any of it matter if she was simply gone?

His laptop sat open on her desk, cursor blinking in an empty search bar. Without thinking, he typed: "Do children go to heaven?"

Thousands of results. Christian websites proclaiming certainty. Jewish perspectives on the afterlife. Islamic teachings about souls. Buddhist concepts of rebirth. Hindu beliefs about eternal consciousness.

Every religion claimed to know. Every faith promised answers.

But which one was right? And how could he know without investigating them all?

Jacob closed the laptop and picked up Jessica's card again. Her drawing showed them holding hands. In every religion he'd researched, love seemed to be the constant, the belief that love transcended death, that connections forged in life continued somehow beyond the grave.

If Jessica still existed somewhere, if God had her, then someone, somewhere, would have more than empty comfort to offer. Someone would have real answers backed by more than faith alone.

Jacob thought about his old religion teacher, Father Doyle. A man who had spoken with such conviction about God and salvation all those years ago. If anyone might have real answers instead of empty comfort, it would be someone who had dedicated his life to these questions.

It had been years since they'd spoken, but maybe that was exactly what Jacob needed. Someone who would remember the questioning young man he'd been, someone who might understand his need for evidence rather than platitudes.

Jacob opened his email and began typing:

Father Doyle,

Jessica died three weeks ago. I am sorry I neglected contacting you sooner. Everyone tells me she's with God now. I need to know if that's true. I need to know where God is. I need to know if Jessica is safe.

I'm not looking for comfort father; I'm looking for a friend's evidence. Can we talk?

Jacob Hinsen

He hit send before he could second-guess himself.

The response came within an hour: *Jacob, my sincerest sympathies on Jessica. Please come to St. Catherine's tomorrow. 2pm. We can talk as long as you need me.*

***

The following day Jacob drove the five hours to St. Catherine's Catholic Church in Millbrook, the church whose Gothic spire had once anchored his restless youth. The building looked smaller than memory suggested, weathered limestone showing stress fractures that spoke of Michigan winters and deferred maintenance. But the carved wooden doors still bore their weight of institutional permanence, promising answers that human reason couldn't provide.

Father Doyle met him in the rectory, emerging from shadows like a figure from Jacob's past made flesh. Older by a decade but carrying the same steady presence that had once guided a confused young veteran through questions that catechism couldn't answer. Broad shoulders beneath the black cassock, silver hair where brown had been, but the same intelligent eyes that had seen through Jacob's intellectual posturing to the wounded soul beneath.

He rose slowly from his reading chair, setting aside what appeared to be Thomas Merton's "Seven Storey Mountain," and embraced Jacob the way a father embraces a son who has come home wounded from a war no one else understands. For a moment, Jacob was twenty-one again, fresh from Vietnam with guilt and rage and a duffle bag full of questions about why God allowed good men to die in rice paddies while cowards lived to profit from their sacrifice.

"Jacob." The priest's voice carried recognition and sorrow in equal measure. "I am so sorry about Jessica. I've been praying for you both."

They moved to the small office where late afternoon sunlight slant-ed through stained glass windows depicting the stations of the cross. Dust motes drifted like slow confessions through colored light that painted everything in shades of burgundy and gold. The room smelled of leather-bound books and decades of careful thought, a sanctuary where doubt and faith wrestled without resolution.

Silence stretched between them, but it was not empty. It held the weight of what had been lost, the magnitude of questions that pressed against the boundaries of human understanding. Jacob sensed tears threatening and forced them back. Crying wouldn't bring Jessica home. Only answers could do that if answers existed.

"You look tired, Jacob," Doyle said softly, settling into the chair across from his old friend.

"I am father," Jacob answered, his voice coarser than he'd intended. "More than tired. Exhausted by people who claim to know things they can't possibly know. I promised Jessica we'd always be together. Now I can't keep that promise without knowing where she's gone."

Father Doyle bowed his head for a long moment; his hands folded in an attitude of prayer or perhaps surrender. When he looked up, his eyes carried the weight of forty years spent counseling the grieving, forty years of standing before families whose faith had been shattered by loss that defied explanation.

"I prayed when I heard about the Jessica," he said finally. "For her soul, for your healing, for the questions that would inevitably bring you here. Some prayers feel like shouting into a canyon. Others feel like conversation. This felt like both."

Jacob managed a small smile at the memory of their first serious conversation decades earlier. The priest listened to his hollow, angry questions about divine justice while body counts from Southeast Asia scrolled across television screens. Doyle had never pretended to have easy answers then, never offered the theological shortcuts that other clergy used to avoid confronting mystery.

"You never tried to convince me that God's ways were beyond questioning," Jacob said. "That's why I respected you. That's why I came back."

"And yet here you are, looking for answers I couldn't provide when you were young and whole." Father Doyle's voice carried gentle understanding. "What makes you think an old priest has learned anything new about the deepest mysteries?"

Jacob pulled a sheaf of handwritten notes from his briefcase, old habits dying hard even in theological crisis. Pages covered with careful questions, biblical references, philosophical objections accumulated during sleepless nights when grief felt like a physical weight pressing against his chest.

"Maybe the answers have changed father. If you don't mind, I would like to begin with the basics," he said, his courtroom instincts asserting themselves despite the informal setting. "Why do Christians insist that salvation comes only through Jesus? What makes that claim different from any other religious tradition's promise of exclusive truth?"

Father Doyle draped his jacket over the back of his chair, as if setting down the weight of institutional authority to speak as one searcher to another. "The short answer is the witness of the Gospels and what the Church has always taught. Jesus' life, death, and resurrection form the center of our hope. Without that center, Christianity becomes just another moral philosophy."

"But why only Christianity?" Jacob asked, his legal training demanding logical consistency. "Abraham spoke with God centuries before Jesus was born. Moses received the law directly from divine authority. Muhammad claimed revelation that billions follow. Are they all excluded from salvation because they named God differently?"

The priest was quiet for a moment, recognizing the challenge inherent in the question. His options, claim exclusive truth and appear arrogant. Admit multiple paths and undermine Christian distinctiveness. It was the theological equivalent of a legal double bind, and Jacob had constructed it with professional skill.

"Simple answers never satisfied you," Father Doyle said finally. "Let me try something more complex. Christianity doesn't claim Jesus as one teacher among many. We claim he is the incarnate Word, God himself entering human existence to bridge the gap between finite and infinite. That claim changes everything."

Jacob's analytical mind seized on the conditional phrasing. But the Word was transcribed in gospels written decades after the events they describe. Paul, who shaped old Christian theology more than anyone, never walked with Jesus during his earthly ministry. The biblical canon was assembled over centuries. How can I trust writings selected by fallible humans claiming divine guidance?"

Before Father Doyle could respond, three measured knocks sounded at the rectory door. The priest stood without surprise, as though he'd been expecting additional company. Through the doorway stepped Cardinal Leopold, a figure from Jacob's childhood who somehow managed to appear both older and more formidable than memory suggested.

Tall and lean with silver hair that caught the afternoon light, Leopold carried himself with the authority of someone accustomed to speaking for an institution that had outlasted empires. His red cardinal's ring caught light as he moved, but his presence was more scholarly than imperial. This was a man who had spent decades wrestling with exactly the questions Jacob was raising.

"Your Eminence," Jacob said, standing out of reflexive respect ingrained since childhood.

Cardinal Leopold took the offered chair and observed Jacob with patient eyes that had clearly evaluated thousands of doubting souls over the decades. His smile carried traces of the schoolmaster he had once been, someone capable of both gentle instruction and merciless intellectual honesty.

"Alfred tells me you have hard questions," the cardinal said, his voice carrying the hint of accent that suggested European education. "I find that promising. Easy questions usually indicate shallow thinking."

Jacob sensed his courtroom impulses sharpen into focus. Here was authority worth challenging, institutional power that claimed divine sanction. If Christianity offered truth rather than comfort, it should be able to withstand rigorous examination.

"Your Eminence, if human beings have shaped scripture and doctrine through diplomatic processes," Jacob said, meeting the cardinal's gaze directly, "why should I endorse the Church's version as the final truth? Isn't organized Christianity simply a human power struggle clothed in divine authority?"

Cardinal Leopold's hand moved as if smoothing an unseen wrinkle from the air, a gesture that somehow conveyed both acknowledgment of the question's validity and confidence in his response.

"Faith is ultimately a trust relationship," he said attentively. "We do not pretend that two thousand years of transmission have been without human error or political influence. But we believe that through prayer, study, debate, and communal discernment, the Church has preserved a reliable witness to divine truth. That requires intellectual humility, not blindness."

"But how do you know?" Jacob pressed, his lawyer's precision demanding concrete answers. "Not what you believe. Not what the

Church teaches. How do you know God exists? How do you know Jessica is with Him? Everyone at her funeral spoke with such certainty, but where's the evidence?"

Father Doyle leaned forward, his voice gentle but firm. "I've stood before parents who demanded answers I could not provide. The day a mother asked me, 'Where was God when my grandson died in Afghanistan?' I prayed for wisdom, and the silence that answered felt like its own kind of theology. Sometimes we serve God most faithfully by acknowledging the limits of human understanding."

"So, you're admitting you don't know," Jacob said. The words came out more sharply than he intended, but he couldn't soften them. "You speak with certainty at funerals. You promise grieving parents their children are with God. But when I ask for proof, you tell me it's a mystery?"

"We're suggesting that absolute certainty may be incompatible with authentic faith," Cardinal Leopold replied, his tone remaining patient. "True assent is not intellectual capitulation but a choice made again and again to trust in something larger than individual reason. You will decide whether that trust feels justified. We cannot make that decision for you."

Jacob felt frustration building in his chest. These men were honest, more honest than he'd expected. But honesty about uncertainty wasn't what he needed. "Let me ask you directly: Does God exist?"

"Yes," both priests answered simultaneously.

"Where is He?"

Father Doyle spread his hands in a gesture that encompassed both everything and nothing. "Everywhere. In all things. The ground of being itself."

"That's not an answer," Jacob said. "That's philosophy. Where was God when Jessica ran into the street? Where was He when the car struck her? Where is He now that she's dead?"

The two priests exchanged glances. Cardinal Leopold spoke first. "We believe God is present even in suffering, even in loss. That His presence isn't always obvious doesn't mean He's absent."

"But I need to know where Jessica is," Jacob said, hearing the desperation in his own voice. "Everyone promises she's with God. You just told me God is everywhere. That doesn't help me. Is she conscious? Is she aware? Is she safe? Can I find her again?"

"The Church teaches that the soul is immortal," Father Doyle said carefully. "That death is not the end but a transition. That those who die in faith are received into God's presence."

"Teaches. Believes. Claims." Jacob's hands gripped the arms of his chair. "But how do you know any of its true? What evidence do you have beyond ancient texts and institutional tradition?"

The silence that followed was long and heavy.

Finally, Cardinal Leopold spoke. "You're asking for empirical verification of metaphysical realities. That's a category error, like asking for the weight of justice or the color of truth. Some realities transcend the categories we use to measure physical phenomena."

"That sounds like an excuse for having no evidence at all," Jacob said.

Father Doyle's voice carried a note of sadness. "Tell me, Jacob. Do you love Jessica?"

The question caught him off guard. "Of course I do."

"Prove it."

Jacob stared at him. "That's not the same thing."

"Isn't it?" the priest asked gently. "Give me empirical evidence that your love for your daughter exists. Show me the neural pathways, the chemical reactions. Even if you could measure the biological components, would that really capture what you mean when you say you love her? Or is love something that exists beyond pure materialism?"

"Love is real because I experience it," Jacob countered. "Because it affects my actions, my choices. I can demonstrate love through behavior."

"And we experience God," Father Doyle said. "Through prayer, through community, through the transformation of lives devoted to following Christ. Millions of believers across centuries have testified to this experience. Is that no evidence of a kind?"

"Subjective experience isn't proof," Jacob argued. "People have subjective experiences of all kinds of things. That doesn't make them real."

Cardinal Leopold nodded slowly. "You're not wrong to demand rigor. But consider this: if God exists as Christianity claims, as the infinite source of all finite reality, how would you expect to verify His existence using methods designed to measure finite phenomena? The very nature of the divine would preclude the kind of evidence you're demanding."

Jacob felt the logic of the argument even as he resisted it. "So, God is conveniently unprovable?"

"Or," Father Doyle said, "God is beyond the reach of proof in the scientific sense, which is not the same as being unknowable. We come to know God through encounter, through relationship, through the slow work of faith seeking understanding."

"But that requires faith first," Jacob said. "You're asking me to believe before I have evidence. That's backwards."

"Is it?" Cardinal Leopold asked. "Think about any meaningful relationship in your life. Did you wait for absolute certainty before trusting? Or did trust develop gradually through encounter and experience?"

The conversation continued for another hour, ranging across questions of scriptural authority, religious pluralism, and the problem of suffering in a world supposedly governed by divine love. When Jacob raised objections, neither priest responded with defensiveness or deflection. They acknowledged difficulties while maintaining that faith remained reasonable despite its mysteries.

"Where will you go from here?" Father Doyle asked finally, his voice softer than any sermon Jacob remembered.

"I don't know," Jacob admitted. "You've been more honest than I expected. You've acknowledged that you can't prove what you claim. But honesty about uncertainty doesn't answer my question. I need to know where God is. I need to know where Jessica is. If Catholicism can't tell me, maybe Islam can. Or Judaism. Or Buddhism."

"You will decide," Father Doyle said. "Not because we convinced you through argument, but because you will choose to believe or not believe. Until you reach that decision, keep searching. God honors honest questions more than dishonest answers."

Cardinal Leopold stood, his movements carrying the weight of his years and his office. "One more thing, Jacob. You're asking where God is. Have you considered that perhaps God is asking where you are?"

Jacob didn't know how to answer that.

***

Jacob stepped back into the cool evening, long after the rectory lights had dimmed, carrying questions that felt heavier rather than lighter. Rain-glossed streets reflected neon like scripture gone sideways, fragments of meaning without clear interpretation. He drove two hours to a cheap motel on the edge of town and spread his scribbled notes across the polyester bedspread.

Answers multiplied objections. Each tradition he'd begun to read about showed glimpses of something true alongside seams where human hands had stitched meaning together. Christianity offered intellectual sophistication and institutional memory but demanded faith in claims that couldn't be verified. The priests' honesty was refreshing, but honesty about uncertainty wasn't the same as evidence.

He sat on the motel bed, staring at pages of theological questions that seemed to breed more questions with each attempt at resolution. Father Doyle's invitation to "keep searching" echoed in his mind, but searching where? How? For how long?

He opened his notebook and began writing.

Outside, eighteen-wheelers rumbled past on the interstate, carrying commerce between known destinations. Jacob envied their clarity of purpose. He had no map for the territory he was entering, no GPS for questions that had puzzled humanity since we first contemplated mortality.

Maybe Jessica was safe in heaven. Maybe life ended with brain death. Maybe love transcended physical existence, or maybe it was just biochemistry dressed up as meaning. Tonight, all possibilities felt equally remote and equally urgent.

He closed his notebook without resolution, uncertainty pressing against his chest like a physical weight. Tomorrow would bring the same questions, the same desperate need for answers that might not exist. But tonight, he would simply carry the mystery, the way Father Doyle suggested believers must carry faith, as a burden that might become a gift, if borne with enough patience and courage.

***

Restless, Jacob picked up the motel phone and dialed his brother. The land line crackled before Michael's voice broke through, steady and familiar.

"Jacob, it's the middle of the night. Are you alright?"

Hearing him pulled Jacob back across decades. Michael had always been trailing a step behind, three years younger, following him through cornfields and sandlots, the kid brother who had once believed Jacob invincible. Even now, Jacob could picture him: softer around the eyes, quick to laugh, hair already peppered gray though he was only forty-five. Where Jacob carried the twitch of war in his left eye and the courtroom's precision in his tone, Michael had always carried ease, the teacher's patience, the storyteller's gift.

"No," Jacob admitted, voice low. "But I don't think I ever will be if I stop here."

"Stop where?"

"At the edge of this. At the questions. I can't stay in limbo. I have to go further. If there's any chance Jessica continues, anywhere, I need to know."

Michael sighed, the sound of someone who had run out of arguments but not of love. "And what if there's nothing? What if you spend years chasing shadows and come home with nothing but more grief?"

"Then at least I'll know I tried."

The silence stretched between them. Jacob realized the burden of Michael's worry pressing through the line, but he also felt the old bond, the younger brother who once followed him everywhere, now refusing to let him vanish completely into grief.

"Just don't lose yourself, Jake," Michael said softly.

Jacob hung up knowing he already had.

***.

For weeks after the funeral, Jacob sat in Dr. Diane Thornton's office and endured what the professionals called complicated grief therapy.

Her second-floor room at the Wellness Center smelled faintly of vanilla. Certificates crowded one wall, neat rectangles of earned authority that could not fill the hollow the size of a child. Dr. Thornton kept a notebook, an even voice, and the practiced patience of someone used to people who would not be comforted.

Her brush-and-scrape metaphor, gently excavating anger, denial, bargaining, felt clinical when he needed a map.

"It's natural to question faith after losing a child," she said once, leaning forward as though offering him a lifeline. "But you can't find Jessica by interrogating every religion on earth. She's gone, Jacob. Accepting that lets you begin to live around her memory."

"How can you be so certain?" he asked. His courtroom instincts sharpened the words into cross-examination. "Can you prove existence ends at death? Can you show that love is nothing more than brain chemistry?"

Dr. Thornton shifted in her chair. Philosophy was not in her training manual. "I can't prove what happens after death. Nor do I need to. The burden of proof rests with those who make supernatural claims."

Jacob leaned back, eyes narrowing. "Then you're making metaphysical assumptions too. You're just calling them practical."

For a moment he thought of his first therapist after Vietnam, a soft-spoken woman with tired eyes who once told him, sometimes survival is the only proof you need. That had felt like enough at nineteen. Now it sounded like evasion.

And then the dam broke.

The rice paddies of Vietnam returned with a smell of wet metal and rot. He was nineteen again, raw, the air thick as a storm. Machine-gun fire stitched the day. Men he had bled with lay scattered in mud, faces already gone pale in a country that smelled wrong.

He knelt and zipped bodies into black bags, one by one, the sound of the zippers rasping like judgment. One of the dead was Corporal Nash, who had traded rations with him two days earlier, promising to introduce Jacob to his sister back home.

The memories had been held behind a cerebral wall for decades. Jessica's death had cracked it wide open, and the flood poured through.

The flash vanished, leaving him hollowed, trembling. He sat in Thornton's office while she watched him with professional concern, but she could not follow him into that place. They occupied the same room, but not the same world.

Weeks of appointments had made a pattern, but no answer. Conventional grief counseling did not speak to the questions that had unstitched him.

***

Family and friends circled him constantly, their presence steady even when words failed. Michael called every night from Chicago, his voice threaded with worry and the blunt concern of a brother who couldn't fix what he hadn't lived. A week later he arrived in person, arms full of groceries, his expression set with the quiet resolve of someone who had come to intervene.

At the kitchen table, surrounded by boxes, Michael said what others hadn't dared. "You're scaring me. You talk like someone about to do something dangerous. Promise me you won't hurt yourself."

"I'm not suicidal," Jacob said. "But I can't promise I won't do something that looks dangerous to people who haven't had their world fall apart."

Michael had spoken to the family about Jacob's plans, the leave from work, the travel, the idea of interviewing scholars and walking holy places. "We think this isn't healthy. You can't just abandon everything in hope."

"I have to try," Jacob said simply. "I promised her. I have to exhaust every possibility. This isn't chasing ideas. It's keeping my word."

For a moment Jacob flashed back to the summer he was twelve, when he'd gotten into a fight with older boys who were picking on Michael at the neighborhood pool. Jacob had come home with a split lip and bloody knuckles, but Michael, only nine then, had looked at him like he'd slayed dragons. "You didn't have to do that," Michael had said quietly. "Yeah, I did," Jacob had replied. "That's what big brothers are for." That same protective instinct was in Michael's voice now, but Jacob knew there was nothing left for him to fight.

They worked through the day, packing Jessica's clothes and toys into boxes. It felt less like tidying a house and more like cataloging a life. Jacob held one of her sweaters to his face.

"You don't have to do it all at once," Michael said gently.

"Yes, I do. I can't live in a shrine. But I can't throw away proof she was here."

Under the mattress they found a small pink diary with a tiny lock. Jacob held it like contraband, torn between honoring privacy and hungering for anything of her. Michael urged him: "Read it. She would want you to know."

Inside were the ordinary chronicles of a nine-year-old: playground alliances, math complaints, party plans scribbled with glitter smudges. And then an entry that stilled him:

Marcus was crying at recess because Tyler called him four-eyes. I told Tyler that wasn't nice. Mrs. Patterson says we should treat people how we want to be treated, so I sat with Marcus at lunch and shared my cookies. He smiled for the first time all day.

Page after page showed a child noticing suffering and responding, in ways small but radiant. Jacob read until his throat closed and the room tilted toward the truth he feared most: a life interrupted mid-growth.

Later that day Michael found the letter Jessica had saved for Father's Day, covered in looping hearts and flowers:

Dear Daddy,

You are the best father in the whole world because you listen to all my questions even when they're weird or boring. You make pancakes that are perfectly round, and you never get mad when I can't figure out math problems. I want to be like you when I grow up, someone who helps people solve problems and makes sure everyone gets treated fairly. I love you more than all the planets in the solar system.

Your daughter forever and ever, Jessica Marie Hinsen

The words blurred as Jacob sobbed into silence. Michael put an arm around him. "She saw you," he said softly. "She wanted to be you."

"Which is why it feels impossible," Jacob whispered. "The world needed what she was becoming."

That conviction, more than ritual or doctrine, hardened what was already forming: he could not accept that someone with such moral clarity simply ceased to exist.

***

The next day arrived without mercy. Jacob stood at the kitchen counter while the coffee maker sputtered. He had forgotten to add grounds. Hot, colorless water filled the carafe. He stared at it as though it were an x-ray of his own chest: liquid without substance.

He dumped the pot, tried again, and watched the brown bloom spread through the water. The house was quiet in the way empty houses are quiet, not silence, but absence. Above the table, Jessica's solar system mobile turned slowly in a draft he couldn't feel.

On the dining table, his legal pad lay open where he had left it the night before: questions in neat columns, arrows to subpoints. Where is Jessica? had been underlined so many times the paper was nearly torn through. He traced the groove with his fingertip as if the pressure might break through the page into answers.

His phone buzzed. A text from Michael, who arrived home early that morning: *Eat something. Call later.* The ordinary kindness undid him more than any sermon had. He set the phone face down and gripped the sink until his arms trembled. In the window glass above, his reflection looked like a man who might pass for whole, if you ignored the eyes.

***

He dressed for work by reflex: white shirt, navy suit. The tie refused to knot straight. He left it crooked and drove downtown. In the elevator he stared at the rising numbers as if they were floors of water, each one harder to breathe. Associates glanced up as he passed their desks, sympathy polite and practiced.

In his office, Jessica's birthday photo still smiled from the credenza. The framed bar commendation still hung straight. He opened a draft motion and felt nothing.

Ellen Kline tapped lightly and asked him to step into the conference room. "We can cover your cases, Jacob. Take the time you need. We'll keep you looped in."

He nodded. How could he explain that "time" had collapsed, that every hour without Jessica stretched like an eternity already?

Back at his desk, he typed a formal leave request. The words came out clean, professional, detached from the tremor in his chest. When he hit send, he sat a long while with both palms flat on the desk, bracing himself against an unseen current.

Michael called. His voice carried both caution and love. "Jake, Ellen phoned me. She said you're stepping back. What's going on?"

"I can't keep practicing like nothing happened. I need to know where Jessica is. If this were a case, I'd leave no witness unexamined, no evidence unchecked. Why should this be different?"

Michael exhaled hard. "Because this isn't a case. You can't put God on the stand. You can't cross-examine the universe."

"Then call it grief," Jacob said. "But I made her a promise. I won't break it without exhausting every possibility."

"And what if you find nothing?" Michael asked quietly.

"Then at least I'll know I tried."

They ended without agreement. Jacob set the phone beside Jessica's photo, her gap-toothed grin suddenly more binding than any contract.

Later, a text from Detective Martinez: Checking in.

He typed: Thank you. Then deleted everything after and sent only the two words.

***

Jacob pressed send on the leave-of-absence email, the screen flashing confirmation. His hands stayed flat against the desk as if holding down a document that might otherwise float away. The silence in his office felt strange, thick, as if the air itself were waiting for a verdict.

A knock at the door broke it. Without waiting for an answer, Tom Mitchell stepped inside. He closed the door softly, but his face was anything but soft. His tie was crooked, his eyes rimmed red from too many sleepless nights, and he carried the weight of someone trying to hold up two men's responsibilities on his own back.

"Ellen said you filed for leave." His voice was controlled, too controlled. The way he spoke in court when he was one question away from tearing a witness apart.

Jacob gestured to the chair. "Sit down."

Tom didn't. He crossed the room and planted his hands on Jacob's desk, leaning in. "What the hell are you doing?"

Jacob leaned back, shoulders heavy. "I can't practice right now. Not like this. You've seen me. I'm useless."

"Useless?" Tom barked a humorless laugh. "You're not useless, Jacob, you're absent. There's a difference. I've been carrying clients, hearings, deadlines, everything. Do you even know how many cases are in freefall because you've checked out?"

Jacob closed his eyes briefly. "I know. And I'm sorry."

Tom slammed a hand down on the desk, rattling the framed photo of Jessica. The sound jolted Jacob more than the words. "Sorry, it doesn't cover it! This firm, we built it from scratch. Remember the nights we slept on the damn office floor eating takeout? The first case we won against Bloomberg & Kline? The day Jessica came in with that drawing." His voice caught, and for a moment the mask cracked. "She drew me with a cape, Jacob. Called me Uncle Tom, the superhero lawyer. And now what? I'm the villain holding the bag while you run off to, what? Chasing unanswerable questions?"

Jacob's throat tightened. He remembered the drawing, the red crayon cape, Jessica's gap-toothed grin when she presented it. "She was nine, Tom. Nine. And now she's gone. How do I go back to depositions and contracts when the only thing that matters is knowing where she is?"

Tom straightened, pacing the length of the office. "You think I don't understand grief? I lost her too. Not like you, I know, but she was my family. She called me Uncle Tom. I'd have taken that car myself if it would've spared her." He turned sharply. "But I didn't. And neither did you. And the world keeps moving, Jacob. Clients keep calling. Staff keep waiting on paychecks. My kids still need braces. We don't get to burn it all down because life broke us."

Jacob rubbed his temple, feeling the twitch in his eye pulse against his fingers. The war-twitch. It hadn't bothered him this badly in years. "You're right. But I can't stop. Not yet. Not until I know."

"Know what?" Tom demanded. "That she's in heaven? Does God exist? That every religion isn't just another story to make us feel better before the lights go out? You won't find that, Jacob. You'll find ruins and old men arguing over scripture while everything we built goes to hell."

The words struck harder because they came from Tom, his brother in every way but blood. They had survived law school finals, impossible clients, nights of bourbon and bad jokes, the first years of fatherhood when neither of them slept more than four hours. Their lives had been braided together for thirty years.

"Tom," Jacob said, his voice raw, "I promised her. In that hospital room. I told her we'd always be together. If there's even the smallest chance she still exists, I have to find it. If I don't, I'll break the only promise that mattered."

Tom's eyes glistened, but his jaw stayed tight. "And what about the promises you made to the living? To Margaret, to me, to every client who trusted you? What about those, Jacob? Do they not matter?"

"They matter," Jacob whispered. "But Jessica matters more."

The silence that followed was unbearable. The hum of the fluorescent light, the muted traffic outside, even the ticking of the old clock on Jacob's shelf seemed too loud.

Finally, Tom nodded once, curtly. "Then this is it."

"Don't do this."

"No." Tom's voice was sharp now, a blade. "You go chase ghosts, Jacob. But understand this: when you walk out that door, you're not just leaving cases. You're leaving me. You're leaving everything we built. And when the malpractice suits hit, and they will, you'll face them alone."

Jacob tried to speak, but Tom was already at the door. He paused, hand on the frame, shoulders tight. Without turning, he said, "You were my brother. That's the only reason I held on this long. But I can't carry you and Jessica's ghost both. Decide who you're going to save, Jacob. Because right now, it's not us."

The door shut behind him with a soft click that sounded louder than any slam.

Jacob sat in the silence, Jessica's photo tilting slightly from Tom's blow. He reached out, straightened the frame, and whispered, "I'm sorry."

***

Near midnight he wandered the house, opening closets, pulling down the suitcase. He set it on the bed but didn't pack. In the bathroom, Jessica's extra toothbrush still stood in the cup, purple handle chewed, as if she had been halfway through brushing. He gripped the sink until his hands ached.

When his anger subsided, he thought about his journey. The decision came not in a moment of revelation but in the slow accumulation of unbearable questions. For weeks after the funeral, Jacob had moved through the motions of ordinary life, returning phone calls, reviewing case files, pretending that legal briefs mattered when the only brief that counted was the brief time he'd had with Jessica.

Dr. Thornton had been gentle but direct during their sessions. "Grief has stages, Jacob. Denial, anger, bargaining, depression, acceptance. You're trying to skip straight to bargaining with God."

"Maybe because the other stages don't lead anywhere," Jacob had replied. "What's the point of accepting something that might not be final?"

"What if it is final? What if death simply ends? What will you do with that reality?"

But he couldn't accept that reality without investigation. He was a lawyer. He examined evidence, interviewed witnesses, built cases from facts rather than assumptions. Why should the most important question of his life receive less rigorous attention than a property dispute?

The breaking point had come during Sunday service at St. Mary's. Father Alcoa had preached about divine mystery, about trusting God's plan even when that plan included unbearable loss. The congregation had nodded with the satisfied expressions of people who found comfort in not thinking too deeply.

But Jacob's mind had rebelled against the easy answers. If God had a plan, why did that plan include nine-year-olds dying for art projects?

If divine love was real, why was its silence so complete? If faith was supposed to provide comfort, why did every religious platitude feel like intellectual cowardice?

After the service, he'd driven aimlessly through suburban streets that suddenly felt foreign. Past the elementary school where Jessica would never finish fourth grade. Past the soccer field where she'd scored her first goal. Past the library where they'd spent Saturday mornings choosing books that would now remain forever unread.

At home, he'd opened his laptop and begun researching with the systematic thoroughness he brought to complex legal cases. Catholic doctrine about the afterlife. Protestant variations on salvation. Eastern Orthodox mysticism. Judaism's diverse perspectives on the afterlife. Islam's detailed descriptions of paradise.

Each tradition claimed exclusive access to ultimate truth. Each promised reunion with deceased loved ones. Each demanded faith without providing the evidence Jacob's analytical mind required.

He had prepared a list of questions:

I need to know if God exists at all. If there's no God, there's no afterlife. If there's no afterlife, Jessica is simply gone. But if God exists and I can't prove it, I'm no better off than if He doesn't. I need verification, evidence that would hold up in court, not just faith, not just hope, but proof.

Do any religious traditions offer verifiable evidence for life after death?

How do competing truth claims resolve into coherent theology?

What distinguishes authentic divine revelation from human religious creativity?

If Jessica continues to exist, which tradition accurately describes that existence. Which path do I follow?

What must I believe or do to ensure eventual reunion?

The list had grown to three pages by dawn. Three pages of questions that demanded answers, not the vague comfort of "divine mystery" or "God's plan." If religious traditions claimed to know these answers, Jacob would investigate their claims with the same rigor he'd brought to every important case.

Tom had tried to dissuade him during a partners' lunch that felt like an intervention. "You're talking about abandoning everything we've built for some kind of spiritual quest. That's not investigation, Jake, that's obsession."

"Maybe obsession is what love looks like when someone you can't live without dies," Jacob had replied. "Maybe the difference between faith and delusion is the willingness to ask hard questions instead of accepting comfortable lies."

"And what if your investigation proves that death is final? What if life simply ends when the brain stops functioning? Will knowing that help you accept Jessica's death?"

The question had haunted Jacob for days. But even devastating truth felt preferable to beautiful uncertainty. Jessica had asked him whether heaven was real, and he'd given her Sunday school answers he couldn't prove. "If she still existed somewhere, she deserved a father who had exhausted every possibility to find her. If she didn't, he deserved to know that truth, no matter how much the knowledge cost."

Margaret had been the most direct in her opposition. "You're planning to abandon your responsibilities here for some kind of religious tourism. What makes you think foreign priests have better answers than Father Doyle?"

"Because Father Doyle has never convinced me he actually knows anything beyond what's written in books that were compiled by policy committees," Jacob had said. "Maybe other traditions have preserved different insights. Maybe someone, somewhere, has evidence rather than just faith."

"And what about your practice? Your clients? The people who depend on you?"

"What about Jessica? The daughter who depended on me to protect her and who died anyway? Don't I owe her the effort to find out if death is final?"

The conversation had ended in stalemate, but Jacob's resolve had only strengthened. Love demanded everything, including the courage to risk everything. If Jessica existed somewhere, he would find evidence of that existence. If she didn't, he would learn to live with that truth. But he wouldn't abandon the search until he'd exhausted every possibility.

The flight reservations had been surprisingly easy to make. Rome first, to examine Catholicism at its source. Then to Florence and Protestants, Bulgaria for Orthodox Christianity, Istanbul for Islam. Then Jerusalem for Judaism. A methodical investigation of humanity's major claims about life after death and divine reality.

Tom had made one final plea the night before departure. "This isn't what Jessica would want, Jake. She loved you because you were present, reliable, someone who showed up when he promised. Now you're planning to disappear for months, maybe longer, chasing something that might not exist."

"She asked me if heaven was real," Jacob had replied. "I lied to her because I didn't know. Now I'm going to find out. If that's obsession, then obsession is what I owe her."

When morning came, June 10th, six weeks after the funeral, Jacob had packed a single suitcase and his leather journal, kissed Jessica's photograph goodbye, and driven to the airport with the desperate hope that somewhere in the ancient cities of faith, someone could tell him whether life survived death, or died with the body that had once contained it.

***

Chapter Two

THE ROAD OF CHRISTIANITY

The departure board at O'Hare glowed with names of cities Jacob had never connected to anything but tourist brochures: Rome, Florence, Sofia. Tonight, they looked less like destinations and more like markers on a map of desperation. Chicago was the point of departure, a city of steel, glass, and cases he no longer cared about. Ahead lay places where people claimed God had spoken, where answers might be waiting if he had the strength to ask.

On the flight, a businessperson in the next seat flipped between spreadsheets, glancing once at Jacob's stack of books: Comparative Christology, The Council of Nicaea: Original Documents, a leather notebook filled with questions in his careful script. Questions that had woken him in the middle of the night, staring into Jessica's empty room:

If God is a loving father, what kind of father watches his children get crushed by cars?

If salvation through Jesus is the only path, why do people die when they follow it?

If the Bible is divine truth, why do Southern Baptists and Catholics read the same verses and reach opposite conclusions?

"Religious studies?" the man asked.

"Personal research," Jacob said. When the man pressed, Jacob added flatly: "Death." The conversation ended there.

By the time the plane descended toward Leonardo da Vinci Airport, Jacob whispered the promise again, the one made over Jessica's still body. I'll find you, baby. I don't know where you are, but I'll keep my promise. We'll be together.

***

Jacob arrived in Rome late in the afternoon, the jet lag draped across him like an unwelcome cloak. At the pensione off Piazza Navona, he dropped his suitcase onto the narrow bed and forced himself to unpack. Shirts into drawers, toiletries by the sink, notebook on the desk, ritual gestures meant to convince himself he was not a man merely passing through, but one beginning something deliberate.

***

Tom Mitchell pressed the phone receiver to his ear until the plastic groaned, a futile attempt to physically contain the anxiety radiating from the man on the other end of the line.

"What do you mean you don't have an update?" Klaus Whitfield's voice was a whipcrack of German-accented impatience. "The appellate deadline is in five weeks, Tom. Five. Where is he?"

"Klaus, I've assured you, I prepared every document before he left," Tom said, forcing a calm he did not feel into his voice. From his desk, he could see Jacob's corner office's closed door. It had been dark for three weeks, a silent, wood-paneled accusation. "The strategy is set. We are on schedule."

"On schedule? Tom, he's vanished! He's on a spiritual walkabout? What am I supposed to tell my investors? That our forty-seven-million-dollar development is in the hands of a man who's gone to find himself?"

Tom closed his eyes, picturing the Whitfield file, a stack of binders two feet high that now felt like a time bomb on Jacob's credenza. "He needed the time, Klaus. For personal reasons."

"We all have personal reasons," Klaus snapped. "But we do not abandon our posts. I expect a call from Jacob by the end of the week. Not from you. From him."

The line went dead. Tom slowly placed the receiver back in its cradle, the silence of his own office rushing in to replace the tirade. He ran a hand through his already disheveled hair and stared at Jacob's door. Chasing ghosts, he thought, the anger a familiar, bitter taste.

A soft knock interrupted him. Margaret stood in the doorway; her ledger held tight to her chest like a shield. She didn't have to ask. Her eyes, filled with a worry that went far beyond accounting, said it all.

"Whitfield?" she asked quietly.

Tom nodded, gesturing for her to come in. "He wants to hear from the man in charge. Apparently, I don't qualify."

Margaret set the ledger on his desk and opened it. "He's right to be nervous. So am I." She pointed to a column of figures. "Billables were down thirty percent last month. With Jacob's major cases on hold, our overhead is eating us alive. At this burn rate, Tom, we have two months of operating capital. Maybe."

The numbers didn't lie. They were cold, clean, and merciless. "I'm trying to cover his hearings," Tom said, the excuse sounding weak even to himself. "But I can't be in two courtrooms at once."

"I know you're doing everything you can," she said, her voice softening. And that was the problem. Margaret's kindness made it worse. She wasn't just their accountant; she was the grandmother of the girl whose death had sent their world spiraling off its axis. They were all orbiting the same empty space.

"He won't answer my calls," Tom admitted, the frustration finally breaking through his professional veneer. "Voicemail. Every time."

Margaret looked toward Jacob's dark office. "Jessica would have wanted him to heal. But she would have hated seeing him leave the people who depend on him behind." She closed the ledger. "I just want you to know what we're facing."

After she left, Tom walked to the window overlooking State Street. Below, the city moved with its usual relentless energy, indifferent to the slow-motion collapse happening on the third floor. He thought of the night he and Jacob signed the lease for this office, young and ambitious, sharing a bottle of cheap champagne and promising each other they'd build something that lasted.

He turned from the window and looked at his partner's empty chair.

"You're chasing ghosts, Jake," he whispered to the silent room. "And you're leaving the rest of us here to drown."

***

The hotel window shutters opened onto a courtyard where laundry swayed in the breeze, scraps of ordinary life untouched by cosmic questions. For a long moment Jacob stood there, listening to the clatter of dishes and the faint ring of a bicycle bell. He felt the pull of the bed, the ache in his bones. But the meeting had been arranged weeks earlier, through a Chicago colleague with Jesuit ties. Weariness could not excuse him from the appointment.

He wandered for a couple of hours before heading across the city. Rome revealed itself in fragments: children playing soccer against a crumbling wall, tourists clustered around gelato stands, priests in black cassocks threading through crowds like shadows. At the Pantheon he craned his neck beneath the dome where sunlight fell through the oculus like a wound in the sky. Awe stirred in him, but he wondered if it was proof of anything, or only architecture's ability to mimic eternity.

When the bells of Sant 'Ignazio struck the hour, he turned toward the Jesuit guesthouse. A seminarian ushered him down a corridor lined with oil paintings, into a quiet parlor.

Father Romano rose slowly from his chair. His cassock was plain, the white-collar stark against dark skin weathered by decades of sun. His eyes carried both intensity and welcome, as if he had been waiting not just for Jacob, but for the questions that trailed him.

"Mr. Hinsen," he said, his Italian accent giving the name a softer cadence. "You've traveled far."

Jacob managed a tired smile. "Farther than Rome, Father. I'm looking for answers no one else has given me."

Romano gestured to the chair opposite. "Then sit. We will begin with questions, as all serious conversations do."

Jacob lowered himself into the seat, journal balanced on his knee. "Then let's begin. Why do Christians believe salvation comes only by accepting Jesus Christ?"

"The straightforward answer," Romano replied, "is that it is written in the Gospels and affirmed through centuries of tradition. For us, it is the heart of the faith."

"But why only?" Jacob pressed, courtroom cadence sharpening his words. "Jews, Muslims, they revere the same God. Are they cast aside because they call Him differently?"

Romano folded his hands. "Simple answers do not satisfy you, I see. The Church rests on two pillars: scripture and tradition. Both affirm that Jesus is not merely a prophet, but God's own Son. As John records: 'I am the way, the truth, and the life. No man comes to the Father but by me.'"

Jacob leaned forward. "Then what of Abraham, Moses, Muhammad? They, too, taught God's love."

"That," Romano said gently, "is the line of division. For us, Christ is not one voice among many, but the Word made flesh. At his baptism, the heavens opened and a voice declared: 'This is my beloved Son.'"

Jacob hesitated. "But those words were written decades later. Names like Matthew and John may not even belong to the authors. Councils decided which writings survived. How can you be sure what remains is truth, and not politics?"

Romano did not flinch. "Because faith is not built on certainty of manuscripts but on trust in the Spirit who guided those who preserved them. Councils did not create truth, they safeguarded it. Yes, they were men, but men moved by something greater."

Jacob shook his head. "So, men grant themselves authority to decide God's word."

"No," Romano said firmly. "They preserve it, even as they interpret it. But you are right in one sense: it requires surrender. Faith is not arrogance. It is trust that God will not abandon His Church to error."

The silence lengthened. Jacob felt the lawyer in him itching to push harder, but something in Romano's steady gaze slowed him. This was not cross-examination; it was an invitation.

At last Jacob said quietly, "Then why does scripture read so ambiguously that hate groups can twist it into violence? Wouldn't the world be better if Christians lived only by two commandments: love God, love your neighbor?"

Romano's mouth curved in something between a smile and sorrow. "Yes. But even then, men would argue what love means. That is why Christ himself is our measure. The rest is commentary, interpretation, and yes, sometimes distortion. But the call remains: love."

Jacob sat back, notebook limp in his lap. The words did not settle him, but they pressed on him with the weight of centuries. He thought of Doyle's weary honesty, of Leopold's iron tradition, and now Romano's dark, steady eyes insisting that love was not suggestion but command.

The ache of fatigue returned, but beneath it lay something else, a recognition that this search may not yield courtroom proof. Only glimpses. Only fragments.

When he finally left the Jesuit house, the Roman night pressed close around him. The city smelled of stone and woodsmoke, its alleys alive with laughter, clinking glasses, scooters flashing past. Jacob walked back to his small pensione with the feeling that something had begun, though he could not yet name it.

***

Early the next day Jacob walked to St. Peter's Square. Crowds of pilgrims lifted rosaries toward the sky, their faith palpable. Jacob sat on a bench beside a woman in a plain habit, her lips moving silently over the beads.

"Good morning, Sister," he said. "I've been asking questions everywhere I go, and I keep finding more confusion."

She opened her eyes, calm and luminous. "The answers are not in the questions, my son. They are in silence. God is not argued into existence. He is found when you stop demanding proof."

Jacob almost challenged her, but something in her serenity disarmed him. He stayed silent for once.

***

The Swiss Guard at St. Anne's Gate examined his credentials with professional thoroughness. Jacob's black suit and conservative tie marked him as serious rather than tourist, someone worthy of institutional attention. He was escorted through corridors that seemed designed to inspire awe through sheer accumulated grandeur, marble floors worn smooth by centuries of pilgrims, frescoed ceilings that depicted biblical scenes with Renaissance confidence.

Cardinal Rossi received him in an office that felt like a library designed by angels. Books lined the walls from floor to ceiling, their leather spines bearing titles in Latin, Italian, German, and languages Jacob couldn't identify. The cardinal himself was smaller than Jacob had expected, a man in his seventies whose authority came not from physical presence but from institutional weight and intellectual depth.

"Mr. Hinsen," Cardinal Rossi said, rising from behind a desk that looked older than America. "During my call with Father Doyle when he suggested I meet with you he spoke highly of your sincerity, if not your conclusions. Please, sit."

Jacob took the offered chair, leather worn smooth by countless other seekers who had come here bearing impossible questions. The cardinal's eyes were sharp behind wire-rimmed glasses, the gaze of someone accustomed to evaluating souls in crisis.

"Your Eminence, I appreciate your time. If I may be direct. My nine-year-old daughter was killed by a distracted driver six weeks ago. I simply need to know two things: Does God exist, and if so, is my daughter with Him? I can't accept 'have faith' as an answer. If God exists, there should be evidence. If there is life after death, there should be verification. I'm examining every major religious tradition of Abraham to find that evidence."

The directness hung in the air between them. Cardinal Rossi's expression softened, his institutional authority giving way to pastoral concern.

"I am deeply sorry for your loss, Mr. Hinsen. To lose a child..." The cardinal paused, gathering his thoughts. "Yes, God exists. And yes, your daughter is with Him now, safe in His perfect love."

Jacob felt his jurist impulses sharpen. "How do you know this? What evidence can you give me?"

"The witness of Scripture, the teaching of the Church, two thousand years of apostolic tradition..."

"With respect, Your Eminence, those are claims, not evidence. If I were in court representing a client, I would need more than institutional assertions. How can you prove God exists?"

Cardinal Rossi leaned back, recognizing the familiar challenge. "Mr. Hinsen, proof of God's existence is not like proving a legal case. Faith involves trust in realities beyond empirical demonstration."

"But surely there must be something more than just faith? Signs, miracles, documented experiences that point to God's existence?"

"There are indeed such things. Miraculous healings verified by medical professionals. Apparitions witnessed by credible sources. The conversion experiences of skeptics who encountered the divine..."

"Which could all be explained by psychology, coincidence, or misunderstanding," Jacob interrupted. "I need something that would convince a skeptical mind, something that proves my daughter didn't just cease to exist when she died."

The cardinal was quiet for a lingering moment. "Mr. Hinsen, what would constitute proof for you? What evidence would satisfy your need to know that Jessica continues?"

Jacob had thought about this question during sleepless nights. "Independent verification that God exists, that heaven is a reality. Multiple credible witnesses to the same phenomena. Physical evidence that can't be explained away. Something that demonstrates we exist beyond this life."

"And if I told you that such evidence exists? That the Church has documented cases of individuals who have returned from clinical death with knowledge they couldn't have possessed? That saints and mystics have described the afterlife in remarkably consistent terms across centuries and cultures?"

"I would want to examine that evidence myself. Meet with witnesses, review medical records, investigate the claims with the same rigor I'd use in any important case."

Cardinal Rossi moved to his bookcase and withdrew a folder. "Then perhaps we should begin with this. These are documented cases investigated by Church authorities, instances where divine intervention seems the only reasonable explanation."

Jacob accepted the folder, his hands trembling slightly. This was what he had come for, not philosophical debate, but concrete information about God's existence and Jessica's fate.

He opened it immediately, scanning the first case while Cardinal Rossi watched. A woman in Lourdes claiming miraculous healing from terminal cancer. Medical records showed tumor regression, but Jacob's legal eye caught the gaps. Experimental treatments administered weeks before the 'miracle', incomplete documentation, no independent verification from skeptical physicians.

The second case: a child's near-death experience describing heaven in remarkable detail. But the account was recorded months later, after extensive religious counseling. Jacob knew how memory could be shaped by suggestion, especially in traumatized children seeking comfort.

Case after case followed the same pattern. Compelling testimonies undermined by missing evidence, miraculous claims diluted by natural explanations the investigators had chosen not to pursue. The Vatican's 'rigorous investigation' would never survive cross-examination in any courtroom.

Jacob looked up at Cardinal Rossi, who was watching him with patient understanding. The Cardinal had offered this folder knowing it wouldn't convince a skeptical lawyer. It demonstrated the Church's diligence, not divine intervention.

"Your Eminence," Jacob said quietly, "this evidence requires the same leap of faith you're asking me to make. These cases have natural explanations that weren't fully explored."

Rossi nodded slowly. "Perhaps that's the point, Mr. Hinsen. Faith isn't about eliminating all doubt. It's about choosing trust despite reasonable uncertainty."

"Your Eminence, I need you to understand that I'm not here as a casual seeker or someone looking for solace. If God exists and Jessica is with Him, I need to know beyond any reasonable doubt. If He doesn't exist and she's simply gone, I need to know that too. I can't live in uncertainty."

"And what will you do with whatever certainty you find or don't find?"

Jacob met the cardinal's gaze directly. "If I find evidence that God exists and Jessica is safe with Him, then I'll know my promise to always be together isn't broken. If I find that God doesn't exist and death is final, then I'll know she's gone forever and I'll have to learn to live with that."

"And if you find something in between? Evidence that suggests divine reality but doesn't provide absolute proof?"

Jacob had not considered this possibility. He demanded clear verdicts, unambiguous conclusions. The thought of remaining in limbo between faith and doubt was almost unbearable.

"Then I'll keep investigating until I find definitive answers," he said. "I owe Jessica that much."

"Your Eminence, I understand our time is short, but if I may just one last question, please." The cardinal nodded. "Jesus commanded his followers to love their enemies and turn the other cheek. Yet the Catholic Church launched Crusades, conducted Inquisitions, burned heretics. Where in Christ's teaching does He authorize such violence?"

Rossi's expression grew somber. "He doesn't. The Sermon on the Mount explicitly forbids it."

"Then which God are we following? The Old Testament God who commanded genocide? Deuteronomy orders Israel to kill every Canaanite: man, woman, child. Samuel has God commanding the extermination of Amalekite infants. How does the Church reconcile the God who ordered infanticide with Jesus who preached nonviolence?"

"The Church teaches definitively that God did not command genocide," Rossi said, his voice carrying the weight of theological certainty. "Modern biblical scholarship, which the Church fully accepts, demonstrates these texts reflect ancient Near Eastern conquest rhetoric and theological narratives written centuries after the supposed events. They tell us how ancient Israelites understood God within their brutal cultural context, not what God actually commanded. The historical evidence shows these conquest stories are largely theological fiction."

"But the text says, 'God commanded.' Either it's true or it's a lie."

"It's neither. It's ancient people interpreting their history through their understanding of divine will. Think of it as a theological interpretation rather than a historical record. When Christ came, He revealed God's true nature completely: nonviolent, merciful, self-giving love. Everything in the Old Testament must be read through that lens."

"Yet Christians still used those old texts to justify violence. Crusaders cited Joshua's conquests. Inquisitors cited Deuteronomy's laws about heresy. The same Bible."

"Yes." Rossi's honesty was amazing. "That is the Church's great shame. Humans have always found ways to make scripture serve power rather than submit to its true message. We took the God revealed in Christ, who died rather than kill His enemies, and twisted Him back into a war god whenever that suited our political purposes. We ignored two thousand years of our own best theology whenever violence was convenient."

Jacob leaned forward, pressing the point. "But Your Eminence, that raises a deeper question. If the Old Testament portrays God commanding genocide, and you're now saying those texts misrepresent His character, how do I know ANY of the Bible represents Him accurately? The God who ordered the slaughter of Amalekite infants seems nothing like the Jesus who blessed children and preached nonviolence. Are we even talking about the same God?"

"Catholics believe Jesus IS God, correct? Through the Trinity, Father, Son, Holy Spirit as one being?"

"Yes. Three persons, one God."

"Then the God who commanded genocide in Deuteronomy is the same God who said 'turn the other cheek' as Jesus? The same divine being gave opposite commands?"

Rossi nodded slowly. "The Trinity is a mystery. But Jesus reveals God's true nature. The Old Testament shows humanity's incomplete grasp of that nature."

Rossi's expression grew reflective, recognizing the philosophical trap. "They are the same God but progressively revealed. The ancient Israelites understood God through their limited cultural framework, a framework that included tribal warfare and divine kingship. Jesus came to show us God's true nature fully. Everything in the Old Testament must be read through the lens of Christ's revelation."

"So, the answer is selective reading," Jacob said, his lawyer's mind cutting to the logic. "You keep the parts that align with Jesus and reinterpret the parts that don't. But who decides which passages reveal God accurately and which are just ancient misunderstandings? When Jessica asked me where she'd go when she dies, am I supposed to base my answer on texts that even the Church admits are culturally improved human interpretations?"

Cardinal Rossi was quiet for a long moment. "You're asking for a level of certainty that faith, by its nature, cannot provide. Yes, we must interpret. Yes, we must discern between cultural context and eternal truth. That requires wisdom, tradition, and the guidance of the Holy Spirit working through the Church."

"Which brings me back to human authority claiming divine backing," Jacob said quietly.

The Cardinal's phone buzzed discreetly on his desk. He glanced at it, then back to Jacob with genuine regret. "I apologize, Mr. Hinsen, but I have another meeting I must attend. The questions you ask have been debated for millennia, but I hope you continue to ask them until you find what you're looking for."

Jacob stood, suddenly worn out. "Thank you, Your Eminence. I will keep searching."

The meeting concluded with Cardinal Rossi's invitation to return, to continue the conversation if Jacob's journey through other traditions left questions unanswered. As Jacob walked back through Vatican corridors toward the ordinary world of Roman streets, he carried both disappointment and relief.

***

The Church had not provided the proof he sought. But neither had it insulted his intelligence with false certainties or demanded belief without acknowledgment of difficulty. Cardinal Rossi had offered the most honest religious response Jacob had yet encountered: we believe, but we cannot prove, and faith requires courage precisely because certainty is not available.

Jacob stared at the crucifix above the desk. Rossi's voice echoed in his head, certainty, authority, map, and compass. Yet the nun's words lingered too, quiet as the turning of rosary beads: God found not in argument, but in silence.

From the window he saw Rome spread out, basilicas, ruins, the scars, and triumphs of two thousand years. He realized he was leaving with two competing Christianity's: one of marble certainty, one of quiet surrender.

The marble saints of the Vatican were cold company. Their polished eyes, fixed on a distant heaven, offered no answers, only an unyielding, silent certainty. Jacob left the grandeur of St. Peter's with the Cardinal's words still echoing in his ears, a faith of unbreakable rules and guarded truths. It felt magnificent, ancient, and utterly hollow. He needed to touch something humbler. Something real, but it demanded something he could not yet give.

Outside St. Peter's Square, crowds of pilgrims lifted rosaries toward the sky, their faith palpable even to Jacob's skeptical eye. He envied their confidence while questioning its foundation. They found peace through surrender, while he demanded evidence before submission.

Jacob found a small cafe and wrote in his journal:

Rome. Cardinal Rossi gave the official answer: God never commanded genocide, those texts are ancient cultural interpretation, Christ reveals God's true nonviolent nature. It's intellectually sophisticated. It handles the contradiction.

But it raises a deeper problem. If the Church can reinterpret genocide passages as "ancient cultural misunderstanding," what stops them from reinterpreting anything else? Resurrection? Virgin birth? Heaven itself? Once you admit scripture contains theological fiction mixed with truth, who decides which is which?

And the practical problem remains: Christians STILL use Old Testament violence when convenient. Rossi admitted it. They claim to follow Christ but reach for Joshua whenever they want to justify war, oppression, or power. If two thousand years of theology can't stop believers from weaponizing their own scriptures, what good is the theology?

The pattern holds: beautiful teachings about love, selective application, violence when power is threatened.

***

That afternoon, he found himself on a bus heading out of the city on the Appian Way, joining a small, multilingual tour group at the entrance to the Catacombs of Callixtus. He stood for a moment under the brilliant Roman sun, then followed the others down a narrow stone staircase into the earth.

The world vanished. The Roman sun was replaced by a cool, damp dark that smelled of stone, earth, and time itself. A single, low-wattage bulb hummed overhead, casting long, dancing shadows down a corridor that seemed to have no end. The passages were tight, the tufa-rock walls lined with thousands of empty, rectangular burial niches, or loculi, stacked five or six high like shelves in a library of the dead.

The guide's voice was a rehearsed undertone, her words about secret worship and Roman persecution blurring into a historical drone. Jacob barely listened. He wasn't here for a history lesson. He was in a place where, for centuries, people had brought their dead, their hope, and their grief.

He ran his hand along the rough wall, his fingers tracing a crudely carved fish. Ichthys. A symbol, a secret. Not a statement of doctrine, he thought, but a desperate password whispered in the dark. Further on, he saw an anchor, the symbol of hope. Hope for what? Reunion? An end to suffering? The simple, raw plea of the symbol felt more authentic than all the gilded crucifixes in the Vatican.

"And here," the guide said, her flashlight beam landing on a niche smaller than the others, at the height of Jacob's waist, "we have the tomb of a young child. The inscription, in simple Greek, reads, 'Aurelia, sweet soul, in peace.'"

The tour group murmured a collective, sympathetic sigh and shuffled forward.

But Jacob was frozen.

The 1,800 years separating him from that tomb collapsed into a single, breathless moment. The name Aurelia vanished, replaced by Jessica. The cold, damp tunnel became a too-bright hospital room. The guide's hushed voice became the steady, merciless beep of a monitor. He saw the hands that had carved that simple inscription, not as historical figures, but as the trembling hands of a mother and father. He felt the weight of the small body they had wrapped in linen and laid to rest in this cold, dark place. Their faith, in that moment, wasn't about councils or canons or papal authority. It was a raw, aching hope that they would see their daughter again.

He waited until the group had turned a corner, their footsteps fading down the corridor. He stepped back to the child's tomb and placed his palm flat against the cool stone that sealed the niche. There was no prayer, no theological breakthrough. There was only a silent acknowledgment that passed between him and the unknown parents across two millennia, a shared, unutterable grief. Here, in the heart of the earth, he had found no answers from God. But he had found a terrible, profound kinship with man.

***

Jacob stayed in Rome longer than he planned; three weeks became five, then seven. He drifted between cafés and side streets, ruins that seemed older than memory itself, asking questions, debating the answers. The city carried faith like a watermark, woven into its rhythm, its architecture, its people.

The Cardinal's words about "protected truth" and a "sure map to heaven" still echoed in his mind, but they felt oddly hollow when set against the ordinary warmth of Romans sharing bread, laughter, or a sundown stroll through piazzas. Everywhere he looked, he saw the paradox: a faith of immense power and rigidity, yet also a faith of quiet, lived connection that needed no institution at all.

***

Early one day, he wandered into Trastevere, ducking into a cramped book shop called Libri Antichi. The air smelled of dust and ink, shelves groaning with centuries of scholarship. He browsed halfheartedly until raised voices from the history section caught his attention.

"You're deliberately misrepresenting the Council's purpose," a woman was saying. "Nicaea wasn't about inventing Christ's divinity, it was about defending established doctrine against Arian heresy."

"Established by whom?" The second voice belonged to a man, sharp with intellectual impatience. "Three hundred bishops, representing a fraction of Christianity's leadership, voting on metaphysical questions. That's politics, not divine revelation."

Jacob rounded the corner to find them facing off over an open book. The woman appeared to be in her sixties, wearing understated academic elegance. The man looked younger, perhaps forty, with the restless energy of someone accustomed to dismantling assumptions.

"The bishops gathered to address theological confusion," the woman said defensively. "Arius was teaching that Christ was subordinate to the Father. They had to clarify orthodox beliefs."

"They had to choose between competing interpretations," the man corrected. "Their choice became 'orthodox' only because they had imperial backing from Constantine."

The woman noticed Jacob's approach and turned with desperate hope for reinforcement. "Perhaps you could settle this? I'm Dr. Francesca Torretti from the Pontifical Gregorian University. This is Dr. Marco Vasquez from the Institute for Secular Studies."

Jacob felt trapped between competing certainties. "I'm not qualified for theological debates. I'm just trying to understand something."

"Which is?" Dr. Vasquez asked.

Jacob hesitated, then pressed forward. "Actually, your discussion is one of interest. If three hundred men in 325 AD voted on Christ's divinity, and their decision shapes how two billion people live today, what does that mean for a novice like me trying to understand what Christianity teaches?"

Dr. Torretti's expression softened. "The Council preserved apostolic truth against heretical innovation."

"But how do I know that?" Jacob's frustration leaked through. "Dr. Vasquez suggests it was political. You say it was divinely guided. I'm supposed to base my understanding of my daughter's eternal fate on a fourth-century committee decision?"

"Your daughter?" Dr. Torretti's voice was gentle.

"She died four months ago. Nine years old." Jacob's voice was flat. "I'm investigating whether Christianity offers reliable answers about what happens after death. But if fundamental doctrines were decided by vote..."

"Faith transcends political processes," Dr. Torretti said carefully. "The Holy Spirit guided those bishops."

"How do you prove that?" Jacob pressed. "And if I can't prove it, how do I distinguish authentic revelation from human politics?"

Dr. Vasquez leaned forward with interest. "You're discovering the central problem with institutional authority."

Jacob looked between them, feeling caught in the same impossible position he'd faced with every religious authority. "So, when my daughter asked me if heaven was real, I was supposed to say, 'Well, three hundred bishops voted that Christ was divine, and if they were right and not politically motivated, then yes?'"

"That's not how faith works," Dr. Torretti said with obvious discomfort.

"Then how does it work?" Jacob's voice cracked slightly. "Because I've been searching for months, and everyone gives me different answers based on different authorities making different claims about the same events."

Dr. Torretti and Dr. Vasquez exchanged glances, the heat of their academic debate suddenly cooled by Jacob's raw desperation.

"Perhaps," Dr. Torretti said carefully, "faith isn't about resolving such questions definitively. Perhaps it's about trusting despite uncertainty."

"But trust in what?" Jacob pressed. "Your interpretation? His interpretation? Some other scholar's theory about what those bishops really meant?"

Dr. Vasquez spoke more gently than before. "Maybe that's exactly the problem you're identifying. Maybe no human religion can provide the certainty you're seeking."

For a moment, the bookshop fell silent except for distant Roman traffic. Jacob stared at the historical text they'd been debating, realizing it represented the same problem he'd encountered everywhere: human beings making decisions about divine truth, then demanding others accept those decisions as divinely guaranteed.

"I have to go," Jacob said calmly. "But thank you for showing me something I hadn't considered before."

"Which is?" Dr. Vasquez asked.

"That maybe I'm asking the wrong question entirely."

As Jacob walked toward the exit, he heard them resume their argument behind him. Outside, Roman traffic moved with familiar chaos, and Jacob found himself wondering whether any human institution could preserve divine truth unchanged, or whether all religious authority was human authority claiming divine backing.

The question followed him through Rome's ancient streets like a shadow he couldn't shake.

***

The coffee in the bank's conference room was cold and bitter, a perfect match for Tom Mitchell's mood. Across the polished mahogany table, Mark Henderson, the bank's vice president of business accounts, steepled his fingers and offered a smile that didn't reach his eyes.

"Tom, we value our long relationship with Hinsen & Mitchell," Henderson began, his tone dripping with practiced concern. "But I'll be frank. The numbers are concerning. Revenue is down forty percent quarter-over-quarter. Your operating capital is shrinking faster than we're comfortable with."

"It's a temporary downturn," Tom said, hearing the hollow echo of the same lie he'd told Klaus Whitfield. "Jacob's absence has created a bottleneck, but we have several major settlements pending."

"Pending settlements aren't cash in hand," Henderson countered smoothly. "The bank needs to see a concrete plan to stabilize your cash flow. We need to see your senior partner back at the helm. Otherwise, we'll be forced to re-evaluate the terms of your business line of credit."

The threat, though professionally veiled, was clear. Re-evaluate meant freeze. Freeze meant they couldn't make payroll. Tom left the bank feeling like he'd just walked fifteen rounds with a heavyweight.

The air felt thin when he got back to the office. The usual hum of activity had been replaced by a tense quiet. He saw the reason immediately. Samantha, their best senior paralegal, was standing outside his office, her expression grim.

"Tom, can I have a word?"

He knew before she spoke. He saw it in the way she wouldn't meet his eyes. She closed the door behind them.

"I've accepted a position at Cutler & Swann," she said, the words coming in a rush. "I am so, so sorry, Tom. My last day is in two weeks."

It was a body blow. Samantha had been with them for a decade. She was the firm's institutional memory. "We can match their offer, Samantha. We can beat it."

She shook her head, tears welling in her eyes. "It's not about the money. It's about stability. I have a mortgage, Tom. My son starts college next year. I hear the whispers. I see Klaus Whitfield's messages. I can't go down with the ship."

There was nothing he could say to that. He wished her well, shook her hand, and watched another piece of the life he'd built with Jacob walk out the door.

He stood for a long time in the center of his office, the silence pressing in. The bank was closing in. The staff was abandoning ship. He walked to his desk, snatched the phone, and dialed Jacob's number. He knew it was useless, but he did it anyway. The automated European voicemail message, cheerful, distant, and utterly indifferent, was a final insult.

When the beep sounded, the control Tom had been maintaining for weeks finally shattered.

"Jake, it's me. Again." His voice was tight with a fury that bordered on despair. "Henderson at the bank is getting ready to call our loans. Samantha just quit. She said she can't go down with the ship. The walls are closing in, you son of a bitch." He was breathing hard now, the words tearing out of him. "For God's sake, pick up the phone. I can't hold this together alone."

He slammed the receiver down, the crash echoing in the empty office. He stared at the dark, silent door to Jacob's office, feeling the siege's full, crushing weight.

***

Christianity wasn't a single revelation but the survivor of theological warfare. The thought was a bitter acid in Jacob's mind as he crossed Campo de' Fiori a week later, his head down as he navigated the crowded market. He was so focused on the bookstore conversation that he didn't see the man burdened with books until they collided, sending volumes scattering across the cobblestones.

"My apologies," Jacob muttered, stooping to help. He picked up a worn copy of Augustine's Confessions and froze as he looked up at the man's face. The features were heavier, the hair thinner and grayed, but the eyes were the same, sharp, intelligent, and now framed by the deep lines of a grief Jacob recognized instantly.

"Thomas?"

The man blinked in disbelief. "Jacob? God help me, I didn't expect this." Dr. Thomas Morrison, once Harvard's brightest star in systematic theology, looked from Jacob's face to the furious scrawl in his open notebook. "You look like you're at war."

"With whom, I'm not sure," Jacob admitted.

"Let's get some coffee and catch up."

"But first," Thomas asked. "You're in Rome so you must be searching for something, maybe I can help?"

"I'm searching for proof that God exists and that my daughter Jessica is with Him. But every tradition offers promises without evidence, demands faith without verification. Catholics say God revealed himself through Christ. But how do I know any of them are right? How do I distinguish authentic divine revelation from human religious creativity?"

Thomas shook his head, a smile touching his lips. "Forget coffee. Walk with me. I've got a meeting to get to but there's something I think you need to see."

He led Jacob through a labyrinth of side streets to the Basilica of San Clemente. From the outside, it was unassuming, but as they stepped inside the 12th-century church, the air grew cool and smelled of incense and stone. Golden mosaics glittered in the apse, depicting a triumphant, glorified Christ.

"Beautiful, isn't it?" Thomas said quietly. "Polished. Certain. The final word."

Jacob, still raw from his discovery about the Council of Nicaea, felt a cynical edge in his own voice. "A version of the final word, anyway. Decided by a committee."

Thomas simply motioned and led him to a small door at the side of the nave. "But this is not where the story begins."

He led Jacob down a flight of stone stairs into a different world. The air grew damper, the light dimmer. They were standing in the vast, ghostly nave of a 4th-century basilica, buried for centuries beneath the newer one. Faded frescoes of saints, their faces half-erased by time and water, flickered in the low light.

"They built their triumph on top of this," Thomas murmured, running a hand over the damp stone. "A simpler, messier faith. Closer to the ground. Closer to the bone." He turned to Jacob, his academic polish gone, leaving only a man bearing his own scars. "I spent twenty years of my life up there," he said, gesturing toward the ceiling. "Teaching theology like it was a chess match. Proving God's existence. Defending the Trinity. I had answers for everything."

He paused, his voice dropping. "Then I buried my son. He was twenty-two. A roadside bomb in Afghanistan. I stood at his grave, and all my arguments, all my elegant proofs, were just noise. Ash. I had been selling answers I'd never tested. So, I left Harvard and came here searching. Not to prove anything. Just to see if faith could still matter when life rips you apart."

The confession hung in the ancient air between them, an offering of shared, unbearable pain.

"I am sorry Thomas; I feel your pain. I lost my daughter, Jessica," Jacob said, the words coming out rough. "Nine years old. Killed by an automobile while she waited for me."

Thomas closed his eyes, and in the gesture, Jacob felt not pity, but recognition. "Then you surely know pain: my sincere remorse Jacob."

Thomas led him down another, steeper set of stairs. The air grew colder still; the only sound was the steady drip of water in the dark. They were in a different age now. The narrow brick corridors belonged to the 1st century. In a small, barrel-vaulted chamber, Thomas pointed to a stone altar.

"A Mithraic temple," he said. "Before the Christians were here, another faith practiced its own mysteries in this same dark place. A rival story." He looked at Jacob, his eyes accustomed to the gloom. "This is what I wanted you to see. Layers of interpretation. Each one covering what came before, each claiming to be the truth. Maybe faith isn't about finding the one, final layer. Maybe it's about having the courage to journey through all of them."

Here, in the deepest, oldest part of the structure, surrounded by the ghosts of a forgotten religion, Jacob finally asked the question that had driven him across the world. "Do you still believe? In life after death? That I'll see her again?"

Thomas was silent for a long time, the dripping water counting the seconds. "I nearly destroyed myself trying to find my son," he said at last. His voice was not the voice of a scholar, but of a fellow survivor. "I stopped eating, stopped sleeping, and pushed away everyone who tried to help me. The search became more important than living. I spent three years demanding God explain why my son had to die, and I got nothing but silence. But I lost three years of my life to that silence." He looked directly at Jacob. "Don't let finding Jessica cost you the life she'd want you to have. Don't become so obsessed with where she is that you forget how to live where you are."

Jacob's eyes flashed. "So, you decided to simply believe and give up your search? Maybe if you'd kept looking, you would have found him?"

Thomas met his gaze without flinching. "That's what I told myself for three years. 'Just one more library, one more scholar, one more vision.' But Jacob, I wasn't searching anymore. I was drowning. I'd convinced myself that stopping meant I didn't love my son enough, that giving up the quest meant abandoning him."

He gestured around the ancient chamber. "You want to know what I found when I finally stopped? The same thing every grieving parent discovers, whether they're Christian, Muslim, Jewish, or nothing at all. We all tell ourselves the same story, that love continues somehow, that death isn't final, that we'll see them again. Maybe we're all right.

Maybe we're all wrong. But we're all saying the same thing because we're all human, and this is how humans survive unbearable loss."

Jacob stood slowly, the weight of Thomas's words settling like sediment in still water. His admission that every grieving parent tells themselves the same story regardless of their faith, cut through his assumptions about finding unique answers.

"Thank you," Jacob said quietly. "For telling me what no one else would say."

"What will you do now?"

Jacob looked around the ancient space, layers of faith built upon layers of faith, each claiming to be the foundation. "Keep looking. I must. But maybe I'll listen differently now." He paused. "You said every tradition tells the same story. I need to find out if that's true for myself. I guess it's a father's matter."

He turned toward the narrow staircase leading back to street level. "If Christianity, Islam, and Judaism all give me the same answers about Jessica, then maybe the answers aren't as important as I thought they were."

Walking up through the layers of buried churches toward Rome's afternoon light, Jacob carried Thomas's warning with him. The search would continue, but the desperation felt different now, less frantic, more deliberate. If Thomas was right about the universality of religious dogma, Jacob would discover it himself in the mosques of Istanbul and the synagogues of Jerusalem.

The Roman sun felt immediate on his face as he emerged from underground. Tomorrow he would fly east, still searching for Jessica, but now wondering if what he found would sound exactly like what he'd already heard.

***

Kevin, a junior associate with an Ivy League degree and the perpetual look of a startled deer, stood trembling in Tom Mitchell's doorway. "Tom? We have a problem. A big one. With the Whitfield appeal."

Tom looked up from a mountain of paperwork, his patience worn to a thread. "What kind of problem, Kevin?"

"I just got an email from opposing counsel," Kevin stammered, holding out a printed sheet as if it were radioactive. "They're filing a motion to dismiss the appeal. For failure to timely file."

The words didn't register at first. Tom snatched the paper, his eyes scanning the legalese until they landed on the date. "That's impossible. The deadline isn't for another two weeks."

"It was last Tuesday, Tom." Kevin's voice was barely a whisper. "It was last week."

Tom shoved past him and stormed down the hall to Jacob's office, which had become a dusty archive of pending disaster. He heaved the top stack of Whitfield binders onto the desk, his hands tearing through files until he found the appellate court's scheduling order. He stared at the date, circled in red by Jacob's own hand months ago. Last Tuesday. Kevin was right. A cold, sickening dread washed over him, the kind that preceded catastrophe.

He stalked back to his own office and dialed the court clerk. "Cheryl, it's Tom Mitchell. I'm fine, thanks. Listen, I have an insane question on the Whitfield case, 22-CH-845. I know it's a statutory deadline, but there must be some kind of exception for cause? Excusable neglect?" He listened, his knuckles turning white as he gripped the receiver. "No, I understand. It's absolute. Right. Thank you, Cheryl."

He hung up the phone and turned slowly to face Kevin, who had followed him like a man on his way to his own execution. Tom's voice was dangerously quiet. "Tell me what happened."

"I thought I calendared it," Kevin stammered, shrinking under Tom's gaze. "Jacob's notes were all here, but I was handling three of his other major clients, and the Henderson discovery was a nightmare, and I just missed it."

Tom stared at the young man, the excuses, the panic, the sheer incompetence. This was what was left of their firm. A skeleton crew overworked and cracking under the strain. He felt a surge of white-hot fury, but it was followed by a wave of profound, soul-crushing weariness.

"Get out," he said, the words flat and dead. "Just get out of my office."

When he was alone, Tom sank into his chair and stared at the wall. Forty-seven million dollars. That was the number on the Whitfield development. A malpractice suit of that magnitude wouldn't just bankrupt the firm; it would bankrupt him and Jacob personally. They'd lose everything. The firm. Their houses. Their savings. His kids' college funds. Everything they had built over thirty years, gone. Erased. Because of a missed deadline. Because Jacob was off chasing ghosts.

The anger was gone, replaced by a grim, cold resolve. He had tried calling. He had tried waiting. He had tried holding it all together. Now, there was only one move left.

He turned to his computer, the screen glowing in the dim office. He opened a browser, the familiar logo of an airline filling the screen. He pulled the sparse, weeks-old itinerary Jacob had left with Margaret from his desk drawer. His next stop was Istanbul.

With steady, deliberate clicks, Tom Mitchell typed the letters into the text fields.

From: ORD. To: ISTANBUL

His finger hovered over the mouse for a single, heavy heartbeat. He clicked. The screen filled with red-eye flights and last-minute fares, a digital bridge to the man who had to be brought home.

He sent a text message to Jacob: "I have your schedule. I will meet you at the Istanbul airport. Must talk, don't disappoint me again."

***

That night in his hotel room, Jacob wrote:

Rome. I went down into the earth today, through layers of history and faith. I thought I was looking for the origin of Christianity, but I think I was just looking for an honest man. And I found one.

Thomas lost his son. He nearly destroyed himself searching for answers, just as I'm doing now. He warned me not to let finding Jessica cost me the life she'd want me to have. But then he said something that cut deeper: every grieving parent tells themselves the same story about love continuing, regardless of their faith. Maybe we're all right. Maybe we're all wrong. But we're all saying the same thing because we're all human.

My phone has seventeen missed calls from Tom. I can't bring myself to listen to the voicemails. I know the firm is struggling without me, I know I'm abandoning people who depend on me, and it aches more than I ever could have imagined. But I can't get drowned with business when I'm still searching for the truth about Jessica. Tom wouldn't understand. He's never lost a child. How can I explain that everything else feels meaningless until I know where she is?

Tom will meet me at Istanbul Airport. He must speak to me. I must meet with him; I owe it to him.

Thomas showed me the layers beneath Rome; church built on church built on temple. He called them layers of interpretation. Maybe that's all religion is. His honesty felt like the first solid ground I've stood on in months, but it also terrified me. If he's right about religious universality, what will I find in Istanbul and Jerusalem?

Is that it? Is all I'll discover just variations on the same human story about love transcending death? It isn't the answer I came for, but Thomas's warning echoes in my head: I'm not searching for Jessica anymore, I'm running from the possibility that this life might be all there is.

Tomorrow: Florence. Tom. Bulgaria. Istanbul. Then Jerusalem. I must finish this, even if every tradition tells me the same thing. Even if Tom never forgives me for choosing Jessica over everything we built together.

He closed the journal and looked out over Rome's skyline, domes and ruins rising like riddles against the dark. His phone buzzed again, Tom calling. Jacob turned it face down. Tears forming, he watched the Roman sunset burn the sky in gold and crimson, beautiful, undeniable, but born of particles and atmosphere, or divine intention.

***

Florence greeted him by train the next morning, the Tuscan countryside giving way to terracotta rooftops and church spires that pierced the sky like ancient prayers. After the ancient, heavy stones of Rome, the city felt like a Renaissance painting sprung to life. Brunelleschi's dome swelled above the medieval streets, its engineering marvel rising from faith and human ambition in equal measure. The Arno curved through the city's heart, its bridges arcing like stone promises that some things could span any divide.

Jacob walked from the station through streets where every corner revealed another masterpiece born from Christian devotion. Giotto's campanile reached toward heaven with mathematical precision. The Basilica of Santa Croce displayed frescoes that had taught theology to the illiterate for centuries. Yet this was also the city where Savonarola had burned books and art in his "bonfire of the vanities," where religious fervor had turned destructive in the name of purity.

The beauty was a sharp, almost painful contrast to his internal turmoil. How could the same faith that inspired this soaring architecture also produce the theological chaos Thomas had described? How could one tradition create both Michelangelo's Pietà and the Inquisition's pyres?

Jacob spent the day wandering Florence's piazzas and galleries, allowing himself to appreciate human creativity without interrogating its divine inspiration.

That night he reviewed the note from Cardinal Rossi who had arranged the meeting with Professor Elena Marchetti before Jacob left Rome. "If you must pursue this path of questioning," Rossi had said with resigned understanding, "Elena can show you where Protestant fragmentation leads. She studies the Reformation's consequences with unflinching honesty."

***

The next morning, Jacob made his way to the University of Florence through Renaissance streets that embodied Christianity's contradictions. Professor Marchetti's office occupied a converted palazzo, its frescoed ceilings now witnessing academic debates rather than noble gatherings.

His appointment with Elena Marchetti was at 8:00 am, before her first class began. She was younger than Jacob had expected, perhaps late thirties, with the kind of restless intelligence that made her seem to be listening to something beyond their conversation.

"Mr. Hinsen." She didn't rise from behind her desk, which was covered with open books, their spines broken from years of consultation. "You're the American lawyer asking uncomfortable questions about certainty."

Jacob settled into the chair across from her, noting how she studied him, not with the pastoral concern he'd encountered from priests, but with the cool assessment of someone accustomed to dismantling illusions. "I'm trying to determine if God exists and whether my daughter survived death. Christianity offers contradictory answers to both questions, not just about afterlife, but about God's very nature and how to know Him."

"Christianity?" Marchetti's laugh was sharp. "There is no such thing. There are thirty thousand Christian entities, each claiming exclusive access to divine truth." She pulled a slim volume from the chaos of her desk. "Martin Luther destroyed unified Christianity in 1517, though he never intended to."

Jacob's pen hovered over his notebook. "How does one man destroy fifteen centuries of religious authority?"

"With a simple idea that proved catastrophic: let every believer interpret Scripture for themselves." She opened the book to a woodcut of Luther nailing his theses to the church door. "No more papal infallibility. No more institutional authority. Just individuals with Bibles, convinced they could hear God's voice more clearly than the Church."

"That sounds democratic, not catastrophic."

Marchetti's eyes glinted with something between amusement and pity. "Democratic, yes. And chaos." She moved to a wall chart showing denominational branches spreading like cracks through glass. "Within fifty years of Luther's revolt, Protestant Christianity had shattered into competing fragments. Today, Baptists disagree with Presbyterians about infant baptism. Lutherans and Reformed churches contradict each other on communion. Pentecostals and Methodists reach opposite conclusions about spiritual gifts."

Jacob studied the chart, his lawyer's mind tracking the logical implications. "But surely they agree on fundamental doctrines: salvation, heaven, hell?"

"Do they?" Marchetti returned to her desk and opened a well-worn Bible. "Your daughter Jessica, if she died as a Baptist, she's in heaven now, conscious and blessed. If Seventh-day Adventists are correct, she's unconscious, sleeping until Christ's return. If Universalists speak truth, her salvation was guaranteed regardless of belief. If Calvinists are right, her eternal fate was decided before creation."

The contradictions hit Jacob like bodily blows. "They can't all be right."

"Yet they all claim biblical authority for their positions." Marchetti's finger traced verses highlighted in distinct colors. "Each denomination insists Scripture clearly supports their interpretation. The problem is, Scripture apparently 'clearly teaches' contradictory things to sincere readers."

Jacob sensed his certainty cracking. "But there must be proper interpretive methods, scholarly consensus."

"Five hundred years of Protestant scholarship have produced more division, not less." Marchetti's voice carried the weariness of someone who'd spent decades watching intelligent people reach opposite conclusions from identical evidence. "Consider Jesus's teachings. 'Turn the other cheek,' he said. Mennonites built their entire faith on nonviolence. But He also said, 'If you don't have a sword, sell your cloak and buy one.' Christian militarists use that to justify warfare."

"Those statements have different contexts," Jacob protested. "Any competent interpreter could reconcile them."

"Could they? Then why haven't they?" Marchetti gestured toward her bookshelves, thick with commentaries and theological treatises. "Every generation of Protestant scholars believes they'll finally resolve Scripture's apparent contradictions. Instead, they create new denominations."

Jacob scribbled notes furiously, his neat legal handwriting deteriorating as the implications mounted. "So, when pastors tell me with absolute certainty that Jessica is in heaven, they're speculating based on texts that have produced thousands of contradictory interpretations?"

"They're offering their denomination's particular reading of ambiguous material, then claiming divine authority for human interpretation." Marchetti closed the Bible with finality. "Luther's revolution didn't clarify Christian truth. It revealed that religious certainty might be a human invention."

The silence stretched between them, broken only by the distant sound of Vespa engines on the street below. Jacob stared at his notes, pages of contradictory Protestant positions that made his head spin.

"What do you believe?" he asked finally. "About Jessica, about the afterlife, about whether any of this searching matters?"

Marchetti was quiet for a moment, her scholarly composure giving way to something more personal. "I believe your love for her is the most real thing in this room. I believe that love has driven you across continents, changed you, forced you to question everything you thought you knew." She paused. "Do I believe she exists somewhere beyond death? I have no idea. But I know that living as if love transcends mortality creates better human beings than living as if it doesn't."

Jacob felt the familiar disappointment rise. "So, you're giving me the same non-answer as everyone else."

"Perhaps because it's the only honest answer." Marchetti's voice was gentle but unyielding. "The Reformation taught us that ultimate questions might exceed human capacity for certainty. That doesn't make the questions meaningless. It makes our response to uncertainty the measure of our character."

After another hour of conversation, Jacob closed his notebook and stood, feeling the weight of another tradition that promised much and delivered mystery. Through the window, the Tuscan light was fading, and somewhere in the gathering dusk, church bells began their evening call, the same bells that had been ringing for centuries, calling the faithful to worship, though no one could agree what they were worshipping or why.

The search would continue, but the pattern was becoming painfully clear: every tradition offered hope dressed as knowledge, certainty that dissolved under examination, love disguised as cosmic guarantee. Perhaps that was the answer that there was no answer, only the choice to love anyway.

He left her office with the Duomo's dome looming over him, its vastness feeling less like a symbol of faith and more like a magnificent question mark. Thirty thousand denominations. The foundations of Christianity felt like shifting sand.

***

Overwhelmed with contrary opinions, he stopped at a trattoria tucked between two shuttered shops. It was an appropriate refuge from Florence's tourist crowds. It was a small, quiet place where he could nurse a glass of wine and process the day's theological wreckage without interruption. Professor Marchetti's words still echoed: thirty thousand Christian denominations, each claiming biblical authority for contradictory truths about Jessica's fate.

He was studying his notes when a familiar laugh cut through the ambient chatter. His head snapped up, and there she was, Abby Pearson, sliding gracefully between tables toward the bar, her auburn hair catching the lamplight exactly as it had twenty-five years ago.

The recognition hit him, transporting him instantly to the University of Chicago Law Library, third floor, northwest corner where she'd always claimed the best study spot. Abby at twenty-four, brilliant and relentless, the only student who'd consistently outargued him in Constitutional Law. While other classmates formed study groups based on social compatibility, Abby had sought him out because, as she'd put it, "You're the only one here who won't let me win just because I'm pretty."

She'd been right about that. Their study sessions had been intellectual warfare, trade law, criminal procedure, civil rights cases dissected with surgical precision. She'd challenged every assumption, questioned every precedent, refused to accept "because the professor said so" as adequate reasoning. Where Brenda had been smooth ambition wrapped in calculated charm, Abby had been raw intelligence that couldn't be bothered with pretense.

He remembered the night before their Torts final, both of them bleary-eyed and caffeinated, when she'd suddenly looked up from her casebook and said, "You know what's fascinating about negligence law? It assumes people should care about strangers' wellbeing. That's either the most optimistic or most naive foundation for a legal system I've ever encountered."

That was Abby, finding philosophical implications in parking violations, moral questions in contract disputes. She'd graduated summa cum laude and disappeared into international law, their paths diverging like cases from different jurisdictions.

Now here she was in a Florentine trattoria, twenty-five years later, ordering wine in what sounded like fluent Italian.

"Abby?"

She turned, her face cycling through surprise, recognition, and something deeper, the kind of immediate understanding that comes from shared history. She approached his table with the same confident stride he remembered, though her eyes carried shadows that hadn't been there in law school.

"Jacob Hinsen." She settled into the chair across from him without waiting for an invitation. "I was wondering when our paths would cross again."

"You were expecting this?"

Her smile was gentle but knowing. "I heard through the alumni network about Jessica. I'm so sorry, Jacob." The direct acknowledgment of his loss, delivered without platitudes or awkward fumbling, felt like mercy. Most people either avoided mentioning Jessica entirely or offered meaningless comfort about God's plans. Abby's straightforward sympathy cut through all that noise.

"Thank you," he managed. "It's why I'm here, actually. Trying to understand what happens when we die, whether there's any chance I'll see her again."

Abby gestured toward his notebook, pages dense with theological arguments and contradictory claims. "And you plan to cross-examine the universe for definitive answers?"

"Something like that. Though the universe isn't cooperating with discovery requests."

She laughed, the same sharp, intelligent sound that had once echoed through study rooms. "You always did think logic could solve everything. Remember Professor Reynolds' class? You spent an entire semester trying to prove that legal precedent alone could resolve any constitutional question."

"And you spent that semester proving me wrong."

"Because precedent is just collective human judgment accumulated over time. It's not objective truth, it's institutionalized opinion." Her eyes sparkled with the old argumentative fire. "Which brings me to religion, Jacob. Have you considered that faith traditions might be the same thing, accumulated human responses to questions that don't have empirical answers?"

Jacob felt his prosecutorial instincts engage. "You're saying religions are just collective guesswork?"

"I'm saying they're human constructions. Sophisticated, meaningful, but still invented." She leaned forward, voice dropping to the conspiratorial tone he remembered from their most intense debates. "Take Mormonism. Perfect case study in religious invention."

"The Mormons?"

"Joseph Smith. Farm boy in 1820s New York claims God appeared to him personally, told him all existing churches had been corrupted. Then an angel leads him to golden plates buried in a hillside, ancient American scripture that would restore true Christianity."

Jacob's analytical mind sharpened. "What happened to these plates?"

"Returned to the angel Moroni after Smith translated them. No independent verification, no archaeological evidence, no way to test their authenticity. Smith claimed he translated them using special stones while hidden behind a curtain. Even his scribes never saw the actual plates."

"So, the entire Mormon faith rests on one man's unverifiable claim?"

"Gets more interesting. The Book of Mormon describes vast civilizations in ancient America, millions of people, epic battles, advanced technologies. But archaeological evidence for these civilizations? Nonexistent. DNA studies of Native Americans? They contradict Mormon claims about Hebrew ancestry."

Jacob scribbled notes, his lawyer's training cataloguing the evidentiary problems. "Yet millions of people believe it absolutely."

"Because it offers something irresistible: eternal families." Abby's voice grew more serious, carrying personal weight Jacob hadn't expected. "Mormon doctrine teaches that marriage and family relationships can be 'sealed' for eternity. Parents will be reunited with their children forever, not just until death do us part."

The promise hit Jacob like oxygen to a drowning man. "Eternal reunion?"

"More than that. Faithful Mormons believe they can become gods themselves, literally divine beings ruling their own planets, creating spirit children, governing universes." Abby watched his reaction carefully. "According to Mormon theology, Jessica wouldn't just be waiting for you in heaven. She could eventually become a goddess with cosmic power over her own realm of existence."

The implications were staggering. Jessica not just surviving death but ascending to divinity itself. "And you believe this?"

Abby was quiet for a long moment, her fingers tracing the rim of her wine glass. "I converted two years ago, Jacob. After David died."

"Your brother?"

"Pancreatic cancer. Twenty-two months of watching him disappear piece by piece." Her voice carried controlled grief that resonated with his own. "I couldn't bear the thought that our relationship simply ended when his heart stopped. Mormon theology promised we'd be together forever if I lived faithfully enough."

Jacob leaned back, processing this revelation. "So, you chose to believe in golden plates that can't be verified because the alternative was losing David forever?"

"I chose to live as if love transcends mortality because the alternative felt like dying while still breathing." Abby met his gaze directly. "Maybe Joseph Smith invented the whole thing. Maybe he was a brilliant storyteller who created elaborate mythology because nineteenth-century America was hungry for new revelations. But if living according to that invented religion gives me a framework for hope, does its historical accuracy matter?"

The question hung between them like incense in a cathedral, beautiful, intoxicating, ultimately insubstantial. Jacob stared at his notebook, pages filled with contradictory promises from different traditions. The Council of Nicaea voting on Christ's divinity. Protestant denominations reaching opposite conclusions from identical scriptures. And now golden plates that conveniently disappeared before anyone could examine them.

"My daughter's eternal fate might depend on a fourth-century political meeting, a farm boy's unverifiable vision, or theological speculation by men who never met her," Jacob said quietly. "How do I choose between competing claims when they all require faith in unprovable events?"

Abby reached across the table, her hand briefly covering his. "Maybe the choice isn't between religious traditions, Jacob. Maybe it's between living as if love matters eternally or living as if it doesn't."

She glanced at her watch and sighed with genuine regret. "I would love to stay and talk more, Jacob. It's been too long. But I have a flight back to the States in three hours and I still need to pack." She gathered her things, then paused, her hand resting briefly on the table between them. "You're searching for Jessica in other people's promises about eternity. But she's already proven love survives death. Look what it's done to you, abandoned everything familiar, traveled across continents, questioned everything you thought you knew. If that's not love transcending mortality, what is?"

She embraced as old friends. "Take care of yourself, Jacob. And if you're ever back in Chicago, call me. I mean it."

Jacob watched her disappear into Florence's medieval streets, carrying her own impossible grief and chosen hope. The trattoria's candles flickered in the gathering darkness, and somewhere in the distance, church bells began their evening call, the same bells that had rung for centuries, calling the faithful to worship though no one could agree what they were worshipping or why.

His notebook lay open before him, filled with contradictory certainties from traditions that couldn't all be true. Yet each offered reunion with the dead, meaning beyond mortality, love that transcended physical existence. Perhaps that consistency itself was significant, not because it pointed to objective truth, but because it revealed something essential about human nature.

The search would continue, but Abby had given him a new lens through which to view it. The question wasn't which religious story was factually accurate. The question was whether he could live meaningfully while acknowledging that all religious stories might be human inventions designed to make mortality bearable.

Jessica's fate remained unknowable. But the choice of how to honor her memory while navigating that uncertainty, that choice was entirely his own.

***

Jacob wandered through Florence at sundown, his mind a battle-field of competing ideas. Marchetti's thirty thousand denominations, Abby's golden plates, all pointed to a faith that was human made, a series of stories built to hold back the dark. The weight of it all left him feeling hollowed out, intellectually armed but spiritually empty.

He was turning down a narrow side street when he heard it, not the soaring notes of an opera or a cathedral choir, but the simple, steady rhythm of a guitar and a handful of voices singing in English. The song was as familiar and worn as an old coat: *"Amazing grace, how sweet the sound..."*

Curiosity, or exhaustion, slowed his steps. He followed the sound to its source: a former storefront, its glass door propped open, a plain wooden cross nailed above the frame. There was no grandeur, no history. Just voices singing as if they meant every word.

He stepped inside. A dozen folding chairs filled the small, bare room. At the front stood a man in his sixties, a worn Bible in one hand, his voice roughened by years of shouting over the noise of the world. His shirt sleeves were rolled, his tie slightly askew, but his eyes burned with a conviction that was anything but tired.

When the hymn ended, he spoke. His name was Pastor Ernie Williams.

"I shouldn't be here," he said, his voice filling the small space. "Not alive, not sober, not in my right mind. I was a dead man for twenty years. I lost my wife, my kids, my business, everything I thought made me a man. I drank my life into a hole in the ground. But one night, at the bottom of that hole, Jesus found me. He didn't give me a lecture. He gave me a hand. He gave me Himself. That's why I stand here breathing."

The room fell into contemplative quiet, broken only by occasional murmured "hallelujahs" from those moved beyond speech. It was the kind of silence born from people listening with their whole selves. Ernie's gaze found Jacob lingering near the back. He walked down the short aisle, not with the showmanship of a performer, but with the quiet gravity of a man who had carried his own coffin and set it down.

"You look like someone carrying a weight, friend."

Jacob's throat tightened. He hadn't intended to speak, but the man's directness left no room for evasion. "My daughter. Nine years old. A car accident."

Ernie closed his eyes for a moment, as if the words themselves required reverence. He didn't offer a platitude. He didn't say she was in a better place. He just nodded slowly. "I can't bring her back," he said. "I can't tell you why it happened. But I can tell you this: Jesus has a place prepared, and if you trust Him, you'll see her again. That's not a doctrine to argue. That's a promise to hold."

The lawyer in Jacob, the skeptic, the prosecutor, rose up. "But how do you *know*?" he pressed, his voice sharper and challenging than he intended. "How do you distinguish faith from the simple need to believe something, anything, to survive?"

Ernie didn't flinch. He placed a hand over his own chest, over the heart that had been restarted. "Because I was dead inside," he said, his voice dropping but losing none of its power. "And now I live. That's all the proof I got. But it's enough."

Jacob had no counterargument. He could not cross-examine the resurrection that had taken place not in a tomb, but in a man's own soul.

He stepped back out into the Florentine night, the echo of the hymn following him. For the first time since Jessica's death, a new, unsettling thought took root: maybe resurrection wasn't only about eternity. It was about whether the broken could live again, right here, right now.

That night, after the Waldensian service invitation arrived, Jacob sat in his hotel room and wrote:

Florence. Three encounters today, each offering a different version of the same impossible promise.

Professor Marchetti showed me how the Reformation shattered Christianity into thirty thousand competing interpretations. No central authority, no way to determine which reading of Scripture is correct. Luther thought he was clarifying the truth. Instead, he guaranteed theological chaos.

Ernie's testimony at that church. He wasn't promising heaven or resurrection after death. He was singing about being raised from despair, about love giving broken people permission to live again. For the first time in months, I felt something besides grief, not hope exactly, but maybe the possibility of it. Maybe resurrection isn't about Jessica's fate. It's about mine.

Abby at the café this morning. She converted to Mormonism after her brother died, now believes in golden plates no one can examine and families sealed for eternity. Another tradition, another unprovable claim, another promise of reunion based on faith alone.

The pattern is unmistakable: Catholics vote on divinity in 325 AD. Protestants fracture into infinite interpretations. Mormons add new scripture from buried plates. Every tradition offers reunion. Every tradition demands belief without verification.

The more I investigate, the harder it becomes to believe scripture survived four millennia unchanged when human fingerprints are visible everywhere; councils voting on doctrines, scribes making copies of copies, translators choosing between competing meanings, church authorities deciding which books counted as sacred and which didn't. Every tradition claims perfect preservation while the historical evidence screams human influence at every step.

But Ernie showed me something different, people who let love resurrect them from the living death of grief, regardless of whether cosmic reunion is guaranteed. And Abby asked a question I can't shake. The issue isn't which story is factually true, but which story helps me live most fully while I'm here.

I still don't know if Jessica exists anywhere. But I'm starting to wonder if that is even the right question anymore.

Tomorrow: Waldensian service. More Protestant theology. More promises I can't verify.

***

First thing the next day, Jacob glanced at his phone at the hotel breakfast table. He reviewed the email: a formal invitation to attend Sunday afternoon service at the Waldensian church in Florence. The wording was polite, almost academic, but Jacob sensed eagerness beneath it, even challenge.

Jacob spent the morning wandering Florence's Renaissance streets, his conversation with Professor Marchetti echoing through every cathedral bell and church facade. Her words about Protestant fragmentation had left him unsettled. Thirty thousand denominations, each claiming biblical authority for contradictory truths. By noon, curiosity overcame his reluctance. If Christianity had truly shattered into competing fragments, witnessing one of those fragments in action would illuminate something Professor Marchetti's academic analysis couldn't capture.

That afternoon, Jacob entered the Waldensian church through heavy wooden doors that opened onto centuries of quiet resistance. The space was deliberately stripped of grandeur, its whitewashed walls bearing no frescoes or golden icons. Simple wooden pews, worn smooth by generations of worshippers, faced a plain altar that seemed almost austere after Rome's marble magnificence. Tall arched windows admitted pale Tuscan light without the filter of stained glass, casting everything in honest, unadorned illumination

A single wooden cross hung at the front, dark against the white wall, stark and unwavering in its simplicity. No crucifix with suffering Christ, no elaborate metalwork, or precious stones. Just two intersecting beams that spoke of sacrifice without ornamentation. The floor was worn stone, polished by countless footsteps of believers who had chosen faith over comfort, truth over beauty.

The air itself felt different here. Where St. Peter's Basilica had been overwhelmed with golden excess and architectural ambition, this space invited contemplation through restraint. Every element seemed chosen to direct attention inward rather than upward, toward personal conviction rather than institutional authority. It was completely opposite of the opulence in Catholic churches, yet somehow no less sacred for its simplicity.

Pastor Roberto Simone greeted him with a firm handshake and eyes that carried the weight of inherited memory. The Waldensian church felt different from other Protestant spaces Jacob had visited, older somehow, as if the stones themselves remembered centuries of hidden worship.

"Welcome, Mr. Hinsen. Professor Marchetti told me about your search." Simone's voice carried a slight accent; Italian inflected with the mountain dialects of the Piedmont valleys. "She thought you might find our perspective... illuminating."

Jacob settled into a worn pew as Simone sat beside him, not behind a pulpit but as equals in conversation. "What makes your perspective different?"

"We never left," Simone said simply. "While other Protestant denominations formed during the Reformation, we've been here since the twelfth century. Peter Waldo began preaching the Gospel in Lyon in 1170, three and a half centuries before Luther posted his theses."

Jacob leaned forward, intrigued. "You predate the Reformation?"

"We are the Reformation. Or rather, we are what the Reformation rediscovered." Simone stood and moved to a simple wooden cabinet, withdrawing an ancient-looking manuscript. "For eight hundred years, we preserved biblical truth while the Catholic Church accumulated power and wealth. We were translating scripture into common languages when Rome forbade it. We were preaching salvation by grace when Rome sold indulgences."

The manuscript was carefully protected in glass, its pages yellowed with age. "This is a fourteenth-century copy of the Scriptures in Occitan, our mountain language. My ancestors died to preserve this book."

"Died how?"

Simone's expression grew somber. "Pope Innocent VIII issued a bull against us in 1487, authorizing violence against Christians in Alpine valleys who dared read the Bible in their own language. Over the next two centuries, thousands were slaughtered for the crime of biblical literacy. The worst came in 1655, when entire Waldensian villages in the Piedmont valleys were massacred in what became known as the Piedmont Easter. Thousands, Mr. Hinsen, were slaughtered for the crime of biblical literacy."

Jacob studied the manuscript, thinking of Professor Marchetti's words about human politics shaping religious truth. "So, the Catholic Church killed people for reading the Bible?"

"For reading it without priestly interpretation. For insisting that salvation comes through Christ alone, not through sacraments administered by an institution. For believing that any Christian could understand God's word, not just ordained clergy." Simone's voice carried quiet intensity. "We hid in mountain caves during winter, worshipping in secret, preserving biblical truth while armies hunted us like animals."

"But couldn't you just be wrong? Couldn't the Catholic Church have legitimate reasons for requiring trained interpretation of Scripture?"

Simone smiled sadly. "That's what they said as they burned our villages. 'Submit to proper authority. Trust institutional wisdom. Don't think you can understand divine mysteries without our guidance.'" He paused, looking at Jacob directly. "Does that sound familiar to your quest, Mr. Hinsen? Have you been told you lack authority to question, lack training to understand, lack humility to accept?"

The parallel hit harder than Jacob expected. His months of demanding proof had indeed been met with calls for submission, trust, acceptance of mystery beyond human comprehension.

"But even you can't prove your interpretation is correct," Jacob pressed. "Catholics could say the same thing, that you're the ones who misunderstood Scripture."

"Perhaps. But here's what eight centuries of persecution taught us: when institutional power aligns with religious authority, ordinary people suffer. When churches accumulate wealth and political influ-ence, the Gospel gets lost in human ambition." Simone returned the manuscript to its case with reverent care. "We stayed poor, stayed hid-den, stayed focused on Scripture alone because we saw what happened when Christianity became a business empire."

Jacob felt something changing in his understanding. "You're saying the issue isn't which interpretation is correct, but what happens when any interpretation gains too much power?"

"Exactly. Whether Catholic or Protestant, Orthodox or Evangeli-cal, when religious leaders claim exclusive access to divine truth and demand unquestioning obedience, the result is spiritual tyranny." Si-mone sat back down, his voice growing gentler. "Your daughter died, and you want someone to guarantee she's safe. But Mr. Hinsen, the moment anyone claims such authority, the moment they insist they alone can verify her eternal fate, you should remember our mountain caves and ask yourself what they're really selling."

"Then what do you believe about Jessica? About eternal life?"

Simone was quiet, staring at the simple wooden cross. "I believe the biblical promise that those who trust in Christ will not perish. I believe your daughter is safe in God's love. But I also believe that if you demand I prove this before you'll trust it, I become like the priests who claimed exclusive access to divine truth. The moment I insist you must accept my interpretation without question, I repeat the spiritual tyranny my ancestors died to resist."

Jacob sat in the silence of the sanctuary, feeling the weight of cen-turies of hidden worship, of people who'd chosen conscience over comfort, truth over safety, biblical faith over institutional authority. "So, what am I supposed to do with my doubt?"

"Talk to God directly. Read Scripture yourself. Pray honestly. Trust that the same Spirit who guided mountain peasants to preserve biblical truth can guide a grieving father to find peace." Simone's voice carried deep compassion. "But don't let anyone, Catholic, Protestant, or otherwise, convince you that spiritual truth requires surrendering your mind or conscience to their authority."

As Jacob left the small church, he carried something he hadn't expected: not certainty about Jessica's fate, but respect for those who'd chosen integrity over authority, who'd preserved the right to question even when questioning cost, them everything. The Waldensians hadn't provided proof of eternal life, but they'd demonstrated something equally valuable; that authentic faith could survive without institutional guarantee, that truth was worth preserving even when power opposed it.

***

Jacob's journey to Sofia required three days and multiple connections along one of Europe's most grueling rail routes. He'd considered flying; a simple four-hour flight would have delivered him directly to Bulgarian soil. But something about the overland journey appealed to him after his months of theological investigation. Flying felt like skipping chapters in a book he was trying to understand.

The train would carry him gradually from Western Catholicism through the religious crossroads of Central Europe to Orthodox Christianity's heartland, letting him watch the spiritual geography shift with the physical landscape.

Florence to Milan on the high-speed Frecciarossa, then the ÖBB Night jet sleeper through Alpine valleys to Vienna. From Vienna, Hungarian Railways carried him to Budapest across the vast Pannonian Plain, then the aging overnight train crawled south through Serbia to Belgrade.

During the long journey through Central Europe, Jacob had struck up conversations with fellow travelers, a Hungarian businessman who dismissed all religion as "medieval superstition," an Austrian grandmother who clutched her rosary and insisted "faith needs no proof," a Romanian student who shrugged and said "maybe there's something, maybe not, who can know?" Each conversation had ended the same way: believe without proof, don't believe at all, or remain forever uncertain. No one offered the verification Jacob desperately sought.

It was on the Belgrade-Sofia train, as the aging carriage crawled through Serbian countryside toward the Bulgarian border, that Jacob encountered Arnold.

The philosophy professor had boarded in Belgrade, settling into the threadbare compartment with the resigned patience of someone familiar with Balkan rail travel. His weathered face and careful movements suggested a man in his late sixties who had learned to travel light. A dog-eared copy of Camus rested on his knee.

The worn copy of Camus caught Jacob's attention. He'd read "The Stranger" in college, wrestling with existential questions that felt theoretical then. Now, searching for Jessica across Europe, Camus's absurdism felt less like philosophy and more like prophecy.

"American?" Arnold asked in accented English, noting Jacob's obvious discomfort with the decrepit train car.

"Yes. Jacob Hinsen." Jacob extended his hand reluctantly, knowing where this conversation would be going.

"Arnold Kellner. Serbian, though I taught philosophy in Belgrade for forty years." Arnold's grip was firm. "What brings you to this particular corner of misery?"

"I'm traveling to Orthodox countries. Investigating religious claims about God's existence and life after death."

Arnold's eyebrows rose slightly. "Ah. Personal loss?"

"My daughter. Nine years old." Jacob's voice was flat, defensive.

"My sincere condolences, Jacob. But you think Orthodox priests will have answers Western Christianity couldn't provide?"

"I'm being thorough."

Arnold nodded slowly. "And what have you discovered so far?"

"Competing claims about God's existence and whether my daughter's soul survived death. Christians promise both, God through Christ, reunion through faith. Everyone offers promises, no one provides proof of either."

"Because neither exists. There is no God, and consciousness is brain activity that ceases at death. Your search for divine reality and your daughter's survival is both quests for comfort, not truth." Arnold assuredly replied.

Jacob anticipated what Arnold would say. "You can't know that definitively."

"I can know it with the same confidence I know this train won't sprout wings. Some propositions are so well-supported that claiming uncertainty becomes intellectual dishonesty."

The train lurched through a curve. Outside, Serbian farmland stretched endlessly under gray skies. "What about near-death experiences? People report seeing deceased relatives, divine light."

Arnold sighed with practiced weariness. "Oxygen deprivation produces predictable hallucinations. Dying brains release DMT. What people report matches what we'd expect from neural chemistry, not divine contact or afterlife."

"But some report accurate information they couldn't have known..."

"Selective reporting and confirmation bias." Arnold pulled out a worn notebook. "I've studied this literature for decades, Jacob. The claims of God and afterlife dissolve under scrutiny."

Jacob stood abruptly, pacing as the train swayed. "So, my daughter Jessica asked me if heaven was real before she died, and I lied to her? Nine years of love, curiosity, joy, and it all just vanishes?"

"You gave her comfort when she needed it most. That was love." Arnold's voice softened. "But when her brain died, Jessica ceased to exist. What remains is her impact on you, the changes she created in everyone who knew her."

"That's not enough!" Jacob's voice cracked. "She was so alive, so real. That can't just disappear into nothing!"

"Why must it be more? Why isn't love itself sufficient?" Arnold studied Jacob with practiced patience. "Evolution gave us brains that contemplate mortality but can't accept it emotionally. That's why humans create gods and afterlives, not because they exist, but because we psychologically require them."

Jacob slumped in his seat. "So, existence is meaningless? We love, suffer, die, and none of it matters ultimately?"

"According to whom? Who decreed life requires eternal significance to have meaning?" Arnold pulled out a photograph, a woman with kind eyes, intelligent smile. "My wife Jelena died three years ago. Cancer. I prayed to a God I didn't believe in and begged for her survival. When she died, I desperately wanted to believe we'd reunite."

Jacob saw genuine grief in how Arnold handled the photograph.

"But I can't believe something because I want it to be true. Jelena's consciousness ended when her brain died. That doesn't diminish what we shared. If anything, death makes every moment precious beyond measure."

Jacob tried finally. "If you're wrong about God's existence, the consequences could be eternal."

Arnold laughed without malice. "Which God should, I fear? The Christian deity who might damn me for intellectual honesty? Allah who might punish rejection of Muhammad? Hindu deities offended by my diet? I can't live in terror of every possible divine authority humanity has imagined."

"But what if Jesus really did rise from the dead?"

"Then extraordinary claims require extraordinary evidence. The resurrection accounts were written decades later by non-eyewitnesses. They contradict each other on crucial details." Arnold's voice carried the weight of decades examining these claims. "I've studied the historical evidence with scholarly rigor. It doesn't support the conclusion millions base their lives upon."

The train began slowing as it approached the Bulgarian border. Arnold gathered his few belongings. "Jacob, tomorrow you'll meet Orthodox priests who may promise Jessica waits in paradise with the same certainty I promise she doesn't. Their sincerity will equal mine; their compassion will match mine."

He paused at the compartment door. "The question isn't who's more persuasive. The question is whether you can live meaningfully while acknowledging that ultimate truth about God and afterlife might be unknowable."

Jacob looked up at this man who had systematically dismantled every hope he'd carried. "And you think I can? Live meaningfully while believing there's no God and she's just gone?"

"I think you already are. Your journey across Europe, your investigation of different traditions, your refusal to accept easy answers." Arnold shouldered his worn bag. "You're creating meaning through your choices, honoring Jessica's memory through your actions, living as if love matters even while unable to prove God exists or that it transcends death. That's not nothing, Jacob. That's everything."

Arnold stepped onto the platform at the border crossing, disappearing into the small crowd. Jacob continued alone toward Sofia, carrying hours of systematic atheistic argument that felt more honest than months of religious comfort.

The train pulled away toward Sofia, carrying Jacob deeper into Orthodox lands where faith had survived centuries of persecution, poverty, and foreign domination. But Arnold's final observation echoed in the rhythm of wheels on rails: perhaps he was already living meaningfully despite uncertainty, already honoring Jessica through choices that created significance whether or not the universe guaranteed eternal validation.

Through the night, as the train crossed into Bulgaria and Orthodox church domes appeared silver in moonlight, Jacob sat with the growing recognition that his search might not end with the proof he'd demanded, but with the courage to live fully while acknowledging that some questions might forever remain unanswered.

Outside, the Bulgarian countryside rolled past in darkness, carrying him toward his final theological encounters with a faith tradition that had endured everything history could inflict except, perhaps, the simple demand for verifiable evidence that life survived death.

***

The train wheezed into Sofia Central Station at 6:47 AM, three hours behind schedule. Jacob stepped onto the platform carrying the weight of Arnold's arguments along with his travel bag, breathing the crisp mountain air of a city ringed by snow-capped peaks. Sofia was different from Rome's ancient grandeur or Florence's Renaissance elegance, older somehow, more weathered, bearing the accumulated scars of Byzantine empires, Ottoman occupation, and communist rule.

The station itself told the story: a hodgepodge of architectural eras layered like geological strata. Ottoman-era stonework gave way to interwar Bulgarian construction, overlaid with Soviet-era concrete platforms, while newer EU-funded renovations attempted to modernize what centuries had complicated. Cyrillic script dominated the signs, reminding Jacob that he'd entered a world where even the alphabet spoke of different spiritual traditions."

He caught a taxi driven by a chain-smoking Bulgarian who spoke three words of English but understood "Hotel Bulgaria" well enough. The early morning ride through Sofia's streets revealed a city still awakening from its communist slumber. Stalinist apartment blocks stood shoulder-to-shoulder with Ottoman-era mosques, while golden-domed Orthodox churches rose like Byzantine promises amid the urban confusion.

The Hotel Bulgaria occupied a converted 19th-century mansion in the city center, its facade bearing the elegant decay common to Balkan capitals. The lobby retained traces of Ottoman elegance mixed with European influences, marble floors worn smooth, crystal chandeliers, oil paintings of Bulgarian merchants watching modern travelers.

Jacob's third-floor room overlooked Vitosha Boulevard, where morning vendors set up stalls selling Orthodox icons beside knock-off handbags. Through tall windows, the Vitosha Mountains rose beyond the city's southern edge, while Alexander Nevsky Cathedral's golden domes dominated the skyline, catching morning light like beacons.

The neighborhood pulsed with divergences, Italian espresso shops beside traditional taverns, businesspeople in suits hurrying past grandmothers who crossed themselves at every church. Jacob unpacked his single bag, months of travel having reduced his possessions to a few shirts, journals filled with unanswered questions, and Jessica's photograph.

Somewhere in this city, priests would offer the same promises he'd heard from Catholics and Protestants, wrapped in liturgies that pre-dated both traditions.

But Arnold's voice echoed in his memory, systematically disman-tling every hope he'd carried across Europe. "Consciousness is brain activity. When the brain ceases, consciousness, and therefore life ends." The words felt heavier here, surrounded by evidence of faith that had endured everything except, perhaps, the simple demand for scientific verification.

Jacob showered in the small bathroom, its Soviet-era fixtures pro-viding lukewarm water that nonetheless felt like baptism after the long train journey. As he dressed, he could hear church bells beginning their morning call across the city, the same bronze voices that had summoned believers through Byzantine glory, Ottoman darkness, and communist suppression.

"Today he would meet Orthodox priests who claimed to preserve Christianity's most ancient traditions, who insisted their church had maintained apostolic truth unchanged since Christ's apostles, unbro-ken and uncorrupted by Western innovations. Would they promise him a reunion with Jessica with the same certainty every other Chris-tian tradition had offered?"

But Jacob found himself wondering if the question he'd been ask-ing was wrong. The issue wasn't which tradition possessed truth, but whether truth itself was the kind of thing any tradition could possess. Perhaps Arnold was right that life ended with brain death, that love created meaning without requiring eternal validation, that living fully despite uncertainty was the only honest response to cosmic indifference.

Outside his window, Sofia's morning traffic began building toward the chaos that characterized Balkan cities where Byzantine patience met post-communist urgency. Jacob watched businesspeople hurry toward offices while women made their way slowly toward churches, each group carrying different assumptions about what mattered most in the brief span between birth and death.

He gathered his notebook and prepared to descend into Sofia's streets, ready for what might be his final investigation into Christianity's oldest promises about surviving the grave.

Whether those promises proved true or false, whether Jessica waited somewhere beyond death with God or had simply ceased when her heart stopped. Jacob was beginning to understand that his search had taught him something unexpected: how to honor love without requiring proof of its eternal significance.

***

St. Alexander Nevsky Cathedral pierced the gray sky. Jacob stood at the steps, feeling the weight of centuries. Inside, incense thickened the air. Chants in Church Slavonic reverberated through the stone, low and resonant, until they seemed to vibrate in his chest. Icons covered every wall, Christ Pantocrator, the Virgin Theotokos, saints painted with sorrow and mercy combined.

A priest emerged from the shadows near the iconostasis, his black cassock blending with the dimness before he stepped into a shaft of colored light. His beard was long and silver, his movements deliberate, as though he carried the weight of liturgy in his bones. He studied Jacob for a moment, the way a shepherd might assess a lost traveler.

"You are the American." It was not a question. His English was thickly accented but precise. "Father Dimitri Petrov. The monastery in Florence sent word you were coming, that you search for God in the face of unbearable loss. Come."

He led Jacob to a side chapel where icons gleamed in candlelight, away from the main sanctuary where the faithful came and went like tides. Here, the air was quieter, more intimate, a place for harder questions.

You have traveled far to ask your questions," Dimitri said in careful English. "What is it you seek here in Sofia that you have not already found?"

Jacob had prepared his talking points across three countries. "My daughter Jessica died several months ago. She was nine. Before she died, she asked if heaven was real. I told her yes." His voice caught. "I need to know if I lied to her. Does God exist? Does her life survive death? Will I see her again?"

Dimitri studied Jacob's face with the intensity of someone reading sacred text. "You sound like you come not as a seeker, but someone demanding evidence that would satisfy a nonbeliever."

"I'm a lawyer. Evidence is how we determine truth."

"In courts, perhaps. But some realities exceed legal verification." Dimitri gestured toward the icons. "I understand you have investigated Catholic claims, Protestant claims. What have you discovered?"

"Conflicting promises. Catholics say 'faith plus works' is the way. Protestants say faith alone but fracture into thousands of contradictions. Everyone promises they are the path to God, and a reunion with my daughter. No one proves God exists, or that Jessica is waiting for me somewhere."

"And so, you come to Orthodox Christianity expecting verification others could not provide?" Dimitri's smile was gentle. "I must disappoint you. We offer no courtroom proof. But we offer something the West has forgotten, theosis."

"Theosis?"

"Becoming like God. Participating in divine nature. Not salvation as a legal transaction but as healing, transformation. We don't just escape hell; we become partakers of divine life itself."

Jacob's mind engaged immediately. "Wait, I've heard this before. My friend Abby converted to Mormonism after her brother died. She told me Mormon doctrine teaches humans can become gods, ruling their own worlds. You're saying the same thing. How is this different from Mormonism?"

Dimitri's expression sharpened. "Mormons teach humans to become independent gods with their own divine authority, their own worlds to rule. This is pride dressed as theology. Orthodox theosis is completely different. We become like God not in His essence, that remains forever transcendent, but in His energies, His activities. Think of iron placed in fire. The iron becomes fire-like, glowing with heat and light, but it never becomes fire in its essence. It participates in fire's energies."

"That sounds like semantic gymnastics."

"Or precise distinction between participation and identity." Dimitri moved toward an icon of Christ. "God's essence is absolutely unknowable. No creature can comprehend what God is in Himself. But God's energies, His love, creativity, presence, these we can experience. Not grasping God as an object of knowledge but being grasped by God as beloved children."

"Philosophy isn't helping me, Father. I need to know where God is. You're telling me His essence is unknowable, but if He has Jessica, I need to find Him. Where is He? How do I verify He exists at all?"

Dimitri smiled. "Human beings are a holistic unity, body and soul together. At death, this unity breaks. But in resurrection, it will be restored, transfigured, made incorruptible. What happens between death and resurrection?" Dimitri paused. "We don't know precisely. Some Church Fathers suggest the departed exist in time differently. Others speak of them being present to God outside temporal sequence. Scripture doesn't provide courtroom clarity."

"So, you're admitting you don't know."

"I'm admitting reality exceeds our categories." Dimitris said. "Jacob, you hold Jessica's photograph. When you look at it, is she present to you?"

"Of course not. It's paper and chemicals."

"But something happens. Her love becomes present. The quality of your relationship is renewed." Dimitri gestured toward the icons. "We venerate icons not as idols but as windows. They present the reality they depict. Your photograph functions similarly, not magic, not literal presence, but real participation in love that transcends physical absence."

Jacob felt his frustration building, "Father with all due respect, I need to know if God exists and if Jessica is with Him. Not metaphors about photographs and windows."

"Then perhaps you're asking questions that demand false precision." Dimitri moved toward the cathedral's main doors. "Does your love for Jessica exist? Can you prove it in the laboratory? Measure it? Yet it's the most real thing you've experienced. Perhaps God, perhaps consciousness, perhaps resurrection are realities that exceed binary categories."

"So Orthodox Christianity offers no certainty?"

"We offer different certainty, not legal proof but experiential knowledge. Not argument but participation." Dimitri paused. "You've spent months collecting theological arguments like a lawyer preparing a case. But theology is not law. It's poetry attempting to describe mystery."

The cathedral bells began tolling. Dimitri glanced toward the altar where preparations for evening services began.

"Tonight, come to vespers at six o'clock. Don't cross-examine the prayers. Don't evaluate the theology. Just stand in the liturgy and let it work on you."

"I need answers, not aesthetic experiences."

"Perhaps the answer is that there are realities beyond argumentation." Dimitri's smile was knowing. "In the West, truth must be stated clearly, proven definitely. But what if some truths can only be lived, experienced, participated in? Come tonight. Stop demanding that the universe explain itself and simply be present to mystery."

For the next three hours, Dimitri walked Jacob through Orthodox teachings that differed radically from Western Christianity. Apophatic theology, knowing God by what He is not. The distinction between essence and energies. Icons as windows rather than idols. Salvation not as a legal transaction but as transformation.

Jacob pressed objections at every turn. Dimitri refused courtroom certainty. "Mystery is more honest than false precision," the priest insisted repeatedly.

By afternoon, Jacob's head spun with concepts that felt simultaneously profound and evasive. He left the cathedral as bells called the city to prayer, Dimitri's final words echoing: "Come back at six. Experience what argument cannot convey."

***

Later that afternoon Jacob stepped into Sofia's culture. He wandered randomly through the city center, Dimitri's challenge following him. *Perhaps that is enough.* But was it?

He found himself in a small park near the cathedral, watching Bulgarian families. Children chased pigeons while parents watched with careful attention born from love mixed with mortality's knowledge. A little girl, perhaps nine, Jessica's age, laughed as she fed bread to the birds.

The sound pierced him.

Jessica had loved feeding ducks at the park near their house, insisting they bring the "good bread" because "they deserve something nice too, Daddy." She'd crouch at the water's edge, counting each duck to make sure the shy ones got their share, her small face serious with the responsibility of fairness. That laugh, high and unselfconscious, could have been hers.

Jacob turned away before the girl's parents could notice him staring. He found a bench beneath a linden tree and sat heavily, waiting for his breathing to steady. After a long moment, he pulled out his journal, needing to capture the thought before it dissolved into the general ache of loss.

Sofia. Father Dimitri offered mystery instead of proof, presence instead of answers. He says becoming like God is our purpose, not pride. Says Jessica exists "in God's memory" which somehow isn't the same as being gone. He says I'm asking the wrong questions. That "does Jessica exist somewhere?" is too binary, too Western. But damn it, how else do I ask? Either my daughter is gone forever or she's not. There's no middle ground.

I challenged him about theosis sounding like Mormonism. He distinguished participation from apotheosis. But it still feels like sophisticated evasion.

Yet watching this child feed pigeons, I realize Jessica would have loved this moment. She would have insisted we save bread for the smallest birds. "Daddy, everyone deserves a chance," she would have said.

Is that love transcending death? Not surviving somewhere, but values continuing to shape my choices? Not reunion in paradise, but impact persisting through how I live?

Dimitri wants me at vespers tonight. To stop analyzing and just experience. I don't know if I can do that. My entire search has been about finding answers, and he's asking me to embrace questions. I'll go.

***

The afternoon faded to evening. Jacob returned to Alexander Nevsky as bells called the faithful to evening prayer. He slipped through the cathedral doors into dimness punctuated by hundreds of flickering candles.

The vespers service had just begun. Orthodox priests in ornate vestments moved through rituals that predated the Reformation, predated the Great Schism, predated even the fall of Rome. Their voices rose and fell in ancient Slavonic chants that Jacob couldn't understand but somehow felt in his chest.

There were no pews. The congregation stood, some crossing themselves repeatedly, others simply motionless in prayer. Old women in black headscarves held candles. Young families kept children quiet with practiced gestures. Everyone faced the iconostasis, the wall of icons separating the nave from the altar, glowing with gold leaf in candlelight.

Incense filled the air, thick and sweet, rising in clouds that caught the light like physical manifestations of prayer. A priest emerged from behind the iconostasis swinging a censer, the chains clinking rhythmically as smoke billowed forth. The smell was overpowering, resinous, ancient, carrying centuries of prayers offered in this same ritual.

The chanting continued without break, male voices harmonizing in ways that seemed to bypass Jacob's mind and speak directly to something deeper. There was no organ, no instruments, just human voices offering praise that sounded less like performance and more like breathing, as natural and necessary as life itself.

Jacob stood awkwardly near the back, unsure when to stand or bow or cross himself. But no one watched him. No one evaluated his participation. The liturgy simply continued, wave after wave of prayer washing over everyone present, carrying them along whether they understood the words or not.

A deacon emerged, chanting in a voice that filled the vast space: "Again and again, in peace let us pray to the Lord."

The congregation responded: "Lord, have mercy."

"For the peace from above and for the salvation of our souls, let us pray to the Lord."

"Lord, have mercy."

The petitions continued, naming every human need, the sick, the suffering, travelers, prisoners, the rulers of nations, those who hate us and those who love us. And finally: "For those who have fallen asleep in the hope of resurrection and eternal life, let us pray to the Lord."

"Lord, have mercy."

Jacob's throat tightened. Jessica had fallen asleep hoping. She'd asked if heaven was real. He'd promised her yes. And now, standing in this ancient liturgy, he couldn't prove his promise but couldn't deny the power of these prayers that had been offered for the dead for two thousand years.

He watched an old woman light a candle and place it in the stand before an icon of the Virgin Mary. She stood there weeping silently, her lips moving in prayer for someone she'd lost. Beside her, a young mother did the same, holding a toddler who reached for the flickering flames.

The chants poured over him, not like answers but like presence. For the first time since Jessica's death, Jacob stopped cross-examining the universe and simply stood inside it. The incense rose around him. The voices surrounded him. The candlelight flickered across faces living and painted, the icons seeming to watch with knowing compassion.

When the congregation prayed again for the departed, tears cut down Jacob's face. He moved forward, took a thin candle from the box, lit it from another, and placed it among hundreds of others burning before the icons. He whispered Jessica's name into the incense, not as a demand for proof but as a confession of love.

The vespers service lasted ninety minutes. Jacob stood the entire time, his legs aching, his mind gradually quieting as the liturgy worked on him in ways argument never had. This wasn't evidence. It wasn't verification. It was something else entirely, participation in mystery, standing inside questions rather than demanding they resolve themselves.

As the final blessing was pronounced and the congregation began filtering out into Sofia's evening streets, Jacob remained. The candles still burned. The incense still rose. His candle for Jessica flickered among all the others, one small light joining the prayers of countless others who'd loved and lost and hoped without proof.

Father Dimitri appeared beside him. "Sometimes," the priest said softly, "presence is more honest than explanations."

Jacob nodded, unable to speak. He'd come to Sofia demanding answers. He was leaving with something he couldn't name, not certainty, not proof, but the faint recognition that love creating meaning in the face of loss might itself be a kind of resurrection, happening right now, in this moment, regardless of what awaited beyond death

Evening lights caught the golden crosses atop various Orthodox churches, each one representing the same promise Dimitri had offered: reunion with Jessica through sacramental union with Christ. But Jacob felt no closer to certainty than when he'd arrived in Bulgaria. If anything, his two weeks in Sofia had multiplied rather than resolved his questions.

***

Back in his hotel room, Jacob spread his notes across the writing desk. Catholic authority, Protestant fracture, Orthodox mystery, contradictions scribbled in furious handwriting across pages that documented his journey through Christianity's competing claims. But tonight, another voice intruded, sharp and clear, as if from memory itself.

Daddy, you're not being honest.

Jessica's voice. He froze. She had spoken like this when she wanted him to stop dodging questions.

You're collecting stories to make yourself feel better. But you know they're just stories.

His throat tightened. *'I'm trying to find you, Jess. I promised I would.'*

You're trying to prove death isn't final because you can't stand the thought that it might be. But what if love is all there is? What if that's enough?

Jacob whispered into the empty room, *'So what do I do?'*

Stop looking for me in other people's heavens. If I live anywhere, it's in how you love because of me. In how you let me change you, even if I'm gone.

'Jessica!' His voice cracked, but the silence that followed was absolute.

"Are you disappointed I might not be waiting somewhere with wings and harps?" she asked.

She laughed. *"I'll always love you daddy."*

Then her voice faded. *"Keep searching, Daddy. Not for me, but for who you're becoming because you loved me."*

She was gone. Again.

In his journal that night he wrote:

Was that really Jessica speaking to me, or my mind generating wisdom I needed to hear? And if it was my mind, does that mean there's no God, no afterlife, no divine intervention, just human psychology creating comfort from despair? Or could God work through human psychology to communicate truth? I still can't prove God exists. I still can't verify Jessica survives anywhere. But tonight felt more real than months of theological investigation.

Orthodoxy reminds me: Jews, Christians, Muslims, three traditions, one God. If that's true, I can't stop now. Tomorrow, Istanbul. Tomorrow, Islam.

Met Tom at the airport. Istanbul. I owe him that much.

He closed the notebook, staring at his reflection in the dark window. For the first time, he understood: he wasn't just searching for

Jessica anymore. The search itself was remaking him. Either way he will face reality tomorrow.

***

∾

***

Chapter Three

THE ROAD OF ISLAM

The August flight from Sofia to Istanbul carried Jacob across the Black Sea, its vast darkness broken only by faint constellations above and scattered ship lights far below. He leaned against the cabin window, the hum of the engines pulling him into restless thought. Less than a century after Muhammad's revelations, Islam had spread across these waters like a tide. Could an illiterate seventh-century merchant have received humanity's final message from the same God worshiped by Jews and Christians? Or was that, too, another story polished into certainty by human need?

When the plane broke through dawn clouds, Istanbul revealed itself as a city of collisions. Byzantine domes still bore faded crosses, while Ottoman minarets pierced the skyline like sharpened declarations of faith. The Hagia Sophia dominated the horizon, its layered identity, cathedral, mosque, museum, embodying centuries of rivalry over who spoke most truly for God.

A taxi carried him through Sultanahmet's narrow streets as the call to prayer echoed from every direction. Not a single voice but a chorus, one muezzin after another, the sound swelling into a tide that lifted the stones themselves. His body tensed with the old Marine reflex, assess, react, defend, but there was nothing to defend against. It was only prayer. And yet it stirred something in him, not belief but recognition, a reminder that millions could live as if the unseen were more real than the visible.

At the hotel overlooking the Blue Mosque, he unpacked slowly, checking closets and drawers with unconscious precision. Habit, or paranoia? His first formal appointment, with Professor Amira Hassan at Istanbul University, wasn't until the following afternoon. That gave him time to see Islam not in books, but in practice.

He spent the afternoon wandering Istanbul's old city, past the Blue Mosque's minarets, through the Grand Bazaar's covered corridors, watching Muslim merchants pause their bargaining to spread prayer rugs toward Mecca. At sunset, he stood outside a neighborhood mosque as men filed in for maghrib prayers, their shoes lined up outside the entrance like evidence of devotion requiring physical humility.

By evening, months of travel caught up with him. He returned to the hotel, fell into bed fully clothed, and slept through the night.

***

5:30 a.m., the city woke him. The adhan rose through the dark like a tide breathing against the shore.

"Allahu Akbar, Allahu Akbar..."

One voice, then another, then many, until the call seemed to come from every corner of Istanbul. He moved to the window. Across the Bosphorus, Asia stirred beneath a veil of pale light.

Jessica. Christmas morning. She would tug him from sleep toward the tree before dawn. Once, standing at their kitchen window, she had whispered, "It's like God saying good morning to everyone at the same time."

Now, listening to the chorus of prayer, Jacob whispered: Do you hear this too, Jess? Or is it only human voices echoing into emptiness?

The calls faded one by one. Silence returned. Yet he felt strangely steadied, not converted, but moved. Perhaps faith wasn't about evidence. Perhaps it was about beginning each day as if meaning were possible, even without proof.

***

Within a few hours Jacob was in a taxi making his way back through Sultanahmet's narrow streets to the airport. Waiting at the arrival gate, Jacob spotted Tom's familiar figure emerging from the international terminal at Atatürk. His partner's usually immaculate appearance was frayed: shirt rumpled, jaw unshaven, shoulders tight as wire. Jacob's left eye gave a tiny twitch, an old reflex from Vietnam that surfaced now whenever his world was crowded with too many contradictions.

"You look like hell," Jacob said, trying for levity that didn't land.

"I feel worse." Tom's voice was granite. "We need to go somewhere private. This can't wait."

They found a corner table in an airport café. Tom ordered black coffee, no sugar, the way he'd taken it since college, and folded his hands around the cup like a man bracing for unwelcome news. His stare was the same tool that had once made hostile witnesses crumble: hard, unblinking, precise.

"Hinsen & Mitchell is hemorrhaging clients," Tom said flatly.

The words hit like body blows, but worse than the sentence was the echo behind it. "You didn't leave me a firm," Tom went on, voice low. "You left me a battlefield."

"We've lost sixty percent of revenue. Laid off three associates. Roberta cried in the bathroom yesterday. We've got three weeks before eviction notices start flooding my office." Tom's hand trembled as he lifted his cup. "Three weeks, Jacob."

Jacob felt his throat go tight. It wasn't just a firm at stake; it was the family, young lawyers, paralegals, clients, whose lives were threaded into everything he and Tom had built. He'd thought grief excused neglect; now he saw the people who paid his price.

"I know Jessica's death broke something in you," Tom said, softer now, pleading. "I've been with you through every high and low since we were kids. But are you really going to burn everything we built because you can't stop chasing ghosts?"

"I need you home, Jacob. Now. Not after another priest or imam. Now!"

"And if I don't?"

Tom's face hardened into a law partner's final judgment. "Then I dissolve the fucking partnership. I take what I can. You will face malpractice suits alone. You'll lose the firm, the house, everything. And you'll lose me as a friend."

The sentence struck deeper than any courtroom loss. Losing clients could be survived; losing Tom felt like a moral death.

"I need forty-eight hours," Jacob whispered.

"You have twenty-four." Tom stood, shouldered his bag, and without looking back walked toward the gate.

Jacob sat frozen in the chair Tom had vacated, staring at the patch of floor where his oldest friend had been seconds before. For the first time since he'd left Chicago, he wondered if the search for Jessica might cost the only living family he had left.

His mind flashed to the boy Tom had always been. Jacob saw him suddenly, seventeen again on a cracked Chicago sidewalk behind St. Mary's, mitts slapping palms, dreaming bigger than their block, that same kid who'd taken a fall for a water-gun prank Jacob had engineered. He remembered cheap champagne after their first big win, the cramped office over a deli where they'd sworn never to go back to being small. The memory hurt with the intimacy of a shared sin.

Hands trembling, he fished his phone from his pocket and dialed Margaret, their accountant of fifteen years. Her voice answered on the second ring, steady, then fraying at the edges.

"Jacob, thank God you called. I've been trying to reach you for weeks."

"Margaret, I'm so sorry. Tom just left. Are you okay?"

The question broke her composure for a fraction of a second. "I'm worried, Jacob. We have serious problems and only you can fix them. Tom gave me an overview, but you need to hear the numbers yourself." She inhaled, then laid them out like evidence. "Jake, you left in July. It's been over two months of hemorrhaging clients."

"Your monthly overhead with reduced staff is forty-three thousand. Revenue for the past two months, seven thousand total." She let the figures hang. "At this burn rate, your accounts are empty in six weeks."

Jacob pressed his palm into his temple as if he could press the math back into a kinder shape. "Personal assets?"

"Mortgage balance two hundred thirty thousand, estimated value about four twenty. Retirement accounts total one eighty-five but cashing out early nets one forty after penalties. Your daughter's college fund, thirty-seven thousand, protected by statute. You can't touch it for business."

The number lodged in him like a stone. He'd set that money aside when Jessica was two, talking about universities in a voice that had been all promise. Now it read like a gravestone for a life that would not include a college dorm room.

"What are my options if I don't return immediately?" he asked, though he already feared the answer.

"Personal bankruptcy in three months. Lose the house, the savings, the firm's reputation. And Jacob, abandoning a law practice for six months creates malpractice exposure I can't even calculate. Missed deadlines, client damages, this is catastrophic." Her tone, usually so clinical, turned urgent. "Tom said you have twenty-four hours to decide. Don't wait until twenty-three hours and fifty-nine minutes."

The phone buzzed with an incoming call from the mortgage company, a creditor, or automated reminder about a filing deadline. They were small mechanical things till they weren't the slow machinery of ruin turning inside a man's life.

Jacob closed his eyes. In the hollow moments that followed, memories drifted up. Tom's hand on his shoulder the night they won their first big case, the two of them in a cheap apartment celebrating with lukewarm champagne. Roberta crying in the bathroom. Margaret's practical voice counting down possibilities. Jessica's small hand waving goodbye at the school curb. Each memory was a thread in the net he might now cut.

"Margaret," he said finally, voice numb, "I'll try to be home. I can't promise when. But I'll try."

"Jacob," she said softly, "Jessica is gone, come now. Please."

He ended the call and sat there a moment longer, the airport's hurry going on around him. The left corner of his mouth trembled; his eye twitched again, the little sign of a man fraying at the edges.

Then, slowly, he reached for his journal. The pages that had been maps and questions became something else: a ledger of love, a list of obligations, a record of debts both moral and financial. He knew the choice ahead would make him either noble or ruin him outright. The fact that he could imagine both outcomes did not make the decision easier.

Outside the terminal glass, Istanbul spread before him, minarets and domes, water and light reflecting off the Bosphorus. Inside, Jacob still felt the sting of Tom's words, the weight of professional ruin he'd left behind in Chicago.

He wanted to stop. To process Tom's accusations, the partnership dissolving, the clients abandoned. To sit with everything that had happened in Sofia, Dimitri's mysticism, the vespers service, Arnold's relentless materialism. To figure out what any of it meant before continuing this search that was costing him everything.

But Professor Hassan expected him that afternoon. His appointments were scheduled for the next few days, his investigation incomplete. He'd sacrificed his practice, his partnership, his reputation to find answers about where God was and where Jessica was. Stopping now, with Islam and Judaism still unexplored, would make all of it meaningless.

His search needed to continue, even as the life he'd left behind collapsed around him.

***

The conversation with Professor Amira Hassan took place in her office at the university, overlooking Istanbul's skyline where minarets punctuated the horizon like exclamation points in a theological argument. She was younger than Jacob expected, mid-forties, wearing a hijab but Western professional attire beneath it, her desk cluttered with academic journals in multiple languages.

"Thank you for seeing me on short notice, Professor," Jacob began.

"Your inquiry intrigued me," she replied, gesturing for him to sit. "A father seeking to know if his daughter still exists after death. Most who come to me want to debate politics or critique Islam. You want something deeper."

Jacob appreciated the candor. "My daughter died four months ago. She was nine. I've investigated Christianity's claims about God and the afterlife across three countries. Now I need to understand what Islam claims about both. Does Allah exist? Can you prove it? And if He exists, where is He? Where is my daughter? Is she with Him somewhere I might find her?"

Professor Hassan's expression softened. "I'm deeply sorry for your loss. Islam teaches definitively that your daughter still exists. Death is not the end; it is a transition. The Quran is explicit that each person continues after physical death, and that you will be reunited with those you love in the hereafter if you both submit to Allah's will."

Jacob leaned forward. "But where is Allah? How do you know He exists?"

"The Quran is the word of Allah, revealed to Prophet Muhammad, peace be upon him," she replied with quiet certainty. "It describes what lies beyond death with detail that human imagination could not produce. Surah Al-Baqarah, Surah Al-Mu'minun, Surah Al-Qiyamah, all speak clearly about life after death, resurrection, and reunion with the righteous."

"The Quran was compiled by human beings over twenty-three years," Jacob said, his diplomatic patience from Rome now worn thin after months of searching. "Standardized under Caliph Uthman decades after Muhammad's death. Variant versions existed; he ordered them destroyed. Just like Christians at Nicaea decided which gospels were scripture and which were heresy. So far, every religion does this, humans decide what's divine, then cite their own decisions as proof."

Professor Hassan's expression tightened. "You speak of the sacred Quran with disrespect, Jacob."

"I speak of historical fact," Jacob replied softly. "You're telling me Jessica still exists because the Quran says so. But when I ask how you know the Quran is divinely inspired, you'll tell me because it's Allah's word. And when I ask how you know it's Allah's word, we're back to the Quran itself. That's circular reasoning. Christians do the same thing with the Bible. I assume Jews do it with Torah. How is this proof?"

"Faith is not subject to your standards of empirical proof, Mr. Hinsen."

"Then you don't have proof," Jacob said, hearing the sudden sharpness in his own voice. "You told me definitively that Jessica still exists. That's a claim about reality. But when I ask for evidence, you point to a book compiled and edited by humans. I can't tell my daughter 'yes, heaven is real' based on what men decided to write down and call divine revelation."

Professor Hassan was silent for a long moment. When she spoke again, her voice was understanding but no less firm. "The Quran's authenticity has been preserved with extraordinary care. The chain of transmission, the memorization by thousands of companions, the linguistic miracle of its Arabic, these testify to its divine origin."

"Preserved by humans," Jacob countered. "Memorized by humans. Compiled by a caliph who destroyed competing versions. And 'linguistic miracle' is subjective, I don't speak Arabic. I can't verify that claim. What I can verify is that humans made choices about what to include and exclude, just like every other religious tradition."

"With all due respect, Professor, every tradition claims divine revelation for its scripture. How do I know which one is correct? They all can't be right, they contradict each other. Christianity says Jesus is divine, Islam says he was only a prophet. You can't all be telling the truth."

Hassan nodded slowly, this wasn't the first time she had this debate. "You're correct that we make different claims. Islam understands itself as the final correction of earlier revelations that were corrupted over time. The Quran confirms the truth in Torah and Gospel while correcting their errors."

"But Christians claim the opposite," Jacob said. "They say the New Testament fulfills and supersedes portions of the Old Testament. Its competing claims all the way down, each citing their own scripture as proof that everyone else's scripture is wrong. How does that help me answer my daughter's question about where she is now?"

"It helps," Hassan said carefully, "if you accept that Allah's final revelation is the Quran. Then you have your answer, yes, she continues, yes, you will see her again."

"But I can't accept it," Jacob said calmly. "You're asking me to take it on faith. And faith means believing without proof. Which means you're admitting you can't prove Jessica still exists or that Allah exists. You believe it. That's not the same thing."

Professor Hassan studied him with something that looked like sympathy. "No scholar can give you the kind of proof you seek, Jacob. Not Muslim, not Christian, not Jewish. What you're asking for, empirical evidence that God exists and that a specific person survives death, is beyond human capacity to provide. We have revelation, tradition, the testimony of billions across centuries. But not courtroom proof."

"Then why do you all speak with such certainty?" Jacob's voice cracked slightly. "Cardinal Rossi told me with absolute conviction that Jessica is in heaven with God. You're telling me with absolute conviction that she continues in Allah's presence. But when I ask for proof, suddenly it's 'faith isn't subject to empirical standards.' You can't have it both ways. Either you know she still exists and God exists, which requires evidence, or you believe they do, which is faith, not knowledge."

Hassan was serene for a moment. "You're right to press the distinction. We speak with more certainty than we should. What I know is this: I believe, based on Quranic revelation, that your daughter continues and that Allah exists. I cannot prove it to you. I can only tell you that this belief has sustained billions of people through loss, that it transformed how I understood my own father's death, that choosing to live as if it's true has made me more compassionate, more just, more fully human."

"But if it's not true?" Jacob asked. "If death is just the end and there's nothing after, then I've spent six months and destroyed my law practice chasing a comforting lie."

"Then you will have lived as if love transcends death," Hassan replied gently. "And that choice itself is meaningful, whether or not it corresponds to metaphysical reality. But I don't believe it's a falsehood, Mr. Hinsen. I believe Allah's revelation is true. I simply cannot prove it to you in the way you need."

The conversation continued for another hour, ranging across Islamic philosophy, the problem of competing truth claims among religions. But the core remained unchanged: she believed based on faith in Quranic revelation. Jacob needed evidence faith couldn't provide.

As he prepared to leave, Professor Hassan walked him to the door. "Mr. Hinsen, may I offer one observation?"

"Please."

"You're searching for proof your daughter survives because you love her. That love is real. It transformed you, shaped you, continues to drive you across continents asking questions that have no certain answers. Whether or not you find proof of Jessica's survival, your love for her is evidence that something in human experience transcends mere biology. Love itself is metaphysical. You can't weigh it or measure it, yet you know it's real. Perhaps start there."

Jacob nodded slowly. "Thank you, Professor. For your honesty and your time. That matters more than you might think."

As the afternoon call to prayer echoed across Istanbul, Dr. Hassan suggested they continue their conversation after prayer time. "Would you be interested in observing Islamic worship? Not as a conversion attempt, but to experience the communal aspect of submission that individual study cannot provide?"

Jacob hesitated, remembering similar invitations from Christian authorities that had felt manipulative. But Dr. Hassan's intellectual honesty and lack of evangelical pressure made the invitation feel genuine rather than coercive.

"I'd appreciate that," he replied. "But I should be clear, I'm observing as an investigator, not a potential convert."

"Of course. Islamic teaching prohibits forced conversion or emotional manipulation in religious matters. The Quran says, 'There is no compulsion in religion.' Authentic faith must emerge from conviction, not pressure."

The afternoon call to prayer echoed across Istanbul as Jacob made his way through the university campus with Dr. Hassan toward a small neighborhood mosque. Men streamed toward the entrance, removing their shoes in a practiced rhythm that spoke of daily devotion.

The interior was simple, almost austere. No icons, no crucifixes, no stained glass. Geometric patterns covered the walls, Arabic calligraphy flowing in elegant script. The space felt designed not for visual grandeur but for focused attention on the unseen.

Men arranged themselves in straight rows, shoulder to shoulder. Jacob watched from the back as a university professor stood beside a street vendor, a businessperson next to a janitor, all facing Mecca in identical postures of submission.

The imam began. The congregation moved in unison, standing, bowing, prostrating, rising. The synchronized movement carried power, collective surrender to something beyond individual will.

As foreheads touched the ground in ultimate humility, Jacob thought of Jessica's questions about prayer. "Does God hear everyone at the same time, Daddy?" He'd given vague answers about God being everywhere. Now, watching this ritual repeated by millions across time zones, he wondered if the universality itself was the point, not God hearing but humans practicing collective acknowledgment of something beyond themselves.

The prayer concluded with worshippers turning their heads. "As-salamu alaykum." Peace be upon you.

Outside, Dr. Hassan found him. "What did you observe?"

"Discipline," Jacob said honestly. "Community. But I didn't feel God's presence. I saw humans performing a ritual they believe connects them to the divine. That's not proof the divine exists."

"No, it's not proof," she agreed. "But what you witnessed happens five times daily for 1.8 billion Muslims. That collective practice shapes societies, transforms individuals. Is that not worth considering?"

"You're saying social utility matters more than truth claims?"

"I'm saying perhaps truth has more dimensions than empirical verification."

Jacob had heard this argument from every religious figure he'd encountered. It always felt like changing the subject from "does God exist?" to "doesn't it feel better to believe?"

Back at her office, she handed him several books on Islamic approaches to grief and comparative religion. "Whether or not Islam provides the answers you seek, I hope our discussion has expanded your understanding. Your daughter was blessed to have a father who loves her enough to search the world for evidence of her continued existence."

"Go with peace," she said. "And may you find what you're searching for, even if it's not what you expect."

***

Walking through Istanbul's streets, Jacob realized atheists made the same mistake Hassan did. They claimed death was the end with the same certainty Hassan claimed Jessica still existed somewhere. Neither could prove their position.

He thought of Arnold on the train, the philosophy professor who'd dismissed all religion as wishful thinking. But Arnold couldn't prove there was nothing after death any more than Hassan could prove there was something. Science could explain how the brain worked, but it couldn't tell him whether Jessica simply stopped existing or continued somewhere. Couldn't explain what came before the Big Bang or what it was expanding into.

Science hit its own wall, just like every religion did. Different walls. Same inability to answer the question that mattered: Does my daughter still exist, and will I see her again?

Nobody knew. They all just claimed certainty about things they couldn't prove.

***

The café in Beyoğlu was crowded with students and writers, its air thick with tea and tobacco. At a corner table, a woman in a scarlet headscarf bent over a worn Quran, her notebook dense with commentary in Arabic and English. Her focus radiated seriousness. She motioned to him to join her.

When Jacob introduced himself, she rose, offered her hand, and gestured for him to sit. Her eyes assessed him quickly, as though measuring motives as much as words.

"Your reputation precedes you, Mr. Hinsen. My name is Muhja...."

"Yes, Dr. Hassan said you specialize in comparative religious philosophy,"

"Ah," Muhja said, her voice direct, almost cutting. "The American attorney who abandoned his practice to chase certainties. Tell me, Mr. Hinsen, what would your daughter think of a father who walked away from his duties to others just to chase her shadow?"

The words struck harder than Tom's had. Jacob shifted in his seat, his phone buzzing in his pocket, relentless, insistent. Seventeen missed calls glowed on the screen when he glanced. Creditors. Clients. The mortgage company. A silent indictment.

"Are you expecting something urgent?" Muhja asked.

He stood, nodded stiffly. "Excuse me."

In the corridor by the bathrooms he stared at the screen, frustration rising. The cascade of numbers wasn't just business, it was his life unraveling, call by call. He tapped the phone to his forehead, then shoved it back into his pocket and returned to the table.

He didn't offer excuses. He simply met her gaze. "Professor Hassan told me true love for the dead should inspire righteousness toward the living. What if my love has become a selfish obsession instead? What if it's destroying the people who depend on me?"

Muhja closed her Quran. Her eyes softened, but her words cut clean. "Then it isn't love, Jacob. Not the kind that reunites families in Paradise. It is self-indulgence dressed as devotion."

His voice cracked. "But how can I care about mortgages, payroll, contracts, when I don't even know if Jessica still exists? How can I pretend those things matter?"

"Because that is exactly what faith demands," Muhja said. "The Prophet, peace be upon him, received revelation while running a business, leading a community, and caring for his family. He didn't abandon earthly responsibilities to seek God. He fulfilled them. In that fulfillment, he worshiped."

Jacob's phone buzzed again. He turned it off. For once, silence felt heavier than answering.

"So, you're telling me to give up the search? To go home?"

Muhja's dark eyes never wavered. "I'm telling you there is no choice between the search and your duties. Both are one path. If your quest for Jessica leads you to abandon the living, it is not faith, it is despair. Your daughter is not lost, Jacob. She has returned to Allah, who loves her more than you do. The question is not whether you will find her, but whether you will live in a way that honors her now."

"Jacob, you are seeking answers, but your questions are one of a skeptic. You do not want to discover; you want to assault. I cannot help you." Abruptly she rose and left. He stayed seated, staring at the empty chair. Around him, laughter, arguments, the clink of tea glasses filled the café. Inside, he heard only Jessica's laugh, Tom's weary voice, Margaret's warning.

He felt alone and confused. What if this financial disaster was the test itself? Not whether he could find Jessica, but whether his love for her would make him more faithful to the living or more willing to abandon them?

Jacob lowered his head, unsure if he had just received his harshest judgment or his clearest guidance.

***

That night, at his hotel desk, Istanbul's lights glittering on the Bosphorus, he opened his journal and pressed pen to page.

Tom says the firm has three weeks left. Margaret says bankruptcy is inevitable. My phone is a ledger of missed calls, creditors, clients, voices I can't bear to answer.

I left Chicago to prove Jessica didn't vanish with a broken body. I wanted evidence she still exists. But maybe the test isn't finding heaven. Maybe the test is whether I let love make me faithful to the living.

Would Jessica have wanted Margaret crying in her office? Tom carrying the weight alone? Clients ruined because I cannot accept finality? I promised Jessica, I would find her, not burn everything she loved to ash in the process.

Today Muhja said: "If your love for Jessica leads you to abandon the living, it is not faith. It is despair." I can't shake it.

Hassan says reunion is promised if we submit. Dimitri says mystery must be entered, not solved. Romano admits the Church is a paradox. Muhja says submission should look like responsibility. Ernie says Jesus saved him. Abby clings to Joseph Smith's plates no one ever saw. All point beyond themselves. None give proof. Only stories. Only faith.

I don't know if Jessica is in Paradise. I don't know if I will ever see her again. But love changed me once. The question now is whether that change will be enough to save what remains.

And where is God?

He closed the book. Then reopened it, scrawling one last line:

Tomorrow I must decide. Maybe the real test of faith is not whether God exists, but whether I can live as if love endures, even without proof.

He whispered into the silence: "Jessica, if you're there, show me. If you're not, help me understand how to live like your love is all that matters."

***

The next day, Jacob woke to morning prayers drifting through his window. He dressed and made his way to a simple café near his hotel, where he shared breakfast of olives, cheese, and strong Turkish coffee. The quiet meal gave him time to reflect on his conversations and what he hoped to learn from the day ahead.

After breakfast, he made his way to the garden courtyard of a cultural center where Dr. Hassan had arranged an interfaith gathering. Lanterns glowed in the jasmine air despite the bright sunlight. Around a low table sat Dr. Anjali Sharma, a Hindu scholar; Lama Tenzin, a

Buddhist monk from Tibet; Master Li Wei, a Taoist sage; and Joseph Crow Feather, a Lakota elder.

The moderator introduced Jacob as "a seeker from a distant land, burdened by loss, searching for his daughter's presence with God."

Dr. Sharma spoke first: "In Hinduism, the soul, the Atman, is eternal. It never dies, only moves. The love you feel for your daughter connects your Atman to hers across lifetimes. There is no true separation, only change in perception."

"But that's the problem," Lama Tenzin interjected gently. "Buddhism teaches that this permanent self is an illusion. Suffering arises from clinging to who we call 'Jessica.' When you release attachment, you discover she was never separate from the vast ocean of consciousness."

Jacob felt irritation rising. "So, one dogma says she continues as herself, the other says 'herself' never existed? Which is it?"

Master Li Wei traced circles in the air. "Taoism sees death and life as alternations, like day and night. Your daughter has returned to the source, the Tao from which all things emerge. Fighting this natural flow creates your suffering."

"Natural flow?" Jacob's voice sharpened. "There's nothing natural about children dying before their parents."

Joseph Crow Feather spoke quietly: "In Lakota tradition, we don't separate life and death so sharply. Your daughter has crossed to the spirit world, but the great web of all relations keeps her connected. She exists in every sunset you watch remembering her, in every act of kindness you perform in her honor."

Jacob looked around the circle. "So, I have four different answers. Reincarnation, dissolution, cosmic flow, and ancestral spirits. How do I know which is true?"

"Perhaps," Dr. Sharma suggested, "you're assuming truth must be singular. What if reality encompasses multiple valid perspectives?"

"Because my daughter's fate depends on which one I choose!" Jacob's grief erupted. "If reincarnation is real and I follow Buddhism, I might miss finding her. If Buddhism is right and I pursue reincarnation, I'm chasing an illusion. I can't afford to guess wrong."

Lama Tenzin leaned forward. "Jacob, your love for Jessica, can you prove that scientifically? Measure its weight? Yet you know it exists. Perhaps life operates beyond physical laws, in ways science cannot detect but hearts experience."

Master Li Wei nodded. "The Tao that can be spoken is not the eternal Tao. Some realities exceed human categories."

"More riddles," Jacob muttered.

Joseph Crow Feather smiled sadly. "Not riddles, recognition that love transcends proof. The ancestors taught that grief is love with nowhere to go. But love always finds a way, through dreams, through signs, through wisdom that grows where loss has broken us open."

Jacob's voice cracked: "So none of you can give me certainty?"

"No," admitted Dr. Sharma. "But we witness love persisting beyond physical death, even if we describe the mechanism differently."

The moderator, who had listened in silence, finally spoke: "Jacob, you came seeking proof. Instead, you've discovered that even outside the Abrahamic faiths, human beings recognize love's transcendence of mortality. Perhaps that recognition itself is significant."

Jacob looked at each face around the table: Hindu, Buddhist, Taoist, Native American, all offering wisdom accumulated across millennia, all acknowledging mystery rather than claiming certainty.

"What you're telling me," He said slowly, "is that whether I explore Christianity, Islam, Judaism, or several of these paths, I'll find testimony about love surviving death, but no observed proof."

"Yes," Lama Tenzin replied simply. "And perhaps that uncertainty is where faith begins, not in knowing, but in loving deeply enough to act despite not knowing."

As the gathering dispersed, each representative offered Jacob contact information, but he realized this detour had served its purpose. These traditions provided beautiful frameworks for understanding mortality, but they didn't change his fundamental question: did the God of Abraham, Isaac, and Jacob, the same God claimed by Christianity, Judaism and Islam, offer any more definitive answers?

If Jessica existed in some form beyond death, it would likely be through the God she'd been taught about in Sunday school, the God Jacob had abandoned but never quite forgotten.

These Eastern and indigenous paths had confirmed his suspicion: every tradition grappled with mortality's mystery, but none offered the legal certainty he craved.

His search would continue, but it would focus where it always should have, on the three faiths that claimed to know the same God personally, the God who might be caring for Jessica's soul or might not exist at all.

***

That evening, back at his hotel, his phone rang. The number froze him. Klaus Whitfield. He had to answer. If only to maybe change Tom and Margarete's fate.

"Hello."

"Hinsen," Klaus's clipped German accent cut like steel. "I trust you are enjoying your extended vacation while my company collapses."

Jacob's throat went dry. "Klaus, I understand there's been an issue with the appellate deadline."

"An issue? Your firm missed a statutory deadline circled in red on every calendar. The zoning commission's rejection stands. Our forty-seven-million-dollar development is dead. Four hundred jobs, gone."

"Klaus, I prepared every document. I left instructions."

"Your partner told me he's never handled an appeal. He filed only in circuit court. The deadline is absolute. We are filing malpractice Monday. Forty-seven million, plus punitive."

Jacob's hand shook. Even with insurance, the gap would bankrupt him, strip his house, retirement, everything.

"Klaus, we've worked together for twelve years."

"And twelve years ago, you told me to trust you. Now my board asks why I relied on a man who abandoned his post for religious tourism."

The phrase hit like a slap. From the outside, that's all his search was.

"What would it take to resolve this?"

"Restitution. Termination. Written acknowledgment of malpractice, by Friday. Or we file."

The line went dead. Jacob sat motionless, ruins closing around him.

***

At dawn, the muezzin's call rose again across the city. Days earlier it had moved him. Now it sounded like another human poem elevated to divinity because people needed meaning more than truth.

He opened his laptop to flight schedules home. Tom and Klaus's ultimatums gave him hours. He could end this, return, and face the wreckage.

But stopping wouldn't answer Jessica's question. If he quit now, he would never know if the truth waited just beyond.

"What if it's all fiction?" he whispered. "What if death is just the end?"

Jessica's voice came back to him, a memory from one of their bedtime conversations: *"Daddy, what if the people who say, 'I don't know' are more honest than the people who claim to know?"* The words cut deeper than any theology. Maybe not knowing wasn't cowardice but honesty.

He closed the flight page and opened his journal.

I don't know if God exists. Every faith gives beautiful answers, but beauty isn't proof. Maybe the quest isn't about discovering truth but about living as if love and justice matter, whether eternal or not.

He wasn't sure. But he owed his friend and Margaret an answer. Soon!

***

That afternoon Jacob went to the Galata Mevlevi Lodge, home of the whirling dervishes, for what he'd been told would be a two-part experience: afternoon dhikr practice followed by evening teaching. Through the open doors he heard chanting, "La ilaha illa Allah," the syllables folding over themselves until they became texture rather than argument. The repetition pressed against his dread like balm.

The lodge occupied a restored Ottoman building where centuries of seekers had worn the wooden floors smooth with their devotional practices. Prayer rugs formed concentric circles around a central space where dervishes would spin in their mystical dance, though this afternoon was dedicated to seated dhikr, the rhythmic remembrance of divine names that quieted analytical thinking and opened hearts to spiritual experience.

Fatima, a young guide with a steady smile, found him hesitating at the doorway. She wore modest dress and carried herself with the serene confidence of someone who had found peace through spiritual practice. "You must be Jacob," she said warmly. "Shahid Baba told me to expect you for both sessions today. This afternoon we practice dhikr: breathe, repeat, don't analyze. Just be present." The invitation carried neither proselytizing nor pity, just genuine welcome for a fellow seeker struggling with life's hardest questions.

He took a place on a worn prayer rug among twenty other participants. The foreign Arabic syllables felt awkward in his mouth at first but gradually softened into rhythm that bypassed intellectual resistance. His breath slowed, shoulders loosened, and the relentless chessboard of his legal mind, always calculating, always strategizing, began to recede into something quieter.

For precious minutes, everything that had been crushing him dissolved into pure sound: the lawsuits threatening his practice, Margaret's voice demanding explanations he couldn't provide, Klaus's legal threats that felt like stones in his chest, the endless weight of professional obligations abandoned in pursuit of answers about Jessica's fate. All of it temporarily lifted, replaced by something he hadn't experienced since her death: a moment of peace that asked nothing of him except presence.

It was not revelation so much as reprieve, a temporary unclenching of a chest that had held grief like an accusation against God, against himself, against the universe's apparent indifference to a father's love.

As the dhikr continued, Jacob found himself wondering if this was what Jessica had felt during her bedtime prayers, not the performance of religious duty, but genuine connection to something larger than her immediate concerns. The thought brought both comfort and fresh sorrow: comfort that such peace was possible, sorrow that he'd discovered it too late to share with her.

When the session ended, participants gradually returned to ordinary conversation, but the atmosphere retained something of the sacred, voices softer than usual, movements more deliberate, faces relaxed in ways that suggested inner transformation had occurred, however subtly.

As Jacob prepared to leave, Fatima approached him with gentle concern. "How was that for you? Your first time with dhikr can be intense."

"Different from anything I've experienced," Jacob admitted. "Peaceful, but also emotional. I wasn't expecting that."

"The heart recognizes what it needs," Fatima replied. "Shahid Baba will want to hear about your experience tonight. He says the afternoon opens the heart; the evening teaches the mind how to understand what the heart discovers. Will you return for sohbet?"

Jacob nodded, feeling drawn back despite his uncertainty about mystical practices. "Yes. I think I need to."

"Good. Take some time to walk, to reflect. Let what happened this afternoon settle. Shahid Baba's teaching will help you make sense of it." She smiled with the warmth of someone who had guided many seekers through similar experiences. "The lodge serves tea at sunset if you'd like to return early."

***

By sundown, Jacob returned to the lodge as promised, finding the sohbet gathering in a low-lit room of rugs and cushions. Fatima greeted him at the entrance and led him to a place near the front. "Shahid Baba will be glad you came back," she whispered. "He says the afternoon, and evening together complete the experience."

The space felt intimate despite accommodating thirty people, with Islamic calligraphy adorning the walls and the faint scent of rose water creating an atmosphere conducive to contemplation. Jacob noticed several familiar faces from the afternoon dhikr, suggesting that many participants, like him, had chosen to stay for both sessions.

Shahid Baba, an older teacher whose presence suggested both iron will and a long habit of mercy, took his place at the room's front. His weathered hands and lined face spoke of decades spent guiding spiritual seekers through their darkest questions, while his eyes held depths that seemed to recognize the particular pain Jacob carried.

Before beginning, he caught Jacob's eye and nodded slightly, a teacher's acknowledgment of a student's return, suggesting that Fatima had already informed him about Jacob's afternoon experience.

He opened by reading a couplet of Rumi, the great Persian mystic whose name the lodge bore: "Come, come, whoever you are, wanderer, worshiper, lover of leaving, this door is open. Ours is not a caravan of despair."

The words seemed aimed directly at Jacob's situation: a wanderer indeed, a lover of leaving who had abandoned everything familiar in pursuit of answers that remained maddeningly elusive.

Shahid Baba addressed the room with a voice at once plain and precise, the tone of someone who had wrestled with ultimate questions long enough to speak about them without pretension. "We spend our lives trying to prove what will not submit to proof. The mind demands evidence; the heart wants an encounter. But there is a third faculty: the way we act in the world. Love knows without proof."

He paused, allowing the words to settle before continuing with laser focus on human experience. "You knew your child in ways no ledger can measure. You didn't demand DNA samples to validate breakfast hugs or require philosophical arguments to justify bedtime stories. That knowing is a way of being, not a conclusion reached through reasoning. The question is not whether love proves God's existence, but whether your love proves itself through your actions in the world."

Jacob knew the point landed like a verdict: not intellectual surrender, but ethical recognition that he'd been asking the wrong questions. His certainty about Jessica's reality hadn't required external proof. It emerged from relationship, from shared experience, from the daily practice of loving someone more than his own comfort or convenience.

Shahid continued, sharpening the lesson with a teacher's bluntness born from years of watching seekers get lost in spiritual bypassing. "Mystical states can be joyful illusions or they can be doors to authentic transformation. How to distinguish? By examining the fruit. Does your experience make you more patient with difficult people? More generous with your resources? Does it send you back to the table where your obligations wait, or does it give you excuses to abandon those who depend on you? The tree is known by its fruit, not by the beauty of its blossoms."

The teaching felt like a direct challenge to Jacob's approach to grief. Had his months of religious investigation produced greater love for others, or had it become elaborate justification for abandoning the responsibilities that connected him to the human community?

Someone in the circle, a middle-aged woman Jacob hadn't met, asked the question that haunted all spiritual seekers: "But how do we know when our experiences are authentic versus wishful thinking and self-deception? How do we avoid the trap of seeing what we want to see?"

"Community," Shahid answered immediately, as if he'd been waiting for precisely this question. "We test experience against life lived in relationship with others who can observe our character changes. Practice without accountability breeds fantasy and spiritual pride. Practice with humility and community oversight tends to open hearts that serve others rather than serve the ego's need for special experiences."

He leaned forward slightly, his gaze finding Jacob among the gathered seekers. "If your seeking yields increased pride, isolation from those who knew you before, or harm to people who trusted you with their welfare, then you have not found God. You have found a mirror reflecting your own desperate desires."

The words cut deep because they contained the truth Jacob had been avoiding. His spiritual quest had indeed isolated him from Tom, from Margaret, from professional colleagues who had every right to expect reliability from their law partner. Had his search for Jessica become an elaborate justification for abandoning the community that needed him?

"You come to us seeking proof for reunion with your cherished loved one," Shahid continued, his voice gentle but uncompromising. "Perhaps such a reunion awaits. Allah's mercy encompasses more than human minds can fathom. But you must not allow the search to become an excuse to neglect those you promised to care for in this life. The path to divine reality runs through human responsibility, not around it."

As the gathering dispersed, men filing out into Istanbul's night while offering quiet farewells, Shahid approached Jacob, who had remained seated, processing what he'd witnessed.

"You came here seeking answers about your daughter," Shahid said quietly, settling beside him. "I could see it in your face during the dhikr, the desperate hope that we might offer what Christianity could not."

Jacob nodded, too exhausted to deflect.

"Such a reunion may await. Allah's mercy encompasses more than human minds can fathom. But I sense you have sacrificed much in this search. Have you considered whether this investigation honors the living you've left behind, or abandons them?"

Tom's accusations at the airport echoed in Jacob's memory.

"The path to divine reality runs through human responsibility, not around it," Shahid continued. "My friend Omar Sayyid and his family live that integration: prayers woven between meals, devotion practiced inside daily duty rather than separate from it. Perhaps stay with them for a week if you will accept the invitation. Watch how authentic faith sanctifies the ordinary rather than providing escape from it."

Jacob hesitated. "I appreciate the offer, but I have appointments scheduled in Jerusalem. One more tradition to investigate before I can go home."

Shahid nodded slowly. "Then may you find what you seek. But remember: the answers we need are often different from the answers we want."

As Jacob left the lodge and walked back through Istanbul's night-time streets, Shahid's words followed him. The path to divine reality runs through human responsibility, not around it. Had his entire search been an escape from responsibility dressed as spiritual investigation?

***

That night, back in his small hotel room with the Bosphorus glimmering beyond the glass, he opened his laptop and his journal in quick succession. Words came raw and immediate.

In his journal he wrote:

I still don't know if God exists. I don't know if Jessica exists beyond memory. Every faith offers beautiful answers, but beauty is not proof. Maybe the quest is about living as if love and justice matter, whether eternal or not. But 'feel good' sensations do not answer my questions about God, or Jessica. I have to go on. There are too many unanswered questions.

He turned to his laptop and opened a blank email message he dreaded having to send.

As he began to type, his mind flooded with a childhood memory: summers behind St. Mary's, twelve years old, Tom with the battered mitt, Jacob with a water gun tucked beneath his shirt like contraband. The principal's office smelled of lemon cleaner and nervous authority. Tom had been marched in, red-faced and silent, taking the scolding meant for both because he'd covered for Jacob's prank. On the walk home Tom had said, "Don't let me take the fall alone, Jake." It had been a pact, brotherhood sealed by small acts of loyalty that counted for everything.

Now the fall he'd set in motion was different. This time it wasn't a principal's rebuke but a collapsing practice, families at risk, reputations fraying. The boy who once took a beating for him deserved better than a partner who ran halfway around the world.

Jacob fought to hold back the tears. Hands shaking, he typed:

Dear Tom,

There's no way to soften this: I'm so sorry. I'm sorry for what I've put you, your family, Margaret, and the firm through. I know I've broken your trust and our friendship.

But I cannot stop this search. It has nothing to do with not caring about our work or our friendship. It has everything to do with Jessica. She asked me once if heaven was real. I gave her a Sunday-school answer I wasn't sure I believed. I can't live with that lie anymore.

When I get back, I will face every lawsuit, every consequence. I'll take them on. I'll try to repair what I've broken. But I have to see this through, whatever it costs. Jessica deserves that much.

You are my brother. If this ends us, I am sorry. But I can't quit. Not here. Not now.

Jacob

He read the lines twice, feeling each syllable like a small bone under his ribs, then pressed send. The whoosh of the outgoing message sounded final, like a gavel dropped on a case that had no good verdict.

He shut the laptop, let the silence settle, and watched the Bosphorus lights fracture across the water. This wasn't an escape. It felt like a certain kind of surrender, not defeat, not victory, but a deliberate choosing to love in the only way he felt left.

For now, he had a daughter to find

***

Jacob checked the schedule Hassan had prepared over dinner the previous evening. The professor had been thorough:

9:00 AM - Imam Al-Masri, Fatih Mosque complex. Sunni perspective on God's existence, paradise, path to salvation. He's agreed to discuss your questions about afterlife and requirements for reaching it. Be respectful but ask what you need to know.

2:00 PM - Yasmin al-Khafaji, teahouse near Fatih district (address attached). Shia scholar, expert on Karbala and Ahl al-Bayt theology.

She'll provide the other perspective. Warning: She's passionate about Hussein's martyrdom and will challenge Sunni claims directly. Don't mention Al-Masri's name unless necessary.

Note: These are not just different schools of thought, they represent fourteen centuries of theological and political division. Listen to both before drawing conclusions. Neither will give you proof God exists, but both will show you what Muslims believe and why we disagree.

Jacob studied the schedule as morning light filtered through his hotel window. Two conversations, five hours apart. Sunni order versus Shia passion. Community consensus versus family devotion. Both claim the same God, the same Prophet, the same paradise.

Hassan's final line nagged at him: *Neither will give you proof God exists.* After months of investigation, that sentence had become the refrain of his entire search. No one could prove God existed. No one could verify Jessica's soul survived. Everyone offered hope dressed as certainty, faith disguised as knowledge, unprovable claims wrapped in theological authority.

He showered, dressed, and prepared for another day of collecting beautiful promises he couldn't verify.

***

Jacob made his way to the Fatih Mosque complex where Imam Al-Masri had agreed to meet him. The imam's study overlooked the courtyard where men performed ablutions before prayer, water splashing against ancient stone.

"As-salamu alaykum." Al-Masri gestured to cushioned seating. "Professor Hassan mentioned your search. Your daughter, you want to know if she's with Allah."

"Yes, I want to know if Allah exists, and if Jessica's survived her death." Jacob settled across from him. "I've spent months investigating Christianity. Every tradition makes promises about God and reunion with the dead. None provide proof. What does Islam claim, and what evidence supports it?"

"Islam provides what Christianity lost, clarity." Al-Masri's voice carried quiet certainty. "Allah exists. The Quran proves this through its miraculous nature, its literary perfection, its scientific foreknowledge, its preserved transmission across fourteen centuries. No human could have authored it."

"That the Quran proves Allah exists, because it is written in the Quran?"

"The Quran's existence itself is a miracle. Your daughter Jessica, her ruh, her soul, continues in Barzakh, the realm between death and resurrection. On Judgment Day, Allah will resurrect her bodily and grant her paradise. Children who die innocent enter paradise without question."

"How do you know this is true?"

"Because the Prophet Muhammad, peace be upon him, received these truths directly from Allah through the angel Jibreel. We have preserved his teachings without corruption."

Jacob leaned forward. "Christians claim Jesus revealed God. You claim Muhammad revealed God. Both can't be right. How do I know who actually spoke for God?"

"Christians corrupted their scripture, Catholics invented the Trinity, worshiped a man instead of God. Islam restored the original monotheism of Abraham." Al-Masri's certainty was absolute. "Muhammad is the final prophet, completing God's revelation."

"Assuming I believed that, what would I need to do to reach paradise? To see Jessica again?"

"The five pillars." Al-Masri counted on his fingers. "First, shahada, testify that there is no god, but Allah and Muhammad are His messenger. Second, salat, pray five times daily facing Mecca. Third, zakat, give charity to purify wealth. Fourth, sawm, fast during Ramadan. Fifth, hajj, pilgrimage to Mecca if you're able."

"That's the path to paradise?"

"That, plus following authentic Islamic teaching preserved through the rightly guided caliphs and verified hadith collections. The Prophet, peace be upon him, showed us the way. We preserved it through community consensus, the ummah's collective wisdom."

Jacob pulled out his notebook. "But Professor Hassan told me Islam has major divisions. If Muslims can't agree among yourselves, how do I trust these requirements for paradise?"

Al-Masri's jaw tightened slightly. "You're referring to the Shia."

"Yes. Do they teach a different path to paradise?"

"They add requirements the Prophet never mandated." Al-Masri's voice hardened. "They claim you must love and pledge allegiance to Ali and his descendants, the Ahl al-Bayt, the Prophet's family. They say this devotion is essential for salvation."

"Is it? To pledge allegiance to a family line for perpetuity?"

"No. We honor the Prophet's family, but salvation comes through following Allah and His messenger, not through devotion to any human bloodline." Al-Masri pulled out a photograph, millions of pilgrims circling the Kaaba. "Look at this unity. Sunni Islam preserved what the Prophet actually taught. The Shia created new requirements based on political disputes and family loyalty."

"What disputes?"

"After the Prophet's death, peace be upon him, the community needed leadership. Most Muslims chose Abu Bakr, the Prophet's closest companion, through consultation and consensus. A minority insisted it should be Ali, the Prophet's cousin, and son-in-law. They claimed bloodline succession. We said: leadership through community wisdom, not dynastic inheritance."

"So, it's a political disagreement, not theological?"

"It became theological when they made Ali's family central to salvation itself. When they let grief define their entire faith." Al-Masri's voice carried both conviction and something like regret. "Ali eventually became the fourth caliph, but after his death, his son Hussein challenged the corrupt ruler Yazid. At Karbala in 680 CE, Yazid's army slaughtered Hussein and seventy-two followers, including women and children."

Jacob felt ice in his chest. "They killed children?"

"Yes. We Sunnis also honor Hussein's courage and mourn Karbala's injustice. But the Shia make that suffering sacred. They commemorate it every year during Ashura, beating themselves bloody, reenacting the pain. They turned Hussein's martyrdom into a requirement for paradise, you must love Hussein, weep for Hussein, stand with Hussein to reach Allah."

"But if Hussein died fighting tyranny and injustice...."

"He died unnecessarily!" Al-Masri's composure cracked slightly. "Negotiation was possible. Compromise could have preserved Muslim unity. But Hussein chose principle over survival, and it shattered the community. The Shia worship that choice. They make suffering itself a path to God rather than something to endure with patience."

Jacob pressed: "So if I wanted to honor Jessica's memory by following Islam, you're saying I should follow Sunni teaching because it preserves the authentic path to paradise?"

"Yes. Follow the five pillars. Follow the Quran. Follow the Prophet's verified example. Don't add human requirements based on family devotion and historical trauma."

"But how do I know you're right and the Shia are wrong? You both claim the same Prophet, same Quran, same God."

"Because we preserved what Muhammad actually taught through verified chains of transmission and community consensus. They added requirements after he died, requirements based on loving specific people rather than following authentic teaching." Al-Masri stood. "Your daughter is with Allah, Jacob. If you seek her in paradise, follow the path the Prophet walked, not the path others invented after his death."

Jacob remained seated. "One more question. You and the Shia both claim Muhammad as prophet. The Quran says killing one innocent person is like killing all humanity. Yet Sunni and Shia have killed each other for fourteen centuries. Karbala was Muslims killing Muslims. Modern sectarian violence, car bombs in mosques, assassinations, civil wars. Where does Allah authorize Muslims killing other Muslims over who should have succeeded Muhammad?"

Al-Masri's face darkened. "He doesn't. The Quran commands: 'If two groups of believers fight, make peace between them.' Allah never authorized sectarian violence."

"But it's been happening since Karbala. Hussein's killers were Muslims. Yazid claimed Islamic authority. Modern extremists on both sides cite hadiths and issue fatwas declaring the other side worthy of death."

"Then they lie." Al-Masri's voice was steel. "The Prophet, peace be upon him, said the blood of a Muslim is sacred. Those who kill

Muslims over sectarian identity violate Islam itself. What happened at Karbala was injustice, condemned by Sunni scholars across centuries. Modern extremists betray Islam when they kill each other, their violence is political, dressed in religious language."

"So, whose side is Allah on when Sunni and Shia kill each other claiming His authority?"

Al-Masri met Jacob's eyes. "Neither. Both violate His commands. But understand, the Shia make victimhood central to their faith. They sanctify Hussein's death, cultivate grievance, teach that standing with the oppressed requires violence against oppressors. We Sunnis say: work within the community, preserve unity, avoid fitna, division that destroys the ummah."

"Even when the community tolerates injustice?"

"Even then. Because the alternative is endless cycles of revenge, each side claiming divine authorization for human brutality." Al-Masri moved toward the door. "I must prepare for prayer, Mr. Hinsen. But remember, Allah commands peace among Muslims. Those who cite Karbala to justify modern violence dishonor Hussein's actual sacrifice."

Outside, his phone buzzed. A text from Father Doyle glowed on the screen: *Jacob, unity built on fear cannot be of God. Remember, truth without love is only noise.* Jacob stared at the words, uncertain if they were comfort or indictment. He replied with a thumbs-up emoji and slipped the phone back into his pocket.

***

Before 2:00 PM he arrived at the small teahouse buzzing with conversation. The space was crowded with locals playing backgammon and sharing plates of baklava, the air thick with tobacco smoke and sweet tea.

An elderly woman in the back corner raised her hand slightly, catching his eye. Two tea glasses already sat prepared on her table.

Jacob navigated through the crowd toward her.

"Mr. Hinsen." Not a question. "Professor Hassan described you well. I am Yasmin al-Khafaji." She gestured to the seat across from her, pouring tea with hands that trembled slightly with age. "Hassan said you spent this morning with a Sunni imam who I am sure told you we worship suffering and cannot forget the past."

Jacob settled into the chair and smiled. "He didn't use those exact words."

"But that's what he meant." Her eyes held knowing fire. "They always do. Drink. Let me tell you what the Sunnis won't."

"The Sunni imam told you we add requirements Muhammad never mandated." Not a question. Her eyes held fire. "That we worship suffering. That we should forget Karbala for the sake of unity."

Jacob hesitated. "He said both Sunni and Shia believe in Allah and paradise, but the Shia make Hussein's martyrdom a requirement for salvation that the Prophet never taught."

"Requirements." Yasmin's voice cut. "Let me tell you about requirements. Yes, your daughter is in paradise, all innocent children are. But if you want to reach her there, you must follow the complete path, not the Sunni's convenient half-truth."

"What's the complete path?"

"Everything they teach, faith in Allah, five pillars, righteous living. But also love and allegiance to the Ahl al-Bayt, the Prophet's family." She leaned forward intensely. "The Prophet, peace be upon him, said at Ghadir Khumm: 'Whoever I am his master, Ali is his master.' He designated Ali as his successor. The community ignored this and chose Abu Bakr through political maneuvering."

"I'm afraid I don't know the significance of Ghadir Khumm. And why does succession matter for reaching paradise?"

"Ghadir Khumm was near the end of the Prophet's mission, where he made his final declaration about leadership. He used the word *mawla*, the Sunnis interpret this as 'friend,' 'loyal supporter,' or 'one whom I love.' We believe it means 'master,' 'leader,' 'guardian.' One word. Two interpretations. Fourteen centuries of division."

Jacob felt a chill of recognition. "So, the entire Sunni-Shia split, all the violence, the competing claims about paradise, comes down to how you interpret one Arabic word?"

"Not just interpretation. Divine command versus political convenience." Yasmin's voice was firm but not angry. "As for succession and paradise, Allah commanded love for the Prophet's family. Quran 42:23: 'I ask no reward except love for my near kin.' The Sunnis claim you can reach Allah while dishonoring those closest to His messenger. We say loving Ahl al-Bayt is essential to authentic Islam."

"But Al-Masri said you can honor the Prophet's family without making them requirements for salvation."

"They honor them as historical figures. We honor them as spiritual guides chosen by divine designation. The difference is everything." Yasmin poured more tea. "Your Christians split over how to interpret Jesus's words about Peter being the rock. We split over how to interpret Muhammad's words about Ali being the mawla. Same pattern, one ambiguous statement, centuries of bloodshed."

Jacob opened his notebook. "So, to reach paradise, to see Jessica again, I need to pledge allegiance to Ali's descendants?"

"You need to recognize that spiritual guidance comes through the Prophet's family, the Twelve Imams who preserved authentic teaching. The Sunnis followed political leaders chosen by consensus. We follow spiritual guides chosen by divine designation." Her hands trembled slightly. "And you need to stand with Hussein against tyranny, even if it costs you everything."

"Tell me what happened at Karbala."

Yasmin pulled out a photograph, a shrine, mourners in black, hands raised in anguish. "Hussein was Muhammad's grandson. When Yazid claimed power through power and corruption, Hussein refused allegiance. Not from ambition. From principle. Yazid represented everything Islam opposed, tyranny, injustice, the powerful crushing the weak."

Her voice strengthened with suppressed fury. "Yazid's army of thousands surrounded Hussein's seventy-two followers. Cut off the Euphrates River. Children died of thirst within sight of water. When Hussein carried his dying infant son to negotiate, they shot arrows at the child."

Jacob's throat constricted, Jessica's face flashing before his eyes.

"On the tenth day, Ashura, they slaughtered everyone. Decapitated Hussein and carried his head on a spear to Damascus. Took the women and children as prisoners, parading them through streets." Tears blurred her vision, but her voice never wavered. "Tell me, Jacob, does time erase such injustice? Your daughter died months ago in a senseless accident. Should you 'move on'? Should you forget?"

"No."

"Then you understand why we commemorate Hussein every year. Why we weep for him, stand with him, make his sacrifice part of our path to paradise." She gripped his hand. "Love that refuses to forget injustice. This is what the Sunnis cannot accept. They say: preserve unity, don't dwell on the past, accept what happened. We say: some wounds should never heal because healing requires forgetting, and forgetting makes evil possible."

"So, you're saying the Sunni path to paradise is incomplete because it ignores Hussein's sacrifice?"

"I'm saying they preserved the ritual but lost the soul. They follow five pillars but ignore the foundation, love for those who died defending Islam against corruption. The Prophet's family suffered so Islam would remain pure. The Sunnis accepted political compromise. We chose fidelity to truth over communal convenience."

"But Al-Masri said negotiation was possible at Karbala. That Hussein's stand destroyed Muslim unity unnecessarily."

Yasmin's eyes flashed. "Negotiated with child-murderers? With an army that shot infants? What negotiation exists with evil that is absolute?" Her voice rose. "The Sunnis say this because they descended from those who accepted Yazid's authority, who chose political stability over justice. They built their 'unity' on the blood of the Prophet's family, then ask us to forget for the sake of peace."

"So, whose version of Islam leads to paradise, Sunni consensus or Shia devotion to Ali's line?"

"Both claim to lead to the same paradise. But ask yourself: what path honors your daughter? The Sunni path that says, 'accept what happened, don't dwell on injustice, preserve the community'? Or the Shia path that says, 'love demands we never forget, justice requires we stand with the oppressed even unto death'?"

Jacob leaned back, recognizing the impossible choice. "You both claim Muhammad as prophet. You both follow the Quran. You both believe in Allah. Yet you prescribe different requirements for reaching paradise, and neither can prove your interpretation is correct."

"If you want proof that satisfies courts, no faith provides it." Yasmin's voice softened slightly. "But the question isn't courtroom verification. The question is: what does love to require? What does justice demand? The Sunnis chose order. We chose memory. Both are responses to the same divine reality, but only one refuses to forget innocent blood."

Jacob set down his teacup carefully. "Let me ask you what I asked Al-Masri. The Quran forbids killing innocent people, 'whoever kills a soul, it is as if he killed all mankind.' Yet Sunni and Shia have killed each other for fourteen centuries. Karbala was Muslims killing Muslims. Modern sectarian violence, car bombs, assassinations, civil war. Where does Allah authorize Muslims killing other Muslims over succession disputes?"

Yasmin's face hardened. "He doesn't. The Quran forbids it absolutely. But understand who started the killing, Yazid's army at Karbala, murdering the Prophet's family. We don't kill Sunnis for being Sunni. We remember that Sunnis supported the rulers who killed innocents."

"But sectarian violence continues. Shia militias, Sunni extremists, both sides killing each other, both claiming religious authority."

"Those are political conflicts wearing religious masks." Yasmin's voice was firm. "Extremists on both sides betray authentic Islam. The Quran says: 'There is no coercion in religion.' Allah never authorized Muslims to kill each other."

"Then whose side is Allah on when Sunni and Shia kill each other claiming to defend Islam?"

Yasmin was quiet for a long moment. "Neither side, if they're killing. Both sides, if they're pursuing justice through lawful means. But here's what the Sunnis won't tell you, when they say, 'preserve unity, avoid division,' what they mean is: accept injustice quietly, don't demand accountability, forget what the powerful did to the powerless."

Her voice strengthened. "We refuse that false unity. If standing for justice means division, then division is righteous. If remembering Hussein means we cannot reconcile with those who honor his killers, then we choose memory over convenient peace."

"So, you're saying the Shia path justifies violence against oppressors?"

"I'm saying Hussein showed us that some compromises destroy the soul even as they preserve the body. That love for justice matters more than political unity. That standing with the oppressed is part of the path to paradise, even when it costs everything." She met his eyes directly. "Your daughter died because someone chose convenience over care. That injustice connects you to Hussein, to all who suffer meaninglessly. The Sunnis say: accept it, move on, trust Allah's plan. We say: never forget, demand justice, stand with those who suffer."

Jacob changed position in his chair, his mind reeling. "You're both claiming the same God, so whose side is Allah on when you kill each other, neither answer satisfies."

"Because you're asking the wrong questions." Yasmin said decisively. "You want certainty, which path is correct, whose interpretation Allah endorses. But what if the real question is: what does love require when faced with injustice? The Sunnis chose stability. We chose fidelity. Both claim divine warrant. Neither can prove it."

For the next hour, Jacob and Yasmin set aside theology. They exchanged stories about families, daily struggles, small joys that sustained them. Yasmin spoke of her grandchildren with fierce pride. Jacob found himself laughing at her description of teaching her teenage grandson to make proper tea.

The conversation felt like oxygen after drowning. No competing claims about God's existence. No requirements for paradise. Just two people who'd lost loved ones, finding brief connection in shared humanity.

When Jacob finally stood to leave, Yasmin gripped his hand. "You came seeking answers about God and your daughter. I gave you theology. But this hour, this laughter, this connection, perhaps this is the only proof we have that something transcends death. Love creating meaning between strangers."

***

Jacob left the teahouse as the call to prayer echoed from rival minarets, Sunni and Shia mosques calling to the same Allah, following the same Prophet, unable to agree on the path to the same paradise.

He walked through Istanbul's old city as afternoon faded to evening, his mind churning. Al-Masri had prescribed five pillars plus community consensus. Yasmin had prescribed the same five pillars plus love for the Prophet's family and standing with Hussein's sacrifice. Both claimed their path led to paradise. Both claimed the other's path was incomplete or corrupted. Neither could prove Allah existed or that their requirements came from divine command rather than human interpretation.

And when he'd asked whose side Allah was on when they killed each other, both claiming Quranic authority while violating Quranic commands, neither had given him satisfaction. Al-Masri blamed Shia cultivation of grievance. Yasmin blamed Sunni acceptance of tyranny. Both condemned extremist violence while defending their tradition's theological framework that made such violence conceivable.

It was Christianity all over again. Catholics requiring faith plus works plus sacraments. Protestants insisting on faith alone. Orthodox teaching transformation through theosis. All claiming the same God. All promising reunion with the dead. All fractured over what God required, none able to verify their claims.

Now Islam: Sunnis require five pillars plus consensus. Shia require the same pillars plus devotion to Ali's line. Both claim Muhammad as prophet. Both follow the Quran. Both unable to agree on what Allah demanded or whose interpretation He endorsed.

His phone buzzed. Michael: *Jake, you've been gone over four months. Tom says the practice is finished. When are you coming home?*

"Not sure, Mike, I'm on my way to talk about Judaism and Jessica. Maybe shortly after that?"

Jacob stared at the message. Four months investigating God's existence and his daughter's fate. Four months collecting promises from traditions that fractured into competing certainties. Four months watching humans claim divine authority for interpretations they couldn't verify, requirements they couldn't prove, violence they couldn't justify.

He found a bench near the Hagia Sophia, that ancient church turned mosque turned museum that embodied every contradiction he'd witnessed. Christians had worshiped here claiming exclusive truth. Muslims had prayed here claiming the same. Now tourists photographed both traditions' remnants, neither able to verify whether God existed or cared which prayers were offered in His name.

Jacob pulled out his journal, and for the next two hours he wrote about his journey through Islam:

Istanbul. Met Sunni imam and Shia scholar. Both claim Allah exists, no proof. Both claim Jessica's soul continues in paradise, no verification. Both prescribe different requirements for reaching that paradise: five pillars vs. five pillars plus love for the Prophet's family.

Al-Masri says Shia add requirements Muhammad never taught, that they worship suffering, that Hussein died unnecessarily. Yasmin says Sunnis preserve ritual but ignore justice, that loving the Ahl al-Bayt is Quranic command, that Hussein's sacrifice must be remembered.

I asked both: whose side is Allah on when you kill each other? Neither gave a satisfying answer. Both condemn extremist violence while defending theological frameworks that make violence conceivable. Both claim the Quran forbids killing Muslims while their 1,400-year history is written in Muslim blood.

Christianity fractured over interpretation too: Catholics vs. Protestants vs. Orthodox, all claiming the same God, all promising reunion with the dead, none proving their requirements correct. Then they killed each other for centuries: Crusades, Inquisition, religious wars, violating Christ's command to love enemies.

Islam fractured the same way: Sunnis vs. Shia, both claiming the same Allah, both promising the same paradise, neither proving their path correct. Then they killed each other for centuries, Karbala to modern sectarian violence, violating Quran's prohibition on Muslim blood.

Every tradition fractures. Every faction claims divine authority. Every group eventually justifies violence against those who disagree. Not because God commands it, scriptures explicitly forbid it, but because humans claiming to speak for God find theological justification for political brutality.

I came to Islam hoping for clarity Christianity couldn't provide. Instead: same pattern, different prophet, competing requirements, unprovable claims, violence justified by those claiming divine authority while violating divine commands.

Where is God? I don't know. Where is Jessica? I can't prove she continues anywhere. Would following Sunni or Shia Islam lead me to paradise? Both claim yes, neither can verify, and their disagreement suggests neither knows for certain.

Four months. Three countries. Multiple traditions. One pattern: humans making unprovable claims about God's existence and requirements, fracturing over interpretations they can't verify, demanding faith without proof, then killing each other while claiming divine authorization for violence their own scriptures forbid.

Maybe that's all religion is: humanity's desperate attempt to make mortality bearable, to give suffering meaning, to promise reunion with the dead. Beautiful, necessary, unprovable. And when competing groups claim exclusive truth, deadly.

He closed the journal as evening prayer began, dozens of mosques across Istanbul calling the faithful to worship Allah, some through Sunni interpretation, some through Shia devotion, all claiming the same God, none able to prove He existed or cared which path they followed.

Jacob sat alone on the bench, watching Muslims file into mosques, Christians visit Byzantine ruins, tourists photograph it all, everyone searching for meaning in a city where empires had risen and fallen, where religions had conquered and converted, where humans had killed and died claiming God endorsed their particular vision of truth.

He would continue his investigation. Judaism awaited in Jerusalem, the tradition that had birthed both Christianity and Islam, that had its own fractures and competing interpretations, that would likely offer the same pattern he'd witnessed everywhere: unprovable claims about God, competing requirements for salvation, human authority claiming divine warrant.

If God existed, He was watching His followers kill each other over whose interpretation of His will was correct. If God didn't exist, humans were killing each other over competing interpretations of texts they'd written themselves.

Either way, Jacob couldn't find where Jessica was, and no tradition could prove otherwise.

But tonight, Jacob simply sat with the recognition that months of searching had revealed not answers but patterns: the same human responses to mortality repeating across cultures, the same fractures over interpretation, the same violence justified by those claiming to speak for God while violating everything God supposedly commanded.

His phone buzzed. A message from Shahid: The Sayyid family expects you tomorrow evening for iftar. Come hungry. Come willing to see faith lived rather than debated. Your mind needs rest from questions it cannot answer.

Jacob stared at the invitation. After the intellectual brutality of Al-Masri and Yasmin's competing certainties, the thought of simply witnessing ordinary Muslim life felt like mercy. No theological debates. No competing claims about God's existence or requirements for paradise. Just a family breaking their Ramadan fast together.

He typed back: I'll be there.

***

The next evening, Jacob arrived at the Sayyid apartment in a modest neighborhood away from Istanbul's tourist center. The building showed its age: cracked tile in the stairwell, paint peeling near the windows, but the sounds of family life echoed warmly through thin walls.

Omar Sayyid opened the door before Jacob could knock, as if he'd been watching for him. "As-salamu alaykum. Welcome to our home. You're just in time."

The apartment hummed with organized pre-iftar activity. His wife Zahra moved efficiently between kitchen and dining room while four children helped with final preparations. The smell of lentil soup and freshly baked pide filled the small space. Prayer mats were already laid out facing Mecca.

The youngest daughter, maybe nine years old, was setting the table with careful precision, counting out plates, and adjusting their positions until everything aligned perfectly. The sight stopped Jacob cold. Jessica's age. Jessica's careful way of doing tasks. The sharp pain in his chest threatened to buckle his knees.

Zahra noticed his expression. "That's Amina. She takes her responsibilities very seriously." Her voice carried both pride and the knowing look of someone who recognized grief when she saw it.

Jacob couldn't speak. He just smiled and nodded.

"Mr. Jacob!" Amina called when she noticed him in the doorway. "Mama says you lost your daughter. I'm very sorry. I will share my dolls with her when I see her in Paradise."

The innocent certainty in her voice, when I see her, not if, struck Jacob like a physical blow. Here was a nine-year-old who accepted Jessica's continued existence with the same matter-of-fact confidence she showed in setting dinner plates. No theological complexity, no intellectual struggle, just the simple assumption that death was separation, not ending.

"That's very kind of you, Amina," Jacob managed, his voice rougher than he'd intended. "Jessica would have liked that. She loved sharing her toys with other children."

Khalid Sayyid, Omar's father and the family patriarch, welcomed Jacob with the warm hospitality Islamic culture demanded of guests. But Jacob detected something else in his manner: a protective watchfulness, as if he'd heard about Jacob's reputation for challenging religious certainty and was prepared to defend his family's faith if necessary.

Over dinner, as the family shared the simple joy of breaking their daily fast with dates and water, Omar explained their approach to Islamic practice. "We are not scholars like Shahid Baba," he said in careful English. "We are simple believers who try to follow the path Allah has given us through His Prophet."

"What does that look like practically?" Jacob asked, genuinely curious about how ordinary Muslim families navigated daily life according to religious principles.

"Five prayers each day, charity to those in need, fasting during Ramadan, pilgrimage to Mecca if we can afford it," Omar replied. "But more than ritual, we try to live with kindness, honesty, and justice. The Quran teaches that faith without good actions is meaningless."

Jacob watched the family's evening routine unfold homework supervision conducted between prayer times, gentle correction of children's behavior according to Islamic ethics, discussion of neighborhood concerns through the lens of community responsibility. This wasn't theology as an intellectual system but as practical guidance for ordinary moral decisions.

Amina's homework involved memorizing Quranic verses in Arabic, a tradition that connected Muslim children to the sacred language regardless of their native tongue. She recited the verses with careful pronunciation, her young voice carrying syllables that had been repeated by billions of believers across fourteen centuries.

Watching nine-year-old Amina recite Arabic prayers with careful precision transported Jacob instantly to Jessica's bedroom, to the nightly ritual they'd shared since she was four years old.

"Now I lay me down to sleep, I pray the Lord my soul to keep..." Jessica would begin, hands folded with the seriousness of someone conducting important business with the Almighty.

But formal prayer was only the opening act. Jessica's real conversations with God came after, when she'd list everyone who needed divine attention that day: "Please help Mrs. Rodriguez's cat get better, and help Tommy Morrison stop being mean to the new girl, and help Mommy's headache go away, and help Daddy's back stop hurting from carrying all those law books..."

Her prayers were inventory lists of love, cataloguing every person and creature that had crossed her path with kindness worth remembering. She prayed for strangers glimpsed on the street, for characters in books, for the mouse family living in their garage wall, for her teacher Mrs. Patterson who had a cough that wouldn't go away.

"Don't you ever pray for yourself?" Jacob had asked one night.

Jessica had considered this seriously. "Sometimes I thank God for making you my daddy, and for Mrs. Rodriguez next door who makes me cookies, and for having our house. Is that praying for me?"

The memory was so vivid Jacob could smell the lavender soap from her nightly bath, could feel her small hand finding his in the darkness as she settled into sleep. Now, watching Amina's careful recitation, he wondered if God heard nine-year-old prayers in all languages, or if such prayers simply dissolved into the same silence that had swallowed Jessica's voice.

"Amina, what do those words mean to you?" Jacob asked her tenderly.

"They say Allah loves children and protects them," Amina replied confidently, though Jacob suspected her understanding was simplified for her age. "When children die, they go straight to Paradise because they haven't done anything bad yet. That's why your daughter is safe and happy now."

The religious precision of her explanation, children dying before moral accountability automatically achieve salvation, reflected sophisticated Islamic jurisprudence translated into child-appropriate terms. But Jacob heard something else in her words: the absolute confidence of someone who'd never doubted that love transcends mortality, that death is transition rather than termination.

"Amina," Jacob said softly, "how do you know those things are true?"

"Because the Quran says so, and the Quran is Allah's words," she replied with the matter-of-fact certainty that only children could achieve. "And because Mama and Papa told me, and they learned from their mama and papa, and they learned from the Prophet, who learned from Allah."

The chain of transmission, Islamic scholars called it isnad, that connected this nine-year-old girl's bedtime certainties to seventh-century Arabian revelations. Fifteen centuries of parents telling children that death was not the end, that love survived mortality, that good people would be reunited in Paradise. Whether true or false, the tradition had provided comfort to countless families facing the same loss that had shattered Jacob's world.

Amina finished her recitation, and Omar tucked her into bed, the universal language of parental love requiring no translation.

That night, Jacob lay in the Sayyid family's guest room listening to the sounds of a household at rest: children's quiet breathing, parents whispered prayers, the distant call of a muezzin marking the night's final prayer time. For the first time since Jessica's death, he felt embraced by something greater than his own sorrow, sustained by traditions that had helped countless families navigate similar losses.

***

"You look sad," Amina observed the next morning, appearing beside Jacob's chair at the breakfast table like a small ghost in her white nightgown.

"I miss my daughter very much," Jacob admitted.

"Missing is hard," Amina said with the profound simplicity that children sometimes achieved. "But Jessica isn't really gone. She's just in a place we can't see yet. Like when Papa travels for work, we can't see him, but we know he's still Papa and he still loves us."

Jacob felt tears threatening. This child's effortless acceptance of Jessica's continued existence, her casual assumption that death was temporary separation rather than permanent loss, her confidence that love persisted beyond physical presence, it was both comforting and heartbreaking.

"How do you know that's true?" Jacob asked, though he wasn't sure whether he was questioning Amina's certainty or hoping she could transfer some of it to him.

"Because love doesn't stop," Amina replied as if explaining something obvious to a confused adult. "When you love someone, you love them forever. Death can't make love stop, because love is stronger than everything else."

Over the following days, Jacob observed how Islamic faith shaped the Sayyid family's approach to ordinary difficulties. When Omar lost a construction job due to economic slowdown, the family increased their charitable giving rather than reducing it, trusting that generosity during hardship would be rewarded by divine providence. When Zahra's mother fell ill, they organized community support while submitting to Allah's will regarding her recovery.

Their approach to suffering differed markedly from the theological explanations Jacob had encountered among Christian leaders. Instead of trying to justify why a loving God permitted tragedy, they emphasized submission to divine wisdom beyond human understanding while focusing on practical responses that served community welfare.

"When bad things happen," Omar explained during one of their evening conversations, "we don't ask why Allah allowed them. We ask what Allah wants us to learn or how He wants us to help others who suffer similar difficulties."

"But surely you wonder about divine justice when innocent people suffer?"

"Of course. But wondering is different from demanding answers that might be beyond human capacity to understand. The Quran teaches that Allah's wisdom exceeds human comprehension, so we focus on what we can control: our responses to difficulties."

Jacob was both admiring and frustrated by their approach. The Sayyid family prioritized practical charity and community engagement over theological debate, leading lives of genuine service. However, their intellectual humility regarding ultimate questions left his concerns about Jessica's fate unanswered. He was here to observe their faith, not challenge it.

On his final night with the family, Jacob helped Amina with homework that involved drawing pictures to illustrate Islamic stories. She was working on the story of Prophet Muhammad's night journey to Paradise, a mystical experience that took the Prophet through seven levels of heaven to encounter divine presence directly.

"Why do you think Allah let the Prophet see Paradise?" Jacob asked as Amina colored angels with careful attention to detail.

"So, he could tell everyone what it's like," she replied without looking up from her drawing. "So, we wouldn't be scared when we die because we'd know it's beautiful there."

"Are you ever scared about dying?"

Amina looked up from her artwork with the expression of someone considering an interesting but abstract question. "Sometimes. But then I remember that Paradise is where all the people who love me are waiting, and I won't be scared anymore because everyone will be there."

Jacob studied her drawing: angels surrounding a central figure representing the Prophet, gardens filled with rivers and fruit trees, children playing in meadows where no danger could reach them. Islamic Paradise as imagined by a nine-year-old: a place where love persisted, families were reunited, and the sorrows that complicated earthly existence were finally resolved.

"Amina," Jacob said carefully, "do you think my daughter Jessica is in Paradise now?"

"Of course," Amina replied with absolute confidence. "She was a child, so she didn't do anything bad enough to go anywhere else. And you love her so much that Allah wouldn't want you to be sad forever. Paradise is where love goes when people die, so Jessica is definitely there waiting for you."

Whether her certainty reflected accurate understanding of cosmic realities or simply Islamic cultural conditioning, it had produced a nine-year-old who faced mortality without terror, who understood death as transition rather than termination.

***

That night, Jacob sat in the Sayyid family's guest room. For the first time since Jessica's death, he felt embraced by something greater than his own sorrow, sustained by traditions that had guided countless families through similar losses.

In his journal, Jacob wrote:

Still in Istanbul. Living with the Sayyid family has revealed Islamic faith not as a theological system, but as lived practice. Amina's unwavering certainty about Jessica's presence in Paradise offers comfort that intellectual inquiry could not provide.

Amina's faith that "love doesn't stop" and "Paradise is where love goes when people die" expresses through childhood simplicity what sophisticated theology couldn't convey convincingly. Whether true or false, Islamic tradition has equipped this family to face mortality with hope rather than despair, to find meaning in suffering through service to others.

I'm beginning to understand that my investigation may have been asking the wrong questions. Instead of demanding proof that Jessica continues to exist, maybe I should be learning how to live as if love transcends mortality, how to honor our relationship regardless of metaphysical uncertainty about life after death.

Tomorrow, I leave Istanbul for Jerusalem, where Jewish perspectives on ultimate questions await investigation. But the Sayyid family's uncomplicated faith has provided something my academic inquiries couldn't deliver examples of people living meaningfully with mystery, finding peace through submission to divine wisdom they can't fully comprehend.

Jacob closed his journal and prepared for sleep, aware that his investigation was approaching its final phase. The intellectual inadequacy of religious truth claims had been thoroughly established, but traditions like the Sayyid family's Islam offered practical wisdom for living hopefully despite uncertainty about ultimate realities.

Whether such wisdom would prove sufficient for someone whose loss demanded more than hopeful speculation remained the central question of his journey. But for the first time since beginning his investigation, Jacob thought he might be approaching answers, not about death or divine justice, but about how human beings could create meaning through choosing to love over despair, hope over cynicism, service over self-protection.

The questions that had driven him across three continents might never receive definitive answers. But perhaps learning to ask better questions, learning to live beautifully with uncertainty, learning to honor love without requiring guarantees about its duration, perhaps these were the only answers available to finite beings wrestling with infinite mysteries.

Jessica would be proud of him for continuing to ask tough questions while learning to live with their complexity rather than demanding simple solutions to life's deepest puzzles. That recognition, more than any theological certainty, felt like progress toward whatever resolution his journey might ultimately provide.

*****

Chapter Four

THE ROAD OF JUDAISM

The overnight flight from Istanbul to Tel Aviv carried Jacob across the eastern Mediterranean, the cabin dark except for scattered reading lights and the soft glow of seat-back screens. He pressed his forehead against the cold window, watching distant lights of ships moving through waters that had carried pilgrims, crusaders, and refugees for millennia.

No matter how much he pushed them to the back of his mind, Tom's confrontation at the Istanbul airport still echoed. The partnership was finished. Margaret's increasingly desperate texts. Clients abandoning them. Associates jumping ship. All of it haunted his thoughts.

He should get on the next flight home. He should salvage what could be saved. But Jerusalem was the final piece, the tradition that had birthed both Christianity and Islam, the root from which two billion believers had grown. If Judaism couldn't provide answers, then his five-month investigation would still be complete. He would have exhausted every major tradition's claim about God's existence and the soul's survival.

Two more months maximum. That's all he needed. Surely the wreckage in Chicago could hold together that long.

***

Jacob landed at Ben Gurion Airport in the early morning, passing through security with the usual questions about his visit's purpose. "Religious research," he answered, which earned him a skeptical look but no further inquiry.

He took a sherut, a shared taxi, from the airport to Jerusalem. The hour-long drive carried him from the coastal plain up through the Judean hills, past checkpoints and settlements, olive groves, and ancient terraces. As the van climbed higher, Jerusalem appeared on the ridgeline: stone buildings catching morning light, the golden Dome of the Rock gleaming above the Old City's walls.

He checked into a small hotel in the German Colony, a quiet neighborhood of restored Templar houses and tree-lined streets. The room was simple but clean, with a window overlooking a courtyard where lemon trees grew in terracotta pots. He unpacked his bag, now lighter after months of travel, and reviewed the schedule he'd arranged before leaving Istanbul.

Through an interfaith academic network, he had secured an appointment with Rabbi Benjamin Golden, director of the Institute for Progressive Jewish Studies in Jerusalem's Jewish Quarter, scheduled for later that afternoon.

His hotel concierge, when asked for directions, had only smiled knowingly. "Ah, Rabbi Golden. You'll be in good hands. Americans usually leave his office with more questions than answers, but better questions."

The narrow cobblestone streets of Jerusalem's Old City compressed centuries of religious struggle into every step. Hasidic men in long black coats brushed past secular Israelis in jeans, while Palestinian merchants called out prices in Arabic to tourists carrying Christian guidebooks. Church bells competed with the Muslim call to prayer, while Jewish prayer shawls hung drying from apartment balconies. The proximity of such different approaches to the divine felt both inspiring and overwhelming.

Jacob paused at a corner where all four quarters met: Christian, Muslim, Jewish, Armenian, each claiming sacred geography, each convinced of exclusive truth. A group of Christian pilgrims carried a wooden cross along the Via Dolorosa. Ultra-Orthodox Jews hurried toward afternoon prayers at the Western Wall. Muslim families emerged from Al-Aqsa Mosque after prayers. All worshipping the God of Abraham. All fractured into competing interpretations. All certain they alone understood divine will.

The pattern he'd discovered across continents seemed concentrated here in a few ancient blocks: unprovable claims about God, fractures over authority and interpretation, violence justified by religious texts. If anywhere held answers, it would be here at the source. If nowhere held answers, he would finally know.

Rabbi Golden's study center occupied a restored Ottoman building tucked between a spice shop and a bookbinder's workshop. The narrow stairwell smelled of old stone and incense. When Jacob reached the second floor, he found a door marked "Institute for Progressive Jewish Studies" in Hebrew, Arabic, and English.

Inside, a man in his sixties rose from behind a desk covered with open texts. No traditional black coat or wide-brimmed hat, just a small, knitted kippah and casual blazer that suggested intellectual engagement over ritual piety.

"Welcome," Rabbi Golden said, extending his hand. "You must be Jacob Hinsen. Dr. Stern in Chicago wrote that you're investigating religious approaches to God and mortality. I am honored to be a small part of your quest."

Something about Rabbi Golden's manner, curious but not defensive, scholarly but not intimidating, made Jacob's story spill out more easily than he'd expected. He explained Jessica's death in detail he'd never shared with strangers: the wind scattering her art project, the teenage driver's phone conversation, the three minutes that separated tragedy from ordinary Thursday afternoon. He described his months of theological investigation, his encounters with Christian and Islamic scholars, his growing frustration with claims that couldn't be verified.

"I'm not sure yet if I'm seeking conversion," Jacob clarified, opening his notebook now heavy with questions from three continents. "I'm investigating. I need evidence that would hold up to the same standards I'd use in court: independent verification, consistent testimony, logical coherence."

Jacob paused. "Rabbi Golden, I've spent months investigating Christian and Islamic claims about where God is and whether my daughter survived death. Neither tradition provided verification I could accept. Judaism gave birth to both religions. I need to understand what evidence you have that the God of Abraham exists and where He is, and whether believing in Him guarantees reunion with deceased loved ones."

"I understand, Jacob. Where would you like to begin?" Rabbi Golden asked, settling back in his chair with the patient attention of someone accustomed to fielding puzzling questions.

"Rabbi Golden, Judaism gave birth to Christianity and Islam, yet those faiths contradict its fundamental claims even while worshipping the same God. Two billion Christians believe Jesus was the Messiah; one and a half billion Muslims believe Muhammad was the final prophet. How do you maintain confidence that your tradition carries divine truth when its own children deny it so vehemently?"

The rabbi leaned forward, a faint smile playing at his lips as if he'd been waiting for exactly this challenge. "An excellent question, but it rests on several assumptions worth examining. First, that divine truth should be measured by popularity rather than faithfulness to revelation. Second, that contradiction between traditions necessarily invalidates all of them rather than suggesting the complexity of divine reality."

Jacob's prosecutor instincts sharpened. "But Rabbi, couldn't any minority religious sect justify itself that way? Claiming that unpopularity proves authenticity rather than error?"

"Absolutely true," Golden admitted without defensiveness. "Which is why we judge traditions not by their claims about themselves, but by their fruits over time. What has Judaism contributed to human civilization despite, or perhaps because of, remaining a small minority? Disproportionate contributions to ethics, education, scientific discovery, social justice movements. We've preserved the radical conviction that questioning authority is holy, that learning is a sacred obligation, that the vulnerable must be defended even at personal cost."

The rabbi stood and pulled a volume from his shelves, a collection of responsa, rabbinical legal decisions spanning centuries. "Look at this tradition of ethical reasoning, Jacob. For two thousand years, Jewish scholars have wrestled with practical questions: How do we balance individual rights with communal obligations? When does preserving life override religious law? How do we pursue justice when power structures oppose it? Whether you attribute this to divine inspiration or cultural evolution, it represents sophisticated moral reasoning that has influenced human development."

Jacob examined the text, struck by its resemblance to legal precedent: case studies building upon previous decisions, minority opinions preserved alongside majority rulings. "But this brings me to another question, Rabbi. Archaeological evidence shows early Israelites worshipped multiple gods: El, Asherah, Baal, alongside Yahweh. Biblical criticism reveals multiple sources, contradictory accounts, editorial modifications over centuries. Doesn't this undermine claims about unique divine revelation?"

Rabbi Golden's expression grew more serious, but he showed no sign of defensiveness. He walked to another shelf and pulled down a volume of Talmud, opening it to a dense page of commentary with multiple voices arguing distinct positions. "You're a lawyer, Jacob. You understand adversarial process, cross-examination, the value of preserving dissenting opinions. Look at this page."

Jacob studied the layout: central text surrounded by layers of commentary, argument stacked beside counterargument, questions generating more questions rather than final answers.

"Our tradition never erased the messiness," Rabbi Golden continued. "Polytheistic influences, inconsistent faithfulness, theological evolution, it's all preserved in our texts. We didn't sanitize our history to create a neat theological package. We wrestle with God, Jacob. That is literally our name: Israel, 'one who wrestles with God.' We don't run from contradiction; we embrace it as the inevitable result of finite beings encountering infinite mystery."

Jacob leaned forward, not ready to let the question go. "But Rabbi, that doesn't answer what I asked. You're telling me Judaism embraces the messiness, but you're not telling me whether that messiness undermines the claim of divine revelation. If early Israelites worshiped Asherah alongside Yahweh, along with three more, and if the Torah shows straightforward signs of multiple human authors editing texts over centuries, then how is this different from any other ancient religion that evolved naturally? Where's the divine intervention? Where's God in all this human theological development?"

Rabbi Golden set the Talmud down carefully, his expression shifting from scholarly to somber. "You're asking whether I believe God literally spoke to Moses at Sinai, whether the Torah is divine dictation or human interpretation of divine encounter."

"Yes. That's exactly what I'm asking."

"Then here's my honest answer: I don't know. I believe our ancestors encountered something transcendent, something that transformed them from a slave people into a nation with revolutionary ethical vision. Whether that encounter was God speaking audibly or human beings experiencing the divine in ways their ancient context could only express through anthropomorphic language, I cannot prove. What I can say is that the encounter was real, that it produced lasting transformation, and that wrestling with its meaning has sustained us for three millennia."

Jacob wrote quickly in his notebook. "So, you're admitting the foundation might be human interpretation, not divine revelation."

"I'm admitting I hold the tradition with humility rather than certainty. Orthodox Jews would say I'm wrong, that every word of Torah is divine. Reform Judaism says the encounter was real, but the expression is human. We're both Jews. We both believe something sacred happened at Sinai. We disagree about what exactly that 'something' was."

"Which means Judaism can't agree on its own foundation."

"Which means Judaism is honest about the limits of human certainty regarding divine revelation." Rabbi Golden's voice carried both sadness and conviction. "We preserved the contradictions, the polytheistic traces, the multiple sources, because we're not afraid of what honest investigation reveals. That's not weakness, Jacob. That's intellectual courage."

"But doesn't that mean the foundational stories, Abraham's call, Moses at Sinai, the giving of the Torah, are more theological construct than historical event? How can I distinguish authentic divine revelation from human religious creativity if the historical foundation is uncertain? With all the changes, even during the last 1000 years, how can anyone believe that pre-biblical stories were passed down orally without change?"

Rabbi Golden's reply was slow, deliberate, delivered with the precision of someone who'd wrestled with this question personally. "You cannot know revelation the way you know a statute or court precedent. But consider what those stories, historically accurate or not, have made of us as a people. The ethical revolution: moving from tribal loyalty to universal human dignity. The covenantal consciousness: understanding relationship with the divine as reciprocal responsibility rather than hierarchical submission. The insistence that this life matters, that justice is a sacred obligation, that each person bears divine image regardless of social status."

He closed the Talmud softly, his fingers lingering on the worn cover. "Perhaps that transformation itself is the revelation, Jacob. Not a clean historical record that satisfies modern evidential standards, but a people continually shaped by encounter with something beyond themselves. The persistence of Jewish ethical vision despite centuries of persecution, maybe that's the miracle worth examining."

Jacob frowned, his analytical mind pushing against the rabbi's approach. "But if the same God spoke to Jews, Christians, and Muslims, why do they contradict each other so bitterly on fundamental questions? Christians claim salvation through Christ's death and resurrection; Muslims insist Muhammad received the final revelation correcting previous distortions; Jews maintain the covenant remains in effect without need for intermediaries. How is such disagreement possible if one divine source is involved?"

"How will I ever know which path God is on?" he quickly added.

Rabbi Golden's smile returned, gentler this time, carrying what looked like hard-won wisdom. "Maybe revelation is like light passing through a prism, Jacob. One source, refracted into many colors depending on the medium it encounters. Different cultures, historical circumstances, human needs, all functioning as different surfaces that bend the light in various directions."

He moved to his window overlooking the Old City, where minarets, church towers, and synagogue domes competed for skyline space. "The tragedy isn't that we see different colors. The tragedy is when people mistake their particular color for the entire light source. When Christians claim exclusive possession of divine truth, when Muslims insist their revelation supersedes all others, when Jews assert permanent chosen's, that's human pride, not divine communication."

"So, you're saying all three traditions contain partial truth?"

"I'm saying all three traditions represent authentic human encounters with divine reality, filtered through different cultural and historical circumstances. The contradictions reflect human limitation, not divine confusion. Maybe the goal isn't to determine which tradition got it 'right,' but to learn from all of them while maintaining humility about what finite minds can grasp of infinite reality."

Jacob fell silent, his pen hovering over his notebook. It was the closest thing to intellectual coherence he'd encountered since his journey began, yet it was no less elusive for its reasonableness. "Rabbi, that sounds intellectually satisfying, but what about practical questions? If my daughter Jessica exists somewhere beyond death, which tradition's description of that existence is accurate? Do I need to convert to Judaism to be reunited with her? Or does it not matter because all paths lead to the same destination?"

Rabbi Golden returned to his desk, his expression showing the gravity Jacob's question deserved. "Those are the questions that make this conversation more than academic exercise, aren't they? Your daughter's fate, your own spiritual condition, the possibility of reunion, these matter in ways that theological speculation doesn't."

He opened a different book, this one containing traditional Jewish prayers, and read quietly in Hebrew before providing translation: "'The soul You have given me, O God, is pure. You created it, You formed it, You breathed it into me, and You preserve it within me. And You will eventually take it from me and restore it to me in the time to come.'"

"But Rabbi, these are prayers and psalms written by men."

"Yes, but inspired by God!" The rabbi replied with annoyance in his voice.

"Jacob, traditional Jewish prayer acknowledges life's survival, but with characteristic uncertainty about details. 'The time to come,' olam haba in Hebrew, is deliberately vague. Some Jewish thinkers describe literal bodily resurrection, others spiritual continuation in divine presence, still others speak metaphorically about living through influence on future generations."

Jacob leaned forward, his frustration evident. "But that doesn't help me, Rabbi. I need to know whether Jessica, specifically Jessica, with her personality and memories and love for me, still exists somewhere I might eventually encounter her again."

"And I cannot give you that empirical assurance," Rabbi Golden replied with the directness Jacob had come to appreciate. "No honest religious teacher can, regardless of their tradition's claims. What I can offer is the Jewish approach to living meaningfully despite such uncertainty."

He pulled out a collection of Holocaust testimonies, opening to a passage he'd obviously marked long ago. "Jacob, during the Shoah, observant Jews faced the ultimate test of faith: how to maintain belief in divine justice while experiencing systematic genocide. Some lost faith entirely, understandably so. Others emerged with faith paradoxically strengthened, not because they received answers about divine justice, but because they chose to act as if human dignity mattered regardless of cosmic guarantees."

"Meaning what, in effect?"

"Meaning they continued protecting the vulnerable, sharing scarce resources, maintaining learning and ritual and community bonds, even when God seemed absent. They chose ethical behavior not because they could prove its ultimate significance, but because the alternative, nihilism, despair, abandoning moral obligation, produced worse outcomes for everyone."

Rabbi Golden stood and moved to his bookshelf again, this time selecting a volume of contemporary Jewish philosophy. "Emmanuel Levinas, a Holocaust survivor and philosopher, wrote that ethics precedes ontology: our obligation to others exists before we can prove why it should exist. Maybe that's the Jewish contribution to your investigation, Jacob. Maybe faith means choosing ethical behavior, choosing love, choosing hope, regardless of metaphysical certainty about their ultimate foundation."

Jacob was both attracted to and frustrated by this approach. "So, you're saying I should live as if Jessica continues to exist and as if I'll be reunited with her, whether or not I can prove either claim?"

"I'm saying you should live in ways that honor your love for her and extend that love to others who need it, regardless of whether cosmic justice guarantees reward for such behavior. If there is life after death, you'll be prepared for reunion. If there isn't, you'll have lived meaningfully anyway."

Rabbi Golden verged forward, his voice carrying both warmth and challenge. "Jacob, I hope you don't believe that somewhere in your journey you'll turn a corner and find God waiting to have a private conversation with Jacob A. Hinsen, lawyer from Chicago. That He'll say, 'Where have you been? I've been waiting to answer all those questions I haven't answered for anyone else in human history.'"

Jacob felt the words land like stones. "That's not what I'm looking for."

"Isn't it?" Golden's eyes held steady. "You're demanding evidence no one else has received. You want God to prove Himself to your satisfaction using standards you've chosen. But every prophet, every mystic, every saint who claimed an encounter with the divine, they all had to choose faith without the proof you're demanding. Why should you be different?"

"Because my daughter died. Because I need to know if she continues somewhere."

"And millions of parents before you have needed the same thing. God didn't give them courtroom proof either. He gave them community, tradition, practices that sustained them through grief. Not answers, sustenance."

Jacob's jaw tightened. "So, faith means accepting I'll never know?"

"Faith means choosing to live as if the answers matter, whether or not you can prove them. That's not surrender, Jacob. That's courage."

The rabbi's approach felt more honest than the confident assertions Jacob had encountered from other religious leaders, but it also felt emotionally unsatisfying. After months of seeking certainty about Jessica's fate, being told to embrace uncertainty as an appropriate religious response left him feeling adrift.

"Rabbi Golden, I appreciate your intellectual honesty, but I'm not sure philosophical comfort is sufficient for someone whose loss demands more than abstract ethical principles."

"Which brings us to the difference between philosophy and religion," Rabbi Golden replied, closing the book and fixing Jacob with a direct gaze. "Philosophy offers concepts; religion offers community, practice, narrative frameworks that sustain people through experiences concepts alone cannot address."

He moved toward his coat hanging by the door. "Enough abstract discussion for today, Jacob. You want to understand Judaism? You need to experience it, not just analyze it. Come tomorrow night to my nephew David's house for Seder. It's a family gathering, but strangers are always welcome. Our foundational story begins with strangers in Egypt."

Jacob hesitated. "I don't want to intrude on family time or mislead anyone about my intentions. I'm investigating, not seeking conversion."

"Not intrusion, participation," Rabbi Golden said with the first genuine laugh Jacob had heard from him. "And don't worry about conversion pressure. Jews don't proselytize. If anything, we're suspicious of people who want to join us. We figure they don't understand what they're getting into."

He opened the door, signaling the end of their formal discussion. "Besides, David's eight-year-old son Benjamin asks enough questions to challenge three rabbis. You'll fit right in. And Jacob? The Seder isn't about converting anyone to anything. It's about remembering that human liberation is possible, that suffering doesn't last forever, that even slaves can become free people. After what you've been through, that might be exactly the story you need to hear."

Jacob left Rabbi Golden's study feeling more intellectually satisfied yet emotionally unsettled than after any previous religious encounter. The rabbi's refusal to offer comfortable certainties about the afterlife, his emphasis on ethical action without metaphysical guarantees, his intellectual honesty about the limitations of human knowledge regarding ultimate questions, all of it felt more truthful than the confident assertions he'd encountered from Christian and Islamic leaders.

But the truth, Jacob was learning, wasn't necessarily comforting.

***

Walking through Jerusalem's Old City as afternoon shadows lengthened, he found himself confronting the possibility that Golden's approach, acknowledging uncertainty while choosing meaningful action, might represent the most mature religious response to ultimate questions. Yet part of him still rebelled against accepting uncertainty about Jessica's fate. His love for her demanded more than philosophical comfort about the appropriateness of not knowing. Although his options were getting scarce.

The Western Wall loomed ahead as Jacob walked through the plaza at dusk. Ancient limestone blocks caught the last light, their surface worn smooth by weather and countless hands pressing prayers into cracks between stones. Hundreds of worshippers approached for evening prayers: Orthodox men in black coats swaying in intense concentration, secular visitors touching the stones with expressions of awe, tourists taking photos from the barriers.

Jacob approached cautiously, aware he was entering sacred space as a spiritual tourist rather than a believing participant. He placed his palm against the warm stone, feeling its solidity amid all his uncertainty. Thousands of written prayers had been inserted into cracks: requests for healing, peace, answers to questions that seemed to have no answers.

"First time at the Wall?" The voice came from beside him, accented English carrying authority.

Jacob turned to find an Orthodox rabbi in his fifties: black coat and wide-brimmed hat, full beard streaked with gray. His eyes held both warmth and assessment, the look of someone accustomed to identifying seekers among tourists.

"Yes. I'm Jacob Hinsen, from Chicago."

"Rabbi Moshe Berkowitz." He extended his hand. "You have the look of a man asking difficult questions. I've seen that expression many times at this Wall."

Jacob felt oddly exposed. "I'm investigating different religious traditions. Trying to understand what they teach about God's existence and my daughter's survival after death."

"Ah. A serious seeker." Rabbi Berkowitz gestured toward a stone bench away from the main crowd. "You've spoken to Rabbi Golden?"

"Today. How did you know?"

"Jerusalem is a small city for those who study these questions. Golden is Reform, brilliant, but Reform. He told you God's existence can't be proven, and Judaism emphasizes ethics over metaphysics. Yes?"

Jacob nodded, impressed by the accuracy.

"Let me give you the Orthodox perspective, the traditional Jewish teaching that sustained our people for three thousand years." Rabbi Berkowitz's voice carried conviction. "God exists. The Torah is His revealed word given at Mount Sinai. The soul survives death and returns to God who gave it. These are the foundations of Jewish faith."

"Can you prove any of that?"

"Prove?" Rabbi Berkowitz smiled. "Can you prove you love your daughter? Can you measure devotion? Some realities transcend courtroom evidence. But I can tell you that Orthodox Judaism rests on the testimony of an entire people who stood at Sinai and heard God speak. That collective witness, passed down through generations, is our proof."

Jacob pulled out his notebook. "But that's faith-based testimony, not independent verification. And it contradicts what Rabbi Golden told me, that Torah reflects ancient people's understanding of God, not literal divine dictation."

"Yes. That's the divide between Orthodox and Reform. We believe Torah is divine revelation. Golden believes it's a human document inspired by an encounter with the divine. We're both Jews, but we disagree fundamentally on authority and truth." Rabbi Berkowitz's conviction was striking. "Judaism fractures over this question just as Christianity fractures over papal authority and Islam fractures over succession."

"So, you follow the same pattern of competing interpretations."

"Yes. And our fractures run deep. Reform rabbis ordain women and LGBTQ clergy. We don't recognize their conversions or marriages. Conservative Judaism tries to bridge the gap and satisfies no one. Hasidic groups won't intermarry with Modern Orthodox. We argue about everything: Sabbath observance, dietary laws, gender roles, Israel. We can't even agree on what God wants from us."

Jacob wrote quickly. "And violence? Do Orthodox Jews justify violence through religious texts?"

Rabbi Berkowitz's expression grew grave. "Some do. Religious settlers cite Torah to claim Palestinian land. Extremists have murdered in God's name: Rabin's assassination, the Hebron massacre. They quote the same scriptures I revere and reach opposite conclusions. That's the danger when humans claim absolute certainty about God's will."

"But you claim absolute certainty that God exists and gave the Torah."

"I claim faith based on tradition and community testimony. But I admit I cannot prove it to you." Rabbi Berkowitz leaned forward. "You asked about your daughter's survival. Orthodox Judaism teaches that the soul, Neshama, returns to God after death. But we're deliberately vague about details. No descriptions of heaven like Christianity offers. No paradise gardens or virgins like Islam promises. Just trust that the soul continues in God's presence."

"That's not much comfort for someone who needs to know his daughter still exists somewhere."

"No, it's not. But it's honest. We don't invent detailed afterlife descriptions to comfort the grieving. We offer trust in God's justice and mercy without claiming to understand the mechanics." Rabbi Berkowitz stood, straightening his coat. "You want proof that cannot exist. You want certainty about mysteries that transcend human comprehension. Orthodox Judaism offers you community, tradition, practices that have sustained millions through grief like yours. Not answers, sustenance."

Jacob looked up at the Wall, at Orthodox men pressing their foreheads against ancient stone, their prayers fervent despite having no more proof than Jacob possessed. "And if I can't accept faith without evidence?"

"Then you'll continue suffering without the resources our tradition offers to ease that suffering. Not because you're intellectually inferior, but because you're demanding what God has never given anyone. Not Moses, not the prophets, not the millions who've stood where you're standing now." Rabbi Berkowitz's voice softened. "Your daughter's soul is with God, Mr. Hinsen. I believe that with absolute conviction. But I cannot prove it to you in our earthly domain. That's the nature of faith."

He walked back toward the Wall, rejoining the evening prayers, leaving Jacob alone with questions that had followed him across continents. The same questions. The same absence of answers. But for the first time, Jacob wondered whether demanding proof was the problem, not the solution.

Jacob pulled out his journal and began writing by the Wall's floodlights as evening settled over Jerusalem:

Jerusalem, Day One. Two encounters today, each revealing something different.

Rabbi Golden (afternoon): Can't prove God exists. Judaism prioritizes ethics over metaphysics. Afterlife is deliberately vague. Admits Torah contains theological evolution, not pure historical record. Honest about uncertainty. "Living as if justice matters" even without cosmic guarantees.

Rabbi Berkowitz (evening, at the Wall): God exists, Torah is divine revelation, soul survives death. But admits he can't prove any of it. Orthodox faith rests on the "collective witness" of people at Sinai, which is still just testimony, not verification. At least he was honest: "I believe with absolute conviction. But I cannot prove it to you."

The pattern completes itself in Judaism too:

- *Unprovable metaphysical claims (God exists, soul survives)*

- *Internal fractures (Reform vs. Conservative vs. Orthodox, can't even agree on basic authority)*

- *Violence justified by religious texts (Rabin's assassin, Hebron massacre, settler attacks)*

But something Berkowitz said cuts deeper: "You're demanding what God has never given anyone. Not Moses, not the prophets, not the millions who've stood where you're standing."

Is that true? Have I been chasing something that doesn't exist, not because God doesn't exist, but because proof itself is impossible for ultimate questions?

Christianity promised heaven with certainty. Islam promised paradise with certainty. Judaism at least admits uncertainty. But all three rest on the same foundation: faith without proof.

Maybe the problem isn't that religions can't prove their claims. Maybe the problem is that I'm demanding a kind of knowledge humans can't possess about ultimate realities.

But that doesn't help me know where Jessica is. It doesn't tell me if I'll see her again. It just tells me I'll never know.

Golden invited me to a Seder at his nephew's house tomorrow night. I should go. Not for answers, for observation. To see how people actually live with these questions rather than just debate them.

He closed the journal and walked back to his hotel through Jerusalem's quiet streets, exhausted by the weight of questions that had no answers.

***

The next day, Jacob spent the morning wandering Jerusalem's Old City. He watched Orthodox Jews hurrying to morning prayers at the Western Wall, Christian pilgrims walking the Via Dolorosa with expressions of devotion, Muslim families emerging from Al-Aqsa Mosque after prayers. Three faiths, one God, endless contradictions.

In the late afternoon, his phone buzzed. *A text from Rabbi Golden: Sarah Rosen can see you Thursday afternoon at 1 pm if you're interested. She's 94 and tires easily, so keep it brief. Holocaust survivor-maintained faith after Auschwitz. Thought you should meet her. Her address below.*

Jacob stared at the message. A woman who maintained faith after watching her mother and children die in gas chambers.

If anyone had earned the right to doubt God's existence, it was her. Yet somehow, she still believed.

Or did she? What did "maintained faith" mean for someone who'd survived ultimate evil?

He texted back: *Thursday 1 pm works. See you tonight. Thank you.*

***

That evening, Jacob took a taxi to the address Rabbi Golden had provided for the Seder. He found himself climbing stairs to David Golden's apartment in West Jerusalem with a bouquet of flowers and a bottle of Cabernet Sauvignon. The building hummed with preparation: cooking smells, children's voices, the clatter of dishes being arranged for ceremony.

David Golden welcomed him at the door with the same intellectual warmth his uncle possessed, though twenty years younger and surrounded by organized chaos. "You must be the investigator Uncle Ben mentioned. Perfect timing, we're just setting up. Benjamin, come meet our guest!"

A boy of about eight appeared, dark hair sticking up in the back, wearing a white shirt already stained with what looked like grape juice. "Are you the sad man Grandpa Rabbi told us about?" Benjamin asked with the directness only children possess.

"Benjamin!" His mother, Leah, appeared, mortified. "I'm so sorry, Mr. Hinsen."

"It's fine," Jacob managed, though it wasn't. "And yes. I suppose I am a sad man."

Benjamin considered this with the gravity of a boy deciding something important. "My friend Noah's dad died. Noah was really sad. But then he got a new dog and he's not as sad anymore. Do you have a dog?"

"Benjamin, go help your sister set the table," David said gently. The boy scampered off, leaving Jacob standing in the doorway trying to remember how to breathe around the tightness in his chest.

"I apologize," David said. "Children at this age have no filter."

"No," Jacob smiled, and said quietly. "Children at this age tell the truth."

The apartment was modest but warm, filled with the accumulated disorder of family life. Toys in corners, drawings stuck to the refrigerator with magnets, shoes kicked off by the door. Life continuing despite tragedy, despite uncertainty, despite everything.

Rabbi Golden arrived as they were setting up, greeting Jacob with a concerned look. "You look like you haven't slept in days."

"I haven't."

The old rabbi squeezed his shoulder but said nothing more.

Twenty minutes later, fourteen people crowded around a table that probably seated eight comfortably. David's wife Leah, their three children, Rabbi Golden and his wife, David's sister's family from Tel Aviv, and Jacob squeezed in at the end next to Benjamin, who'd insisted on sitting by "the sad man."

David began in Hebrew, his voice carrying the melody of prayers said for generations. Jacob didn't understand the words but felt their weight, their history. Four thousand years of this. Families gathering, telling the story of liberation from slavery, choosing to remember suffering while celebrating freedom.

The youngest child asked the four questions in Hebrew, stumbling over the words, prompted by her mother. Benjamin whispered a translation for the first one: "Why is this night different from all other nights?"

Good question, Jacob thought. What made any night different? What made suffering meaningful or random? What made love last beyond death or vanish like breath?

David lifted a piece of matzah, broke it, explained in English for Jacob's benefit: "The bread of affliction. Our ancestors ate this as slaves. We eat it now, as free people."

"The bitter herbs," David continued, passing a bowl of horseradish. "To taste the bitterness of slavery."

Everyone took some. Benjamin made an exaggerated face. His sister laughed. Normal family moments in the middle of ritual remembering suffering.

"Mr. Hinsen?" Benjamin's small voice. "Are you doing, okay?"

Jacob realized tears were gently rolling down his face. He was thinking of Jessica's sacrifice. Everyone at the table had stopped, looking at him with concern and something else. Recognition. Every person here had lost someone. Every person here knew grief.

"I'm sorry," he managed. "I should go."

"No," Rabbi Golden said firmly. "Stay. This is exactly where you should be."

David began the story. Not reading, telling. The slavery in Egypt, the plagues, the angel of death passing over houses marked with lamb's blood, the exodus through the Red Sea. Liberation not by deserving it but by choosing to walk toward freedom even when freedom seemed impossible.

Benjamin leaned against Jacob's arm, following along in a children's Haggadah with pictures. The weight of him, his small shoulder pressing into Jacob's side, the warmth of a child's body trusting enough to lean, hit Jacob like a fist to the chest. Jessica used to do this. Sunday mornings reading the paper, bedtime stories, sitting in church pews. That exact pressure against his ribs. That exact trust.

Jacob's breath caught. For a moment Benjamin *was* Jessica, and she was alive, and none of the last six months had happened.

"That's when God split the sea," Benjamin whispered, pointing at a drawing of walls of water, oblivious to Jacob's hands beginning to shake. "Do you think that really happened?"

Every adult at the table went quiet, waiting to see how Jacob would answer. But Jacob couldn't speak yet. Couldn't push words past the tightness in his throat. A child was leaning against him, and it wasn't Jessica and would never be Jessica again.

"I don't know," he finally managed, voice quivering. "I don't know if God split the sea. But I know people chose to walk through it anyway, not knowing if they'd make it to the other side."

Benjamin nodded slowly. Then asked the question that broke Jacob completely: "Do you think Jessica would want you to be sad forever? Or would she want you to help other people not be sad?"

Jacob couldn't speak. Couldn't breathe. He saw Jessica's face, heard her voice. "That's not kind, Daddy." She'd hate this. Hate that he'd destroyed Tom's practice, cost people their jobs, abandoned everyone while he searched for proof she survived. She'd want him helping people, not hurting them in her name.

"I think," Jacob finally managed, voice breaking, tears visible, "she'd want me to help people not be sad."

"Then you should do that," Benjamin said with the absolute certainty of childhood. "That's what my friend Noah's dad would have wanted too."

He had articulated in a simple statement what Jacob had heard before: "Choose love, choose meaning, and honor the dead by how you live, not by how completely you mourn."

After dinner, the children acted out the ten plagues with props, giggling as they threw plastic frogs at each other. Life continuing. Joy existing alongside remembered suffering. Freedom chosen despite slavery, celebration despite bitterness, hope despite every reason for despair.

As Jacob prepared to leave, Rabbi Golden walked him to the door. "You survived tonight."

"Barely."

"Benjamin has a gift for asking the questions we're all thinking but afraid to voice."

"He's remarkable."

"He's eight. At eight, they haven't learned to lie to themselves yet." The old rabbi squeezed Jacob's shoulder. "You told him the truth. That matters more than you know."

Jacob descended the stairs into Jerusalem's night. The city glowed amber under streetlights, ancient stones holding the weight of four thousand years of people asking the same questions, choosing to live and love and hope anyway.

He thought of the exodus story. The Israelites didn't know if the sea would part. They walked toward it anyway.

Maybe that was faith. Not certainty about cosmic guarantees. Just choosing to walk through the water not knowing if you'd make it to the other side. Choosing to break your bread not knowing if anyone would remember. Choosing to live as if love was holy whether it was or not.

Jessica would want him to help people not be sad. An eight-year-old boy saw that clearly. Jacob had spent six months demanding proof of heaven when the answer might be simpler: honor her by how you live, not by whether you'll see her again.

The thought still didn't comfort him. But it felt true. And for the first time since the accident, truth felt like enough to build on. Like matzah, simple, plain, the bread of affliction that somehow sustained people through wilderness.

He walked through Jerusalem's streets thinking of Benjamin's question, David's choices, Rabbi Golden's friendship. All of it pointing toward the same answer he'd been circling since leaving Rome: You can't prove God exists. You can't prove Jessica survived. But you can choose to live as if love matters eternally. That choice is the only faith available.

And maybe, finally, that was enough.

His journal entry that night captured the shift he felt occurring:

Tonight, I experienced Jewish faith as lived practice rather than theological theory. The Seder's central message, that liberation from oppression is possible, that suffering doesn't define identity, that each person bears responsibility for others' freedom, felt more relevant to my situation than abstract debates about the afterlife.

Benjamin's question haunts me: Would Jessica want me sad forever, or working to help others avoid similar sadness? If I spent my remain-

ing years serving families experiencing loss rather than seeking proof of reunion, would that honor her memory more authentically?

Maybe Jewish wisdom lies precisely here: focusing on answerable questions How should I live? What do I owe others? rather than unanswerable ones (What happens after death? Is there life after death?). Maybe faith means choosing to live as if love and justice matter eternally, whether or not eternity can be proven.

Jacob closed his journal and looked out at Jerusalem's ancient skyline one more time. Tomorrow he would continue his investigation, but something fundamental had shifted. The questions driving him across continents were slowly transforming from demands for cosmic certainty into invitations for ethical commitment.

Whether that transformation represented spiritual progress or failure of nerve remained to be determined. But for the first time since Jessica's death, Jacob felt connected to a community of meaning that didn't require him to abandon intellectual honesty about ultimate mysteries.

***

At 2 pm Thursday, he arrived in Rehavia. Sarah Rosen's apartment occupied the ground floor of a pre-war building. The door opened before he could knock. A woman in her nineties stood there, small and frail but carrying herself with dignity that suffering hadn't broken. Her eyes were a dark abyss that made Jacob look away immediately. He recognized that look from his own mirror.

"Mr. Hinsen. Rabbi Golden said you were coming. Come in. I made tea."

Photographs covered every surface: family from before, survivors after, children and grandchildren born in the country she'd helped build. On one wall hung a faded photograph of a young woman with dark hair and frightened eyes in striped prison uniform.

"That's me," Sarah said. "1945. Three months after liberation. I was nineteen and weighed seventy-three pounds."

Jacob's throat closed. Jessica had weighed sixty-five pounds when she died. Nine years old. Almost the same weight as a nineteen-year-old woman starved nearly to death.

Sarah gestured to a worn sofa. "Sit. Tell me in your own words why you're here."

"My daughter died five months ago. Car accident. She was nine. I'm trying to determine if God exists and where He is. And whether my daughter is with Him. You survived the Holocaust and still believe. I need to understand how you maintain faith in God's existence after witnessing ultimate evil, and how you can be certain about the hereafter when there's no empirical evidence for either "

He couldn't finish.

"After ultimate evil," Sarah finished quickly. She poured tea but her hands trembled, the cup rattling against the saucer. She had to use both hands to steady it. "You want to know how I still believe in God after Bergen-Belsen."

"Yes. Very much."

"Then I must disappoint you." Her voice was steady, but her hands kept shaking. She set the cup down. "I don't know if God exists, Mr. Hinsen. I haven't known since 1944."

Jacob felt something tighten in his chest. "But Rabbi Golden said you maintained faith."

"I maintained practice. Community. Ethics. But certainty about God?" She shook her head sideways. "That died with my mother."

"Then why pray if you don't know anyone's listening?"

Sarah's eyes met his. "Because it gave me hope. Made me feel less alone. When I prayed in that camp, I could pretend someone was with me in the darkness. I don't know if God exists. But praying as if He did, that kept me human when everything around me was designed to make me an animal."

Her hands wouldn't stop shaking now. She pressed them flat against her lap, but they trembled anyway. "Typhus. That's what killed my mother. Not the gas chambers, not bullets, typhus. A treatable disease. She lay dying for three days while I held her hand and begged God to save her."

The shaking got worse. Sarah gripped the armrests. "She weighed maybe sixty pounds. All bone. But she still whispered the Shema with her last breath. 'Hear, O Israel, the Lord our God, the Lord is One.' She died believing. I sat there holding her corpse and felt nothing but rage."

Jacob thought of Jessica on hospital machines, her small body dwarfed by equipment. But at least clean sheets. Morphine. Him holding her hand. Sarah's mother had died on wooden planks among the dying, in her own waste, with nothing but faith.

"My father was shot two months earlier." Sarah's voice dropped. "For sharing his bread with a child who was starving. A little girl, maybe seven, crying because she was so hungry. My father broke his bread and gave her half. A guard saw and shot him in the head. Right there. The child dropped the bread in his blood."

Jacob's hands gripped his teacup so hard he thought it might shatter. How many times did she have to relive her story? Should he thank her for the tea and leave her in peace?

"Your daughter," Sarah said. "How did she die?"

"She was chasing papers from her backpack. An art project. She ran into the street. The driver was on her phone and didn't brake in time."

"So quick. A moment. And she was gone."

"Three minutes," Jacob whispered. "If I'd left work three minutes earlier..."

"My brother died at Auschwitz. Gassed on arrival. Sixteen. Strong, healthy. They killed him anyway. Three seconds. The time it takes to point left instead of right. One guard's gesture, and Aaron was dead within hours."

She stood slowly and moved to the window where children played soccer below. Normal life. Impossible life.

"Do you know what the worst part was?" Her voice dropped to almost a whisper. "Not the adults dying. It was the children. Watching children starve. Watching them realize no one was coming. Watching them die crying for mothers already dead."

Jacob felt anger and compassion rising.

"Then imagine your Jessica." Sarah turned, sudden intensity in her face. "Imagine her in those barracks. Nine years old, starving, covered in lice, watching other children die. Imagine her crying for you while you're in the men's section and can't reach her. Imagine her asking why God isn't answering her prayers."

The image hit Jacob like a fist. Jessica's face. Her small body wasting away. Those bright eyes going hollow with hunger. Reaching for him through barbed wire while guards laughed.

"Stop," he managed, but his voice was breaking.

"I held children as they died, Mr. Hinsen. Girls Jessica's age. Some younger. They'd ask if they were going to heaven. I'd lie and say yes even though I no longer believed it." Tears streamed down Sarah's face, ninety-four years old and still weeping. "There was a girl named

Miriam. Eight. Dark hair, bright eyes before hunger dulled them. She died in my arms asking if her mama was waiting."

Jacob saw Jessica's face on that dying child. Jessica asking him the same question. Jessica dying while he couldn't reach her, couldn't save her, couldn't even hold her properly because he was separated, imprisoned, helpless.

His vision blurred. The teacup slipped from his hand, tea spreading across the floor. He doubled over, gasping, unable to get air into his lungs. The image wouldn't stop: Jessica starving, Jessica asking why, Jessica dying while he watched through barbed wire, believing in a God who wasn't there.

"I'm sorry," he choked out between gasps. "I can't, I shouldn't ha ve..."

"Don't." Sarah's voice cut through his panic. "Don't you dare diminish your grief. You lost your only child. The center of your world. That your pain is singular doesn't make it less than mine. We're both in the same darkness. Just different chambers of the same hell."

Jacob couldn't speak. Couldn't breathe right. The image of Jessica in that camp had broken something loose in him that six months of investigation had kept contained.

Sarah's voice gentled. "You asked how I maintained faith. I didn't. What I maintained was choice. Every morning, I chose to act as if human dignity mattered when all evidence screamed it was a lie."

She moved back to her chair, slowly, age and memory weighing on her. "There was a woman named Rachel in our barracks. She was dying. Starvation. But every day she saved a piece of her bread for the children."

Sarah's hands shook worse now, gripping the armrests. "You need to understand what that meant. The bread was maybe four ounces. That's all. Four ounces to sustain life for twenty-four hours. Rachel was already dying. Every calorie mattered. But she'd break off a piece, maybe an ounce, and give it to a child."

"Why?" Jacob managed.

"I asked her the same thing. We were lying on those wooden shelves. She was so weak she could barely move. I said, 'Rachel, you're killing yourself. Keep the bread.' You know what she said?"

Sarah's voice broke. "'If I don't choose love, Hitler wins completely.'"

She had to stop, overcome. When she continued, her voice was barely audible. "She died two weeks before liberation. Never saw freedom. Never knew the war ended. But that last piece of bread she saved, she made me promise to give it to a child named Leah. Even dying, Rachel was still choosing love."

"I kept that promise. Found Leah and gave her Rachel's last piece of bread. Leah survived. She's seventy-eight now. Lives in Tel Aviv. Has great-grandchildren. Every year on the anniversary of liberation, she bakes bread and gives it to homeless children. She tells them about Rachel."

Sarah's tears came freely now. "Rachels not erased, Mr. Hinsen. She's not gone. Her love continued. It's still continuing. Every loaf Leah bakes. Every child who learns about choosing love when everything says to choose hate."

Jacob couldn't speak. The image of Rachel breaking her starvation rations, choosing to die sooner so a child might live an hour longer, was almost unbearable.

"You want to know if your daughter survived," Sarah said. "I can't tell you that. What I can tell you is her love survived. It's working in you right now. It's in every person who remembers her kindness."

"But that's not enough. I need to know where God is, and where Jessica is."

"And if you never know?" Sarah's gaze held his. "Will you let that uncertainty destroy you? Or will you choose to live as if love matters eternally, whether it does or not?"

Jacob sat shaking. Sarah had watched children murdered by thousands, had every reason to curse God and embrace nihilism. He'd lost one child and spent six months demanding cosmic proof before he could function.

"I don't know how to live with not knowing."

"None of us do. We just choose anyway. Every morning, I wake up and choose to believe human dignity matters. I don't know if God exists. I don't know if my parents and brother exist beyond death. But I choose to live as if love is holy, as if justice is sacred, as if each person bears infinite worth. That choice, that's my faith now."

She reached across, took his hand. Her grip was surprisingly strong. "You can't answer Jessica's question with certainty. But you can answer with your life. You can choose to honor her by becoming someone whose love creates the kind of world she believed in."

"And if there's nothing? If death is just the end?"

"Then you will have lived nobly in the face of meaninglessness. You will have created meaning where none existed." Sarah released his hand. "That's the only answer I found. It sustained me through Bergen-Belsen. Perhaps it can sustain you through this."

Jacob stood on shaking legs. "Thank you."

"Come back if you need to. The darkness is easier to bear with company."

Jacob walked away slowly. The afternoon felt too bright. Children played soccer in the street. Normal life. Impossible life.

He made it three blocks before the smell hit: not Jerusalem's dust but wet metal, rotting vegetation, humid air that clung like oil. His vision tunneled.

The cobblestones became mud.

He was nineteen again, crouched along a dirt road outside Da Nang. Monsoon turning everything to soup. Machine-gun fire stitching patterns. The smothering smell of gun power. Screaming. Pain. Death.

Lance Corporal Nash lay three feet away, face down in mud. They'd been joking about his sister thirty minutes ago. "You'll love Mary. Prettiest girl in Memphis."

Nash was dead. Crying, Jacobs cradled him in his arms. Asking God why? Later, his hands shook, pulling the zipper on the familiar black body bag. The sound: obscene, final. When the zipper snagged on Nash's field jacket, Jacob worked it free with numb fingers. Nash's face disappeared in the darkness; his life sealed away inside the black nylon.

Count them. Zip them. Move to the next one. Pray you're not next.

"Sir? Are you alright?"

Jacob blinked. A woman stood in front of him. Israeli, maybe thirty, concerned. He was leaning against a stone wall in Jerusalem. His hands were empty. No body bags. No Nash.

"I'm fine."

She looked unconvinced but moved on.

Jacob pressed his forehead against the cool stone. Sarah Rosen watched children starve in barracks. He'd zipped teenagers into body bags in rice paddies. Different wars. Different decades. Same question: Where was God?

In Vietnam, he'd stopped asking, just prayed as if someone heard. You couldn't function if you thought too hard. You counted bodies, called coordinates, prayed the next firefight wouldn't have a bullet with your name.

Sarah kept asking for seventy years. Kept wrestling while maintaining custom, community, ethics. No answers. But she chose meaning anyway.

Jacob pushed off the wall and started walking. The smell of wet metal clung to him, mingling with Sarah's stories, Jessica crying over the ant. *"It was just trying to get home to its family, Daddy."*

Nash never made it home to Mary. Sarah's parents never made it out. Jessica never made it past nine. But their love survived. Nash's memory drove him to law school. Sarah's parents' faith sustained her. Jessica's compassion echoed in every memory.

Maybe love transcending death wasn't about souls in heaven but influence outlasting bodies.

Sarah's words kept circling back: "I sang prayers I no longer believed were heard but singing them reminded me I was still human."

Jacob sat in a small café trying to make sense of it. Was that what all of this was? Prayers, scriptures, rituals: humans trying to make sense of suffering they couldn't control or understand?

Torah written by men who'd never imagined Bergen-Belsen. Bible compiled by councils who'd never seen Vietnamese mud or body bags. Quran standardized centuries before anyone could conceive of a nine-year-old girl dying while chasing art projects in the wind.

How could any of them know? How could texts written thousands of years ago answer questions about whether Jessica is somewhere? Were they all just writing down their best guesses, policy agenda, desperate hopes, and calling it revelation?

Sarah had kept the practice but released the certainty. That made her different from Rossi, from Berkowitz, from Hassan, all of whom claimed scripture proved God's existence while admitting they couldn't prove scripture was divine.

But was Sarah, right? Or was she just another voice in the chorus of uncertainty?

Jacob didn't know. That was the problem. Six months, three continents, dozens of conversations with believers and scholars and survivors, and he still didn't know if God existed. Didn't know where Jessica was. Didn't know if any of the confident claims in scriptures were true or if they were all just humans making the same guesses, generation after generation, calling it faith because "I don't know" was unbearable.

***

Jacob spent the next two days wandering Jerusalem like a ghost. Sarah's stories had cracked something open that wouldn't close. He'd wake at 3 a.m. seeing Miriam's face, hearing Rachel's whisper: "If I don't choose love, Hitler wins completely."

He walked without a destination. The question burned in him now, different than before. Not "Does God exist?" but "Where is God?"

He asked everyone.

A Palestinian teenager selling falafel near Damascus Gate gestured at the sky. "My grandmother says everywhere. I say nowhere. We're both right."

An elderly Jewish woman at a bus stop touched her heart. "Here. When I light Shabbat candles and remember my husband's face."

A Franciscan monk on the steps of the Church of the Holy Sepulcher spread his arms wide. "In suffering. In the spaces between our prayers and His silence."

A secular Israeli mother at a café near Jaffa Gate shook her head. "I stopped looking. Now I just try to be the kind of person my daughter can believe in."

Each answer pointed somewhere different. Everywhere. Nowhere. Inside. In the spaces between. In giving up the search entirely.

None of them knew. But all of them had chosen something anyway.

***

As Jacob had prepared to leave Sarah Rosen's apartment she pressed a small card into his palm. "This woman is another way of being Jewish," Sarah said. "Speak with her before you finish." The name was; Hanna Kaplan. "I will tell her you are coming."

A few days later he walked to the Center for Humanistic Judaism, housed in a restored Ottoman building near the New City. Inside, a circular library hummed with layered conversations: Hebrew, English, Arabic; students in kippot and jeans; an elderly woman arguing softly with a young rabbi over a line of Maimonides. The place felt less like a seminary than a laboratory.

"Mr. Hinsen?" said a woman with silver-streaked hair and steady eyes. "Hannah Kaplan." She ushered him to a table piled with Tanakh, Talmud, Spinoza, Heschel, Levinas. "Sarah told me you were asking the right kind of hard questions."

"What kind is that?" Jacob asked.

"The kind that risks community. The kind that makes people uncomfortable at dinner tables." she said. "We get called 'impossible Jews,' people who maintain Jewish identity while admitting that many traditional claims can't be proved."

"How is that different from Sarah's practice?"

"Sarah remembers it as a form of resistance. We question it as a form of fidelity," Hannah said. "Judaism at its best invites scrutiny and then survives it."

"Doesn't relentless scrutiny dissolve what makes Judaism Jewish?" Jacob asked.

"What survives is ethical monotheism, a relentless call to justice, covenantal responsibility, and intellectual honesty," she said. "Those don't require literalism. They require courage."

"How do you decide what adapts and what remains?"

"Study. Community. Conscience," Hannah answered. "We don't discard lightly. But Judaism has endured precisely because it evolves without losing its core."

A young man in a knitted kippah approached, cheeks flushed from debate. "Sorry, Dr. Kaplan. I'm James" He gestured to Jacob. "Orthodox background. Couldn't reconcile certain halakhot with what I know about human dignity. This place lets me stay Jewish without turning my brain off."

"And your old community?" Jacob asked.

"Some call me a heretic," James said with a rueful grin. "But the Talmud keeps minority opinions for a reason, future light."

When he moved back to his study circle, Hannah turned to Jacob. "You've tried to force the universe into court. Maybe change the questions."

"To what?" Jacob said.

"From 'Which religion is correct?' to 'How should I live so that the sacred, if it exists, can find me?'" Hannah said. "From 'Where is God?' to 'How do I become more capable of recognizing holiness in a world like this?' From 'What must I believe?' to 'What will I risk loving and repair?'"

"That sounds like ethics, not metaphysics," Jacob said.

"It's both," she replied. "When people choose truth over convenience, generosity over gain, courage over safety, call it God, conscience, or cosmic moral grain, that choice participates in something larger than the self."

"Evolutionary psychology can explain costly altruism," Jacob said, almost automatically.

"Maybe," Hannah said. "But even if a ladder of biology gets you to the roof, you still have to decide whether to look up."

His phone buzzed once in his pocket. A text from Father Doyle: *Proud of your courage. Remember, God may be silent, but love has a voice. Call when you can.*

A second text, Abby: *Seder sounded beautiful. Keep letting the questions do their work. I'm praying in my way.* He slipped the phone away.

"Dr. Kaplan," Jacob said softly, "if God is the same One at the root of Judaism, Christianity, Islam, why does the One speak so many irreconcilable dialects?"

She considered it. "Maybe the One is larger than any grammar. Maybe we hear what our history tunes us to hear. The humility is to admit partial hearing and still answer."

Hannah stood and reached for a slim volume. "Join us tonight," she said. "Open study till midnight. We argue, we sing a little, we drink too-strong coffee. It won't give you proof. It might give you companions."

Outside, the late light washed the limestone gold. Jacob paused beneath an archway as church bells and the *adhan* braided through the air, the same God invoked in competing cadences. He thought of David's apprenticeship of questions, Sarah's choice to love without guarantees, Hannah's insistence that fidelity could include doubt, and felt the shape of a different kind of answer forming, not a verdict, but a way to walk.

***

Jacob couldn't resist Hannah Kaplan's invitation. Four months into his search, he was bone-weary of clerics offering answers dressed as certainties, yet here was a place where questions themselves were holy. Debate was his native language, and something in him longed for the freedom to ask without apology.

That night, he walked into the Beit Midrash. The study hall buzzed like a hive, words ricocheting in Hebrew, Aramaic, English. Long tables sagged under the weight of Torah scrolls, Talmud volumes, notebooks crammed with centuries of struggle. Jacob slid into the chair Hannah indicated, his pulse quickening. He was happy to ask the first question.

"If the Torah is divinely revealed," Jacob asked, "why preserve minority opinions in the Talmud? Wouldn't God's word settle the matter for the last time?"

One student grinned. "Because the truth isn't simple. God's voice comes through contradiction."

"Or because you're hedging bets," Jacob shot back. His lawyer's edge sharpened. "Like a court keeping dissent on record in case the majority is later overturned. Isn't that just human caution dressed as theology?"

The second student leaned forward, eyes bright. "Or humility. To admit we might be wrong. That God's word might reveal itself more fully to another generation."

"That assumes God speaks at all," Jacob said. His tone carried more bite than he intended, and for an instant Jessica's face flashed before him, asking about heaven. He shoved the memory down and pressed harder.

"Then why call this faith?" he demanded. "Why not just philosophy with Hebrew footnotes?"

The first student's grin widened. "Because philosophy argues to win. We argue to keep the argument alive."

Laughter broke around the table, but not unkind. The woman across from Jacob leaned in. "You sound more like us than you realize. You're arguing as if the process of questioning itself is sacred."

Jacob opened his mouth for a retort, but the words caught. Sacred. The word rattled him. For months he had hunted certainties across sermons, cathedrals, mosques, synagogues. Here the certainty was different: not an answer, but the conviction that asking mattered.

Another student jumped in, eager to press. "If God spoke at Sinai, His voice was fire and thunder. But if God still speaks now, maybe it's in the friction between us, the sparks that fly when we refuse to stop pushing."

"Or maybe it's just noise," Jacob muttered. But even as he said it, something in him quickened. The clash itself had a strange electricity, not unlike a courtroom when truth flickered between opposing arguments. For the first time in months, his mind felt lit from the inside.

The arguments came faster, voices overlapping, hands cutting the air in sharp gestures. Someone slammed a palm on the table for emphasis. Another threw back her head in laughter at a clever twist. The room pulsed with intellectual combat, yet Jacob sensed no hostility, only the joy of collision. They weren't trying to silence him. They wanted him sharper, louder, relentless.

He gave it to them.

By midnight, his throat was raw, and his notes littered with scribbled challenges. He clasped hands with the students who had sparred hardest, their grips warm, firm, comradely. The arguments hadn't ended anything. But they had bound him, for a few hours, to something larger than himself. Yet even that connection couldn't quiet the ache in his chest, the echo of Jessica's laughter that had slipped away months ago.

Walking out into the quiet Jerusalem streets, the night air cool on his face, Jacob felt the weight of the city differently. Church bells and the distant call to prayer braided overhead, a reminder that this same God, if God was present at all, was invoked in countless cadences, each sincere in its own way. Debate had given him allies, sharpened his mind, but left his heart raw. Every question he argued felt like a small rehearsal for a larger, more painful question: how to find Jessica, or at least survive without answers.

He paused beneath an olive tree, pen in hand, and opened his journal:

No one has the answers. Not the priests, not the imams, not the rabbis, not the students of the Beit Midrash. But tonight, I learned that questions can be a form of faith. That arguing without resolution still binds people together. That doubt can create community as much as belief.

But I am not here to debate forever. I came because I had a daughter to find. She asked me about heaven, and I still have no answer. The questions are important, but they cannot end here. Not in argument, not in books, not even in brilliant companionship. I must go further.

He closed the journal, feeling the faint warmth of purpose in his hands. Each step through the alleys carried the echo of debate, but also a tether to his own urgency. Jessica's absence remained a raw ache, threading through his thoughts like a shadow at the edge of every argument. The intellectual clarity of the evening collided with a personal void, sharper than any philosophical puzzle.

Outside the Beit Midrash, under the pool of yellow streetlight, Jacob pulled out his phone. He typed four messages, separate threads, same heartbeat:

To Michael: *Be home soon. Not tonight, not tomorrow, but soon. Spent the evening in a study hall where questions were the point, not a problem. Argued for hours and left as friends. Felt honest. I'm not done, but I'm turning toward home.*

To Margaret: *Coming home soon. Sat with people tonight who understand that some questions don't have answers but still matter. Found something I didn't expect peace without knowing everything. I think Jessica would approve of that. I won't forget what you sacrificed.*

To Abby: *Coming home soon. Sat in a Beit Midrash and debated until midnight. No certainties, no posturing, simply challenging questions held together by respect. It didn't give answers, but it gave oxygen. I can breathe again.*

To Father Doyle: *Tonight, I joined a room where doubt was treated as devotion. No one pretended to know. They wrestled anyway. It felt like a kind of prayer I can live with. Yet my heart still aches for my daughter.*

The replies came quickly, warm, and steady, and Jacob welcomed them like small lanterns in his palm. The questions were still with him, heavy and unrelenting, but now so was a faint sense of direction: a way forward through uncertainty, through debate, toward action, toward Jessica.

He slipped the phone into his pocket and resumed walking, the streets of the Old City carrying both the echo of words and the ache of absence. For the first time in months, he felt less alone in his doubt. Yet the search that had begun as an intellectual quest remained painfully, impossibly personal, threaded with grief that no debate could answer.

***

The next morning, Jacob woke early and walked through Jerusalem's Armenian Quarter, where shopkeepers swept their doorsteps and the smell of fresh bread drifted from bakeries. He passed the Church of the Holy Sepulcher, where pilgrims already lined up before dawn, their faces carrying hope or desperation or both.

At a small café near Jaffa Gate, he ordered Turkish coffee and watched the city wake. An elderly Palestinian man at the next table nodded greeting, and they fell into conversation about nothing important: the weather, the quality of the coffee, how tourists never understood the city's rhythms.

"You have the look of someone searching," the old man said eventually.

"Is it that obvious?"

"In Jerusalem? Everyone is searching. Some find. Most don't. But the searching itself, that changes you."

Jacob spent the afternoon at the Israel Museum, standing before the Dead Sea Scrolls, ancient texts preserved in clay jars for two thousand years. Words about God, written by hands long turned to dust, still arguing across centuries about meaning and purpose and whether any of it mattered.

He thought of the Beit Midrash students, continuing arguments that began before they were born, that would continue after they died. The texts couldn't prove God existed. But they proved humans had been asking the same questions forever, finding in the asking itself something worth preserving.

That evening, he returned to the Western Wall. This time he didn't pray or insert a written prayer into the cracks. He simply stood and watched others do it, their devotion genuine whether God heard them or not.

A young Israeli soldier, rifle slung over his shoulder, stood beside him. "First time here?"

"Second. I came a few days ago."

"What do you think?"

"I think people need to believe their prayers matter, whether they do or not."

The soldier considered this. "My grandmother survived the camps. She prayed every day afterward. When I asked her why, if God let that happen, she said: 'Because if I stop, they win completely.' Maybe that's what this place is. Refusing to let evil win."

The soldier walked away, leaving Jacob with a new angle on the same question. Not "Does God exist?" but "What survives if we act as if He does?"

The next day, Jacob hired a guide to show him both sides of Jerusalem's reality. They walked through affluent Jewish neighborhoods with parks and cafés, then into Palestinian areas where sewage ran in open channels and children played in streets too narrow for the military vehicles that patrolled them.

The guide, a secular Israeli named Yael, spoke with weary honesty. "People ask me if I believe in God. I say: which one? The God who promised this land to Jews? The God who commands justice for the oppressed? They can't be the same God, because they demand opposite things."

"So, you don't believe?"

"I believe humans use God to justify what they were going to do anyway. Compassion, cruelty, both get His name attached. The question isn't whether God exists. It's whether we'll use His name to build or to destroy."

That afternoon, Jacob attended a lecture at Hebrew University on biblical archaeology. The professor, a careful scholar with decades of fieldwork, presented evidence that contradicted traditional narratives: no exodus of millions from Egypt, no conquest of Canaan, no united monarchy under David and Solomon as described in scripture.

"Does this mean the Bible is false?" a student asked.

"It means the Bible is theology, not history," the professor replied. "These stories expressed deep truths about identity, purpose, and relationship with the divine. Whether they happened as written is less important than what they've meant to people for three thousand years."

Jacob thought of Rabbi Golden's words: "Perhaps the transformation itself is the revelation." Not historical accuracy but ethical impact. Not what happened at Sinai but what Sinai made of the people who believed it happened.

On his fourth day of wandering, Jacob found himself in Mea Shearim, the ultra-Orthodox neighborhood where modernity barely penetrated. Men in black coats and fur hats hurried to prayer. Signs warned immodestly dressed visitors to leave. Children in traditional dress played in the streets, speaking Yiddish, living as if the 21st century hadn't arrived.

An elderly rabbi, seeing Jacob's obvious confusion, approached. "You are lost?"

"In several ways."

The rabbi smiled. "This neighborhood confuses outsiders. They think we live in the past. But we live in eternity. The secular world changes every generation. Our way has not changed for centuries. Which is more stable?"

"But the world did change. You can't ignore that."

"We don't ignore it. We reject it. The world offers progress at the cost of meaning. We choose meaning even if it means refusing progress." The rabbi gestured at the narrow streets, the ancient customs. "You think this is backward. I think your world is lost. Both of us could be right."

Jacob spent that evening writing in his journal, trying to process what he'd seen:

Four days of walking Jerusalem's contradictions. Museums that prove scripture is mythology. Neighborhoods that live as if scholarship doesn't exist. Soldiers who pray before checkpoints. Palestinians who pray despite checkpoints. Everyone claiming the same God, all reaching opposite conclusions about what He wants.

The archaeological evidence is clear: the foundational stories are theological interpretation, not historical record. Yet the power of those stories persists. They've shaped civilizations, sustained communities, given meaning to suffering. But also provide justification for war. Killing. Genocide.

Is that enough? If the stories aren't historically true but produce real transformation, does the transformation validate the stories? Or is it just humans creating meaning because meaninglessness is unbearable?

Sarah Rosen chose meaning after the camps. Hannah Kaplan builds community around questions. The Beit Midrash students argue as if truth emerges from friction. Palestinians use faith to endure occupation. The secular soldier respects his grandmother's prayers even though he doesn't share them.

All of them surviving. All of them creating meaning. None of them able to prove the metaphysical claims underlying their choices.

Maybe that's the only honest answer: we don't know, but we choose anyway. We choose love or hate, justice or oppression, meaning or despair. We attach God's name to our choices, but the choices are ours.

Jessica asked me if heaven was real. After six months of investigation, I still can't answer with certainty. But I can answer with how I live. I can choose to honor her memory through actions that would make her proud. Not because I'll be rewarded in heaven, but because that's what love requires.

Is that faith? Or just ethics without metaphysics?

I don't know anymore. But I'm ready to go home.

***

It was Rabbi Golden who, when Jacob stopped by his office to say goodbye, gave him one final name with visible reluctance. "If you want to understand the full complexity of what's happening here, you should speak to Rabbi Rosenbalm. But Jacob, his faith is not easy to hear. He represents a strand of Judaism that frightens me, precisely because it's so certain."

"Where do I find him?"

"In a settlement east of here. I'll give you his contact information. But Jacob, be careful. Certainty in the hands of the faithful can justify almost anything."

The drive into the West Bank was a descent from holy city to hard lines. Concrete walls carved the hills. Barbed wire coiled atop checkpoints. Olive groves sat divided by roads built for some but closed to others. Jacob, a man who once believed in the clean promise of law, found himself in a place where law was a weapon sharpened by scripture.

The settlement shimmered like an apparition: white stucco houses with red-tile roofs, clean sidewalks, children skipping to school. An island of suburban order ringed by military checkpoints.

Behind the neat facades loomed a wall that cut through valleys and villages, separating neighbors, families, histories.

Inside, Rabbi Rosenbalm received him with the calm of a man who believed his cause was already vindicated. "Justice," the rabbi began, "means building God's kingdom on His land. Compassion means guiding even those who resist into alignment with His will."

Jacob's lawyer's ear caught the hinge of the argument. "And those who don't accept?"

"They may live here peacefully if they acknowledge Jewish sovereignty and observe the Noahide laws. If they resist, they become obstacles to God's plan."

"The Noahide laws?" Jacob asked.

The rabbi smiled thinly. "Seven universal commandments given to Noah: prohibitions against idolatry, blasphemy, murder, theft, sexual immorality, cruelty to animals, and the requirement to establish justice. A moral code for all humanity."

"But if they are universal," Jacob pressed, "how can they be a condition for sovereignty under you? If Palestinians already honor justice, does that not satisfy your God?"

Rosenbalm's hand swept toward a map on the wall, colored in neat blocks of expansion. "Every family that settles here fulfills the mitzvah of possessing the land. This is not politics, Jacob. This is a covenant."

The words lodged like stones in Jacob's throat. "And when Palestinians die? When children die? Do you call that covenant too?"

"Murder is forbidden. But those who resist divine sovereignty are not innocent. They choose rebellion. They choose death. We choose God."

Jacob's voice hardened. "Or you choose interpretation. What if the Torah is not God's voice but man's justification?"

The rabbi did not flinch. "You look for God in texts. I look at the land. For two thousand years we were exiled, hunted, scattered. Yet here we stand. The land is the proof. The return is the miracle. Look out that window, Jacob. The hills themselves declare God's promise."

Jacob stared at the hills, dry and ancient, scarred by walls and watchtowers. He wanted to see a miracle, but all he saw was division.

Jacob sensed the rabbi's certainty clinging like dust. It was a certainty he had seen before: Christian preachers, Muslim clerics, each cloaking power in the garments of God. Religion's brilliance and its peril revealed again. It could sanctify compassion, or it could sanctify cruelty.

Jacob left the settlement without much debate. There was no debating extremism. The cab drove back along its sterile streets and barbed-wire walls pressing behind him like a bad dream. Rosenbalm's voice still rang in his ears: The land is the contract. The land is the miracle.

But as the cab wound toward Bethlehem, Jacob's eyes clung to the terraced hills beyond the barriers, ancient olive groves twisting under centuries of cultivation.

He thought of Rosenbalm's map, blue squares of expansion cutting across valleys where families had tended trees longer than America had existed. Whose land? Whose promise? Whose God decides? The same God.

At the first checkpoint, soldiers waved them through, rifles slung casually but always ready. Jacob's Marine instincts kicked in: assess, anticipate, defend. But there was nothing to defend against. Just a wall, higher than rooftops, gray and unbroken but for murals of keys, doves, and names scrawled in defiance.

It struck him that the wall was not only concrete. It was silence poured into stone.

***

Rabbi Golden had given him more than Rosenbalm's contact information. Before Jacob left his office, the rabbi had written down another name, his hand hesitating over the paper.

"If you speak to Rosenbalm, you should also speak to the Nasser family in Bethlehem. For balance. For perspective." Golden's voice carried unusual weight. "Khaled Nasser teaches at Bethlehem University. His wife Mariam volunteers with a women's cooperative. They're people of faith who live on the other side of the wall."

"Will they talk to me?"

"I've already called ahead. They're expecting you tomorrow afternoon." Golden had looked at him directly. "Jacob, if you want to understand what faith looks like in this land, you need to see it from both sides of the concrete."

The next day, Jacob hired a driver who knew how to navigate the checkpoints. The man, a Palestinian Christian from Beit Jala, said little during the drive, but his silence spoke volumes about the daily humiliation of passing through barriers on roads that once connected his village to Jerusalem freely.

The driver stopped outside a modest stone home. The Nasser family welcomed him with Palestinian warmth: bread, olives, and steaming tea. Mariam, the mother, ushered her children forward. The youngest, Aisha, peeked from behind her mother's dress before darting off clutching a doll.

Jacob's chest tightened. For a moment, he saw Jessica there instead, darting through their kitchen with her pink diary tucked under her arm. He imagined her in Aisha's world: growing up behind walls, learning to keep her head down at checkpoints, praying for peace before bed. The image hollowed him.

"You must excuse Aisha," Mariam said gently. "She is shy with strangers. But she likes to share her toys."

Jessica too, Jacob thought, hearing her voice: *I'll share when I feel safe, Daddy.*

Khaled, the father, broke the silence. "My grandfather planted the olive trees you passed. They've stood for more than a hundred years. Every season, the bulldozers come closer. They say the land belongs to others now. But how can you bulldoze memory? How can you uproot graves?"

Over dinner, Mariam's voice carried a steadiness Jacob envied. "Our children ask why we can't go to Jerusalem, why the wall cuts their schoolyard. I tell them Allah is testing us. But at night, when they sleep, I pray alone. I ask where Allah is."

Jacob leaned forward. "And when the silence continues?"

Her gaze didn't waver. "Then I believe anyway. If I don't, my children will grow up with nothing but bitterness. If I tell them God is gone, then the wall wins."

Later, in the cramped study of Imam Youssef, Jacob smelled bitter coffee and dust. The imam's voice was weary but steady. "Here, suffering is not an idea. There is a funeral every week. A boy shot at a checkpoint. A house demolished in the night."

"And Allah?" Jacob pressed.

"In the choice not to give up," Youssef said. "We cry out because He is silent. But still we pray. That is faith. If we stop, we are truly lost."

Jacob felt the weight of the imam's words but did not challenge Youssef's conviction. He knew it was faith born of necessity, virtuous in its refusal to surrender to despair.

Jacob left the imam's study as the call to prayer echoed from a nearby minaret. Walking through Bethlehem's narrow streets, he passed the Church of the Nativity, where Christian pilgrims lined up to see the traditional birthplace of Jesus.

A priest in black robes stood outside, greeting visitors. He noticed Jacob's weary expression.

"You look like a man carrying questions," the priest said in accented English.

"Too many questions. Not enough answers."

"Then you've come to the right city. I'm Father Elias. Come, have tea."

Jacob hesitated, but something in the priest's expression, the same weariness he'd seen in Imam Youssef's eyes, made him follow.

Inside the small church attached to Father Elias's parish house, the priest lit candles as dusk settled over Bethlehem. "This city once heard angels sing 'Peace on Earth,'" he told Jacob. "Now I bury the dead. I preach resurrection while walls rise higher. God's silence may be abandonment, or it may be the test. Whether we choose hatred or love, even when He does not speak."

Jacob sat long after, staring at the crucifix. Mariam's whispered prayers, Youssef's endurance, Elias's weary hope, all pointed to the same reality. Faith here did not solve suffering. It endured beside it. It turned silence into defiance.

That night he wrote in his journal:

Today I saw faith where God does not answer. The settlers say the land proves His promise. The Palestinians say His silence deepens their wounds. Yet cling to Him.

I imagined Jessica growing up here: running with Aisha through alleys, asking why soldiers shout, why God says nothing. What would I tell her? Could I give her Mariam's certainty? Or would I confess I hear only silence?

Maybe that is the lesson: faith is not answers but refusal to despair. Silence itself is the test. The children believe. Perhaps their belief is the last unbroken thing.

***

Jacob's final day in Jerusalem was spent walking through the Old City one las time, processing the week of encounters that had revealed Judaism's extraordinary internal diversity. He had met Sarah Rosen, who maintained Jewish practice without traditional belief. Hannah Kaplan, who emphasized ethical behavior over theological certainty. The Beit Midrash students who made questions sacred. And Rabbi Rosenbalm, who used religious authority to justify territorial expansion.

Each claimed authentic Jewish identity while reaching radically different conclusions about God's nature, human responsibility, and the meaning of being chosen.

The tradition he had hoped would provide foundational answers instead mirrored what he had found in Christianity and Islam: sincere people striving to make sense of existence, constructing frameworks that offered community and meaning, yet could not yield empirical proof.

Yet Judaism had also revealed something unique: a tradition that institutionalized questioning, prescrved dissent, and emphasized ethical behavior over doctrinal conformity. Whether these traits reflected divine election or cultural evolution mattered less than the courage and clarity they produced in those who lived by them.

At a café near the Western Wall, Jacob sat at a small outdoor table and ordered strong coffee. The plaza below swelled with pilgrims pressing prayers into ancient stone, the scent of incense and fresh bread mingling with the dry Jerusalem air.

A man in his thirties, close-cropped hair and military bearing, lit a cigarette beside him, catching Jacob's glance.

"First time in Jerusalem?" the man asked in accented English.

"Yes. And you?"

"I live here," he said, tapping ash into the tray. "I'm secular in a city of religion. No prayers, no yarmulke, no God. But I come here sometimes to sit. It's history, you know? My grandparents died in Poland. My parents built a life here. I don't need God to tell me this place matters. It's in my blood."

Jacob leaned in. "So, for you, meaning comes from history, not heaven?"

The man shrugged. "History, family, survival. You light a candle because your grandmother did. You serve in the army because your father did. Maybe God is silent. Maybe He never existed. Doesn't matter. What matters is that we're still here. That's enough faith for me."

He stubbed out the cigarette and walked off into the crowded street, leaving Jacob with the residue of inherited resilience, a quiet testament to enduring despite absence, loss, and silence.

He thought of Jessica and the questions that would never leave him. Survival was not just intellectual. It was personal, visceral, and aching.

Jacob opened his journal. Words flowed faster than his hand could keep pace:

Judaism hasn't given me proof of God's existence or where Jessica is. But it has shown me something valuable: people who survived by choosing meaning over despair, learning over ignorance, hope over cynicism, despite persecution that could justify nihilism. Whether that survival reflects divine protection or human resilience may matter less than the wisdom it generates about how to live in uncertainty.

He paused, letting the murmur of the plaza filter through his awareness: children tugging at parents' hands, pilgrims bowing at the Wall, a street musician plucking a single, mournful note.

The archaeological evidence suggested foundational stories were theological interpretation rather than history. Philosophy could not prove God. Ethical insights might arise from culture rather than revelation. Yet Jewish tradition had produced people committed to justice, learning, and dignity in ways that transcended self-interest, echoing across centuries.

The evidence remained inconclusive. Judaism offered no more definitive proof than Christianity or Islam, yet each contained wisdom that seemed to transcend mere human invention.

Behind him, Jerusalem's stones caught the afternoon sun, witness to centuries of human struggle with questions that had driven his search. Whether they bore witness to authentic divine revelation or to human attempts at grasping the sacred, they were beautiful, enduring, and somehow holy, like the questions themselves.

The road home stretched ahead. Jacob understood his search was entering a new phase: not the desperate quest for proof that had driven him from Chicago, but the careful, personal work of living meaningfully with questions that might never have answers.

The insights he had gathered through months of investigation would have to prove themselves in the choices he had to make, and in the ways, he navigated absence, loss, and hope.

***

Chapter Five

HOME

The flight from Tel Aviv landed in Chicago on December 8th, six months after Jacob had fled in desperate search of answers. He was returning without them.

At O'Hare, the familiar sounds of American English felt foreign after months of Arabic, Hebrew, and Italian. Travelers rushed past with the urgent purpose that had once defined his own life, everyone supremely confident about destinations that probably mattered far less than they imagined. Jacob moved through customs with the disconnected efficiency of someone observing his former country from a great distance.

The suburban landscape that unfolded from the taxi window seemed like a museum exhibit: "American Middle-Class Life, circa 21st Century." Strip malls advertising nail salons and cell phone repairs. Fast-food restaurants promising efficiency over nourishment. Subdivision homes designed to look distinctive while remaining fundamentally identical. The orderly prosperity that had once felt like civilization's triumph now struck him as profoundly arbitrary, a particular way of organizing human energy that could just as easily have developed differently.

His house on Maple Street looked smaller than he remembered, as if his months abroad had shifted the scale by which he measured significance. The key still turned in the lock. The rooms still smelled faintly of the lavender air freshener Margaret and Jessica had favored. But walking through spaces where he had once lived felt like touring a historical recreation of someone else's life.

The answering machine blinked with unanswered messages: foreclosure notices, final bills, former clients seeking new representation.

Jessica's room remained exactly as he had left it, but his relationship to her absence had changed. The stuffed animals and schoolbooks still carried the weight of interrupted life, but now they seemed less like accusations against cosmic injustice and more like invitations to remember love rather than loss. Her drawings on the refrigerator had faded slightly, but they seemed more precious for their impermanence, more beautiful for being unrepeatable.

The stack of mail on his kitchen counter told the story of a life abandoned: mortgage statements, credit card offers, professional journals he would never read, invitations to legal conferences meant for someone he had been but no longer was. He threw most of it away unopened, keeping only the handwritten notes from neighbors who had worried about his months of silence.

Mrs. Henderson from next door had left three separate cards expressing concern about his welfare. The Kowalskis had offered to maintain his lawn. Even people he barely knew had extended the small kindnesses that held communities together when individual members came apart. Their care felt like evidence of something sacred that persisted regardless of theological certainty: the human capacity to love neighbors despite receiving no cosmic guarantee that such love mattered beyond its immediate effects.

Sleep came fitfully in his own bed, too soft after months of harder surfaces, too quiet after the constant urban sounds of ancient cities. He lay awake listening to suburban silence punctuated by the occasional car door, air conditioning unit, distant television, the soundtrack of lives proceeding on schedule while his own life required complete reconstruction.

Morning brought the familiar sight of commuters leaving for jobs they would return to that evening, secure in routines that created meaning through repetition rather than revelation. Jacob watched them from his kitchen window while drinking coffee that tasted exactly like coffee he had drunk seven months earlier, when he had been someone who believed that suffering could be solved through sufficient investigation.

Tom's business card lay on his desk where he had left it, along with client files that now seemed to belong to a stranger's practice. The legal problems that had once consumed his attention, property disputes, custody arrangements, liability claims, struck him as elaborate games designed to occupy minds that might otherwise confront questions too large for legal resolution.

He understood now that his months abroad had not been a search for Jessica so much as a search for a version of himself who could live meaningfully despite irresolvable uncertainty. The priests and rabbis and imams had offered different maps for navigating mystery, but none had provided the cosmic GPS system he had originally sought. Instead, they had taught him that getting lost was itself a form of spiritual practice, that uncertainty could become the foundation for deeper compassion rather than deeper despair.

The phone rang frequently. Margaret checking on his return, her voice carrying relief mixed with exhaustion from months of holding together both the firm and her own grief for her granddaughter. Former clients wondering if he planned to resume practice. He answered selectively, not from antisocial impulses but from the recognition that he needed time to translate insights gained in foreign contexts into practical wisdom for American suburban life.

Dr. Thornton had left several messages about resuming grief counseling sessions. But Jacob realized that his relationship to grief had fundamentally changed. He no longer needed to process Jessica's death as a problem requiring solution. Instead, he needed to learn how to honor her memory through service to others who faced similar loss, and how to transform personal suffering into communal healing.

The turning point came during a walk through Lincoln Elementary's playground, where Jessica had once mastered monkey bars and mediated disputes between first graders. Watching current students navigate the same challenges with the same mixture of determination and anxiety, Jacob understood that his search for Jessica had led him back to something he could actually affect: the living children who needed adults capable of love without guarantees, service without cosmic insurance policies, hope without certainty about ultimate outcomes.

That night, he opened his laptop and began researching grief counseling certification programs, legal aid clinics that served families in crisis, volunteer opportunities that would allow him to practice what months of theological investigation had taught him: that meaning emerged not from solving life's deepest mysteries but from showing up consistently for people who needed practical help with immediate problems.

The quest that had taken him across three continents had brought him home to a simple recognition: faith was less about believing unprovable propositions and more about choosing to act as if love transcends death and creates meaning that echoes beyond individual lives.

Jessica's death remained inexplicable, but her influence could continue through his commitment to protecting other children, supporting other families, demonstrating the kind of selfless care she had shown to struggling classmates and lonely neighbors.

Jacob knew what he needed to do. There would be time to write the letter he owed Father Doyle, time to put into words what months of investigation had taught him about living faithfully within uncertainty. But not yet.

First, he needed to visit Jessica's grave. He needed to make a different promise than the one that had launched his desperate quest. Not a promise to find her somewhere beyond death, but a promise to live as if her love was still at work in the world through his choices, his service, his willingness to care for others with the same devotion she had shown.

The search was ending. The custom was about to begin.

***

The cemetery felt different now, not the scene of ultimate injustice that had driven him to desperate seeking, but simply a place where a beloved child's body rested while her influence continued working through those who remembered her.

Kneeling beside the headstone, Jacob found himself pulling away weeds that had crept around its base during his absence. The sight stirred his anger initially but then transformed into something like acceptance. Even grave sites required ongoing care. Nothing sustained without conscious attention from those who remained.

"I went looking for you," he said quietly to the engraved marble. "I thought if I could prove God existed, I could prove you continued somewhere, that our love meant something ultimate. I met remarkable people who were absolutely certain you're waiting for me in paradise, in the world to come, in pure lands beyond suffering."

A gentle breeze moved through the cemetery's oak trees, carrying the scent of approaching winter. Jacob brushed dirt from Jessica's headstone, noticing how weather had already begun softening the sharp edges of carved letters.

He pulled Jessica's photo from his wallet, the same picture he'd carried across three continents, her gap-toothed smile now worn soft at the edges from constant handling. "But I had to try every possibility, Jess," he whispered. "Because I promised we'd always be together."

As he placed yellow daisies, her favorite, beside the stone, the bells of St. Mary's rang in the distance. The sound carried him back to the last Sunday before the accident. Jessica had been sick with a cold, feverish and miserable, but insisted she felt well enough for church.

"Daddy, I want to light a candle for Grandma Margaret's friend who died," she'd whispered during Mass, tugging his sleeve with nine-year-old insistence.

During the closing hymn, she slipped away, dropped her weekly allowance quarter into the votive stand, and lit a candle with solemn concentration. When Jacob caught up, she was kneeling before the flickering lights, lips moving in silent conversation.

"What are you praying for?"

"That Mrs. Kowalski isn't lonely in heaven. That she knows people still remember her." Jessica's fever-bright eyes had turned to his. *"Do you think she can hear me, Daddy?"*

"I think love doesn't need words to travel," he'd told her, the truest answer he'd ever given.

Now, standing at her grave, he felt that same truth rising again: maybe love didn't need heaven or proof. Maybe love itself was the evidence.

He was brushing dust from the stone when footsteps sounded behind him.

"Hello, Jacob."

The voice froze his heart before restarting it with painful intensity. He turned slowly.

Brenda stood twenty feet away, more striking than he remembered despite eight years of separation that had etched lines around her eyes and threaded silver through her auburn hair. She wore an expensive black dress and carried white roses, though he wondered how she remembered Jessica had loved flowers.

Jacob had known this moment might come eventually. Brenda had left when Jessica was twelve-months old, unable to reconcile motherhood with her ambitions for international law. She'd taken a position in Geneva, promising it was temporary, that she'd return when her career was established. The months became years. The visits became cards. The cards became silence.

Margaret, Brenda's own mother, had stepped in to help Jacob raise Jessica. The irony wasn't lost on anyone: a grandmother doing the work her daughter had abandoned. Margaret never spoke ill of Brenda to Jessica, but the hurt lived in her eyes whenever Jessica asked why Mommy was always too busy to visit.

"Brenda." Her name felt foreign on his tongue, like a word from a language he hadn't spoken in years.

"I know I have no right to be here," she said carefully, as if rehearsed. "I know I gave up any claim to grief when I walked away. But I had to come."

Jacob studied her face. Polished, successful, the kind of woman who traveled the world for international law and had the wardrobe to prove it. Yet in her eyes he caught something raw: the cost of her choice. The Geneva years hadn't delivered the satisfaction she'd expected. He could see it in the way she held herself, the careful control that suggested someone who'd learned to function despite fundamental emptiness.

"Had to come?"

"My mom called me about the accident. I still have Google alerts set for your name." She exhaled, the admission hanging awkwardly. "I wanted to come to the funeral, but I thought my presence would make things worse."

"You were probably right."

They stood in silence, two people bound forever by a child whose life had been too brief. Eight years ago, Brenda had made a choice. She'd convinced herself that professional success was more important than daily presence, that financial security mattered more than bedtime stories, that Jessica would understand someday.

But someday, it never came. And now there would never be a chance to explain, to reconnect, to rebuild what she'd walked away from.

"She would have turned ten next month," Jacob said softly. "She wanted to study marine biology. Save the whales. She had it all planned out." His voice broke on the word planned.

Brenda blinked, as if hearing of a stranger. "Marine biology. I never knew that."

"There were many things you never knew about her." The words weren't meant to wound, but truth cut anyway.

"I know." Her voice carried no defense, only the hollow exhaustion of someone who'd spent years justifying choices that had never brought peace. "I know my absence created... challenges. But Jacob, the work I've been doing in Geneva, it was supposed to provide opportunities Jessica would never have had otherwise. The connections, the financial security..."

Even now, at Jessica's grave, the rationalizations came automatically, but they sounded tired, worn thin by nine years of repetition.

"She didn't need opportunities. She needed her mother."

"She needed stability more than she needed my confusion." Brenda's voice carried the rehearsed quality of someone who'd had this argument with herself a thousand times. "I wasn't ready to be the kind of mother she deserved. You and Margaret could provide consistency while I built something meaningful..."

But the words rang hollow. Jacob could see the flicker of doubt in her eyes, the recognition that the Geneva position hadn't delivered what it promised. The partnership that never materialized. The prestigious cases that went to others. The slow slide from international law to routine corporate work.

She'd traded her daughter for a career that had ultimately disappointed her, leaving her with neither professional satisfaction nor family connection.

"She asked about you," Jacob said quietly. "Every birthday. Every Mother's Day. Margaret would explain that you were doing important work, that you loved her even though you couldn't be here. Jessica would nod and say she understood. But I'd find her crying in her room, holding the one photo she had of you."

Brenda's composure cracked. Tears began sliding down her carefully made-up face, cutting through foundation like cracks in a mask.

"The last time you called was two years ago," Jacob continued, his voice steady but relentless with truth. "Jessica was seven. She talked about the ant she'd saved, about her friend Tommy who was being bullied, about wanting to learn piano. You listened for five minutes, then said you had a meeting. She sat by the phone for an hour afterward, hoping you'd call back."

"Jacob, please..."

"She wrote you letters. Did you know that? Margaret helped her mail them to your Geneva address. Drawings of our house, stories about school, questions about Switzerland. Most came back 'return to sender' because you'd moved and hadn't sent the new address."

Brenda placed the white roses at the base of the headstone with trembling hands. "I thought... I thought there would be time. That when she was older when she could understand the complexity of my choices..."

"There is no more time, Brenda. All your plans for explaining, for reconnecting someday, for having her understand, they died with her on that street."

The blunt truth hung between them like a verdict. Brenda sank to her knees beside the grave, her expensive dress pressing into the damp grass, her careful polish completely undone.

"I made the wrong choice," she whispered, the first honest words she'd spoken. "I told myself it was temporary, strategic, that I was building something for all of us. But the truth is I was afraid. Scared of losing myself in motherhood, scared of becoming ordinary, scared of being trapped. So, I ran. And I kept running. And now she's gone and I never..."

She couldn't finish. Her shoulders shook with sobs that seemed to come from someplace deep and long sealed.

Jacob stood watching her grief, feeling nothing like satisfaction or vindication. Only sadness for all the moments that could never be recovered, all the love that had waited for a someday that never arrived.

"Margaret never stopped hoping you'd come back," he said finally. "Your mother raised your daughter while you chased a career that didn't even make you happy. She never complained, never made Jessica feel like a burden. But it broke her heart that you threw away what she would have given anything to have, time with Jessica while she was still here."

Brenda looked up at him, mascara streaking her face. "Is Margaret...?"

"She's fine. Destroyed by losing Jessica, exhausted from holding the firm together while I fell apart, but fine. She asks about you sometimes. Wonders if you're happy, if Geneva was worth it."

"It wasn't," Brenda whispered. "None of it was worth this."

She stood slowly, trying to regain some composure, but the mask was broken now. The successful international lawyer had dissolved, leaving only a mother who would never know her daughter, who would spend the rest of her life haunted by a choice that could never be unmade.

"I hope you find peace, Jacob. I hope you find whatever you went looking for across the world. Jessica deserved better than what I gave her." She paused, then added softly, "She was lucky to have you. And Margaret. People who actually chose to show up."

As Brenda walked away, her shoulders bent under the weight of permanent regret, Jacob remained beside the grave. He understood now that some people spent their entire lives learning the difference between strategic decisions and catastrophic mistakes. Some wounds never healed because they were self-inflicted, carved deeper by every day of denial, every missed call, every letter returned unopened.

He looked at the white roses against Jessica's stone. Brenda's failure didn't diminish Jessica's worth or change the questions that had driven him across continents. If anything, it reinforced why those questions mattered.

Love was measured not in future opportunities but in present choice, not in strategic planning but in daily presence. Whether God existed or not, whether Jessica survived death or not, love showed itself in consistency, in sacrifice, in the thousand small moments Brenda had missed while building a future that never materialized.

The search that had brought him to ancient cities and sacred texts was really a search for how to love faithfully when certainty was impossible. And Brenda's absence had taught him, by painful counterexample, what that faithfulness required: showing up, staying present, choosing to love even when ambition called you elsewhere.

He touched Jessica's headstone one more time, then turned toward home. There were questions still to be answered, a letter still to be written, but now he understood that the answers he sought weren't about proving Jessica's survival. They were about learning to live as if the love they'd shared created meaning that transcended individual lives, echoing forward through every choice he made to honor her memory.

***

The first several days back carried the weight of dislocation. His house smelled of dust and stale air, as though it had forgotten him. He went through the motions: paying overdue water bills, sorting a pile of yellowed envelopes, pushing a cart past neat rows of cereal boxes under fluorescent light. Each task was absurdly small. Only weeks ago, he had been pressing rabbis and imams on the nature of God. Now he was comparing expiration dates on milk cartons.

One afternoon, Mrs. Davison from across the street waved from her garden. "Jacob, welcome home," she called, her voice careful. "Did you find what you were looking for?"

The question struck him like a stone. He had found something, many things, but nothing whole. He had searched for God in the silence of prayer mats, in the breaking of matzah at a Seder, in the trembling voice of a woman who had survived Bergen-Belsen. But it was not a single truth, not the answer she wanted.

"I found some answers," he murmured. "And many more questions."

Inside, he wandered to Jessica's room. The door creaked as he pushed it open, and the stillness hit him like a physical force. The curtains were drawn halfway, letting in a narrow beam of afternoon light that cut across the bed. Her bedspread was smoothed, though dust had settled in the folds. A stuffed rabbit slumped at the pillow, one ear bent forward as if listening for her return. On the shelf, her books leaned into each other, the spines bright with colors that looked too alive for a room so silent.

He stood in the doorway, unable to step further. The air felt dense, as if it remembered laughter, secrets, the rhythm of a child's small footsteps. The longer he stood, the more the room seemed less like a bedroom and more like a shrine: objects preserved but hollowed of their meaning.

Finally, he crossed to the window and pulled the curtain wider. Sunlight filled the room, startling in its brightness. It illuminated the dust, tiny particles rising and falling in slow, aimless currents. For a moment he imagined them as fragments of her, scattered yet still moving, still present in ways he could not name.

***

In the days that followed, Jacob tried to imagine returning to his old life. Sitting in court, listening to opposing attorneys argue about property division or child custody arrangements, the legal work he had once found meaningful now felt hollow.

His months abroad had changed him. When he thought about legal practice now, he found himself thinking instead about Father Doyle's patient service despite theological uncertainty, about Sarah Rosen's choice to create meaning without traditional belief, about the Sufi sheikh's teaching that spiritual reality transcended analytical categories.

The legal arguments that had once consumed him seemed trivial compared to the questions he'd wrestled with across three continents.

The hardest adjustment, however, was the carefully maintained distance between him and Tom. They had handled the legal necessities of dissolving Hinsen & Mitchell with professional courtesy, dividing assets, transferring client files, managing the insurance settlement that had, mercifully, covered most of their catastrophic losses. But they hadn't really talked, and the weight of unspoken grievances filled every brief encounter in courthouse hallways or chance meetings at professional events.

When the insurance company's denial letter arrived, Jacob knew he couldn't avoid Tom any longer. He sent a straightforward text: "My house Thursday 8 PM. Discuss insurance denial?" They both understood this would be the conversation that ended everything they'd built together.

Tom's headlights cut through Jacob's driveway at seven-thirty on a Thursday night. When he finally emerged from his car, his movements carried the exhausted resignation of someone delivering bad news he'd been dreading for weeks.

"You look tired," Jacob sincerely said, opening the door.

"Eighteen-hour days will do that." Tom's voice was flat, professional. "We need to talk."

They sat in Jacob's living room, Tom placing a folder on the coffee table between them with the careful precision of someone handling evidence.

"Klaus Whitfield is suing us for forty-seven million," Tom said without preamble. "Our malpractice insurance is fighting coverage, claiming your absence during active litigation constitutes abandonment of professional duties."

Even though he already knew the situation, Jacob felt his stomach drop when Tom said them out loud. "What's our exposure?"

"Everything. The firm, our personal assets, our professional licenses." Tom opened the folder, revealing legal documents and financial statements. "I've managed to keep about sixty percent of our clients by working doubles and bringing in contract attorneys. The ones we lost? They didn't leave quietly. Three bar complaints, two malpractice claims, and a reputation that's essentially worthless."

The weight of practical reality pressed down on Jacob. Not dramatic ruin, just slow professional strangulation. "What are you proposing?"

"Dissolution. I buy out your share, what's left of it, assume the liabilities, and try to rebuild something from what's salvageable." Tom's voice carried no anger, just exhausted pragmatism. "You're done practicing law, Jacob. The bar investigation alone will probably result in suspension. Even if it doesn't, no client will trust you after this."

Jacob stared at the documents that would end twenty-three years of partnership. "I'm sorry, Tom. I know that doesn't fix anything, but I'm sorry."

"I know you are. And I know you were in pain." Tom leaned back, looking older than his fifty-two years. "But Jacob, good intentions don't restore client trust. Being sorry doesn't undo missed deadlines or abandoned cases."

"What happens now?"

"I keep the practice, work sixteen-hour days for the next five years trying to rebuild what we had, and hope Klaus Whitfield's lawsuit doesn't bankrupt us both." Tom gathered the papers. "You sign these, we're legally done. Clean break."

As Jacob signed each page, he felt the weight of choices that had seemed cosmic at the time but now felt simply selfish. His search for Jessica had cost his partner a career's worth of work, damaged vulnerable clients, and destroyed professional relationships built over decades.

"For what it's worth," Tom said as he prepared to leave, "I hope your grief counseling helps people. I hope you find whatever you're looking for."

"I hope you can save the practice. You deserve better than cleaning up my mess."

Tom paused at the door. "Jacob? Next time someone needs you to be present for their worst day, be present. That's what we do. That's what we've always done."

After Tom left, Jacob sat surrounded by the quiet wreckage of a professional life he'd abandoned for answers that couldn't be found. The cost wasn't dramatic, no one sleeping in cars, no families destroyed. Just steady, grinding consequences that would take years to fully understand.

Tomorrow was Sunday. For the first time in ten months, Jacob thought he might be ready to return to church, not to demand answers, but to sit quietly, to listen, and to begin building a life where love mattered more than certainty.

***

Sunday bells tolled as Jacob sat in his driveway, engine off, keys clenched in his palm. For twenty minutes he stared at his house. It looked smaller now, or perhaps he had grown larger on his journey, stretched by questions that offered no answers. His research notebooks, heavy with conversations from across continents, lay untouched in a closet. Finally, he turned the key and eased onto the road, driving the few quiet miles to church.

The parking lot was as it had always been. Mrs. Kowalski's Buick in its crooked spot. Father Alcoa's modest sedan. The Tom's family van, still plastered with soccer-ball stickers. Jacob parked in the back, close to the exit.

Inside, St. Catherine's sanctuary stood unchanged since Jessica's funeral months earlier. Polished pews gleamed. Stained glass scattered sunlight in blues and golds across the floor. The air carried the mingled scents of perfumes, candle wax and hymnals aged by countless hands. Everything was familiar, yet Jacob felt like a stranger entering a country he no longer believed he belonged to.

He slid into the pew where he had sat at the funeral, third row on the right. Jessica's spot. He could almost feel her fidgeting beside him, hear her whispering questions that had once embarrassed him but now felt truer than all the sermons he'd heard since. Her memory pressed closer than any mystical vision he had chased abroad.

Father Alcoa's sermon rose and fell in measured cadences. *"God has a plan for each of our lives,"* he declared. *"Even our suffering serves divine purposes we cannot yet understand."*

Jacob listened with ears sharpened by months of investigation. The priest's compassion was genuine, his desire to comfort real. But sincerity was not truth. Comfort was not evidence.

A young mother in the pew ahead rocked her restless infant. Exhaustion darkened her face, yet joy flickered in her eyes. She adjusted a blanket, offered a bottle, soothed with a quiet rhythm. Jacob studied her, wondering: was such love merely neurochemical programming for survival, or a sign of something transcendent?

Perhaps both. Love could be biological and sacred, evolutionary and eternal, chemical and cosmic. Natural explanations didn't erase the possibility of supernatural meaning. But neither did they prove it.

Jacob opened his leather journal and began writing, a habit that would have scandalized him months earlier. Now it felt like the only honest response.

I have spent months seeking definitive answers about God, about life after death, about justice and eternal meaning. Every tradition I explored offered beautiful responses. But beauty isn't proof. Sincerity isn't evidence. The depth of human longing doesn't guarantee cosmic answers.

Father Alcoa shifted to eternal life, painting heaven in confident strokes: a place of reunion, of joy, of certainty. Jacob thought of Father Romano's admission that such claims could never be proven, of Professor Hassan's unwavering certainty in Islamic paradise, of Rabbi Golden's acknowledgment that God's nature remained unknowable. All had promised a reunion. None had offered proof.

Still, Jacob was moved by the congregation's quiet responses, the couples clasping hands, the families teaching children values that reached beyond self-interest, the single adults choosing community over comfort. Whether or not heaven was real, their faith produced lives bent toward love, justice, and compassion. That was worth something.

He wrote again:

Sarah Rosen survived Auschwitz by choosing to act as if human dignity mattered when all evidence said otherwise. She did not wait for cosmic guarantees. Maybe faith is less about correct beliefs and more about choosing to live as if love, justice, and service matter forever, whether they do or not.

Then came communion. Should he go forward? The ritual required affirming beliefs he wasn't sure he could accept as uniquely true. Yet communion also meant remembering love stronger than death, joining a community that carried burdens together, acknowledging mystery no creed could contain.

He rose and walked with the others.

"The body of Christ, broken for you," Father Alcoa said, placing bread in Jacob's hands.

"The blood of Christ, shed for you," he added, offering the cup.

Jacob swallowed the elements, but as a human ritual binding him to memory, to community, to the ancient refusal to surrender to despair. The uncertainty no longer shamed him. It felt like honesty.

After the service, Jacob lingered while the congregation filed out, their chatter mixing Sunday lunch plans with gentle words of care. Community persisted whether its foundation was divine truth or human invention. Love endured whether it was eternal or temporary.

In the quiet, Jessica's voice seemed to echo, not as the presence he had once begged for, but as a memory, steady and enduring: *Daddy, you don't have to know if heaven is real. You just have to live as if love matters forever.*

Jacob closed his journal and sat for a long time in the pew where he had once said goodbye. He still did not know if God existed. He still did not know if death was final or a doorway. But he knew his love for Jessica had remade him. He knew humility mattered more than certainty. He knew that living toward love, justice, and service shaped a life worth carrying forward.

Whether those truths pointed to God or simply to human resilience, they felt real enough.

The drive home passed in silence.

That night, in his study lined with law books that once promised certainty, Jacob pulled a sheet of paper from a drawer. The desk lamp cast its small pool of light, illuminating a blank page that had waited too long. He uncapped his pen.

It was time to write to his mentor and friend, Father Doyle, the man who had first shown him that honest questions mattered more than comfortable answers.

***

Chapter Six

LETTER TO A FRIEND

My Dearest Father Doyle,

It's late. I'm in Jessica's room. Found one of her hair ties behind the desk. Purple with the silver thread she insisted made everything work better. "Sparkle improves function, Daddy." That's what she always said.

My hand won't stop shaking.

You asked me to write when I knew something. I know this: I'm scared you're reading this deciding you can't stay close to someone who's rejected the faith. That loving me means compromising your witness. That you'll have to let me go.

Don't. Please.

Jessica asked me once if heaven was real. I gave her a Sunday-school answer I never affirmed. That lie drove me across three continents. Six months searching. Rome to Istanbul to Jerusalem. Cardinals, imams, rabbis, philosophers, mystics. Everyone with answers. Everyone is absolutely certain.

Father, none of them know.

In Rome, Cardinal Rossi promised Jessica was with God. Painted heaven in colors so beautiful I wanted to weep. But when I pressed him for proof, he admitted the Church has none. Two thousand years of theology built on texts written by men, copied by scribes, voted into scripture by councils with political interests.

"Trust us," he said.

In Istanbul, Professor Hassan promised paradise with the same certainty. The righteous reunited with loved ones in gardens beneath rivers. When I asked how he knew, he pointed to the Quran, standardized under Caliph Uthman after he burned competing versions. Like Christianity did under Constantine.

In Jerusalem, Rabbi Berkowitz at the Western Wall told me the soul continues. When I asked for verification, he said, "Three thousand years of tradition can't all be wrong."

But tradition isn't the truth, Father. Every religion claims divine authority for texts created by human hands, decided by human votes, preserved by human choice.

Then I met Arnold on a train through Serbia. Philosophy professor. Atheist. He dismissed God with Rossi's certainty in reverse. "There is no God," he declared. "Consciousness is neurons firing. Death is the end."

So, I asked him what I'd been asking everyone: Can you prove that?

Can you prove consciousness ends when brains die? Can you tell me what existed before the Big Bang or why there's something instead of nothing? Can you verify that my daughter was just organized matter that stopped organizing?

He couldn't.

Science explains how things work. It can't tell us why anything exists at all. It can't tell us if consciousness survives death or if my daughter's life meant something beyond the neurons that created her thoughts. The atheists claim certainty about ultimate questions the same way believers do, just with different conclusions.

I don't know if God exists. I don't know if Jessica continues somewhere. And Father, I've realized something that breaks me: nobody else knows either. Not the Pope. Not the mystics or the scientists. We're all making claims about truths we can't approach.

I'm done pretending otherwise.

In Jerusalem, I met Sarah Rosen. Ninety-four. Survived Auschwitz. She told me about a child named Miriam who died in her arms asking if her mama was waiting in heaven. Sarah lied and said yes, even though she'd stopped believing months earlier.

"I chose to act as if human dignity mattered when all evidence said otherwise," she told me. "Not because I had proof. Because the alternative was giving up entirely."

In Istanbul, a Sufi sheikh named Shahid Baba said he spent a year demanding Allah explain his son's death. Got only silence. Finally realized he had a choice: curse the silence or live as if mercy was real even when he couldn't feel it.

"Faith over despair," he said. "Not because I know. Because I choose."

I understand that now. That's what you were doing when I was twelve and my dad died. You told me he was with God. Not because you had proof, but because you chose faith over despair. Because the alternative would have destroyed both of us.

You weren't lying. You were choosing faith.

I respect that choice. I understand it.

But I can't choose faith anymore.

I don't pray. I tried for weeks, sitting in hotel rooms whispering into silence, hoping for something. But I was talking to myself, creating the comfort I needed because loneliness would kill me otherwise.

In Sofia, I heard Jessica's voice. Clear as I'm hearing it now. She told me to stop searching for her in other people's heavens.

Was that really her? Divine intervention? Or just my desperate mind? I can't tell the difference anymore. And if I can't tell the difference, what does that say about every claimed moment of divine presence?

I hold this purple hair tie every night, Father. Wrap it around my fingers until they go numb. It still smells like her shampoo if I press it to my face. That's all I have. A piece of elastic and thread that's losing her scent day by day.

Everyone promised me more. Heaven. Paradise. Resurrection. They promised I'd see her again, hold her again, hear her laugh again.

But they were just saying what I needed to hear. What they believed.

Tom doesn't speak to me anymore. We dissolved the partnership informally before I left Jerusalem. Twenty-three years of friendship ended in an airport. The firm is gone. Margaret had to find other work after carrying everything while I abandoned them. Klaus Whitfield is suing us for forty-seven million. Samantha and three associates lost their jobs.

I destroyed people who trusted me while searching for what nobody has.

Jessica would have hated that.

I saw Brenda at Jessica's grave last week. Eight years gone, chasing a Geneva career that never delivered what she sacrificed Jessica for. She broke down, finally admitted she made the wrong choice. All I felt was sadness for moments that can never be recovered.

It showed me something: love is measured in presence, not promises. You showed up, Father. After Vietnam when I couldn't sleep. When Brenda left and I didn't know how to be both parents. When Jessica died, I couldn't breathe.

You didn't demand I believe what you believed. You just sat with me in the dark.

That's what I have now. No proof Jessica continues somewhere. Just evidence her love still works on people who remember her. Mrs. Henderson told me Jessica defended a boy with autism when kids mocked him. "That's not kind," Jessica said. "He's doing his best." Rachel at school says Jessica shared her lunch every day with a girl whose parents couldn't afford food.

That's who she was. That's what survives.

So, I'm taking a grief counseling job. Starting a foundation in her name. Using my law skills for families in crisis. Not because God commands it or heaven rewards it, but because it honors who she was.

Here's what I need you to hear: I can't sit in Mass anymore. Can't say the Creed. Can't take Communion. Can't pretend I believe what I can't verify.

I can't be Catholic anymore, Father. I can't be Christian. I can't be religious at all.

That's not atheism. I'm not claiming God doesn't exist. I'm saying I don't know. Nobody does. Not believers, not atheists, not scientists, not mystics. We're all standing at the edge of an unknowable mystery, making claims we can't verify.

I've chosen honest uncertainty over comforting claims.

And I'm done searching. Not because I found answers, but because I finally understand nobody has them.

I'll live ethically. Compassionately. I'll serve people in crisis. I'll honor Jessica's memory through action.

The ethical teachings survive my loss of faith, Father. The Beatitudes you made me memorize when I was twelve, blessed are those who mourn, blessed are those who hunger for justice, blessed are the merciful. I don't know who wrote them. Maybe Jesus said them, maybe his followers invented them, maybe councils shaped them over centuries.

Doesn't matter. They work whether God gave them to us or we figured them out ourselves

Same with the prophets calling for justice. The Buddhist emphasis on compassion. The Stoic focus on virtue. The humanist commitment to dignity. Religious traditions contain wisdom without requiring divine origin. I can follow those teachings without believing someone supernatural revealed them.

Not because someone's watching from heaven. Not because the universe has a plan. But because that's the right way to live whether anything beyond this exists or not.

Is that enough? Can I be that kind of person, the kind who lives well without claiming to know what nobody can know?

Or does refusing to choose your faith mean losing your friendship?

Your friendship has mattered more than any theology ever could. After Jessica died, you said, "Keep asking. God honors honest questions more than dishonest answers."

I'm still asking, Father. I'm just no longer pretending anyone has answers.

I'm taking the grief counseling position. Establishing Jessica's foundation. Trying to live honorably without claiming to know whether honor means anything to the universe.

That's how I keep my promise to her. Not by finding her somewhere beyond death, but by letting her love continue working through mine.

If I'm wrong about everything, if there are gates in heaven and someone's keeping score, I hope they'll understand how hard I tried. That I loved her enough to cross continents. That I chose meaning over despair, even when I couldn't prove meaning was real.

Write back. Tell me we're okay. Tell me friendship doesn't require matching beliefs. Tell me you'll still sit with me in the uncertainty even though you've chosen faith where I can't.

I'm not lost anymore, Father. I'm done searching for what nobody has. I'm just trying to live well with questions that have no answers.

Thank you for everything you've been to me. For sitting with a broken kid after Vietnam. For teaching me to love. For showing me that honest questions matter.

I hope you won't give up on me now.

Forever grateful, forever your friend,

Jacob

Jacob sealed the letter and placed it by the door. In the morning, he would mail it.

Tonight, he sat in Jessica's room and held her purple hair tie until his fingers went numb.

The scent was almost gone.

Outside, the suburban night continued its routine. Dogs barked. Cars passed. Someone's television murmured through a window. Life proceeding without cosmic validation, ordinary and irreplaceable.

Jacob wrapped the hair tie around his wrist and went downstairs.

Tomorrow he'd mail the letter. Tomorrow he'd begin the grief counseling job. Tomorrow he'd finish the paperwork on Jessica's foundation. After that

He remembered Abby had texted him last week: *Still thinking of you. Hope you're finding what you need.* For some reason he never answered it. Tomorrow, he'd call her. Tell her he hadn't found what he was looking for, but he'd stopped searching and was ready to live anyway.

Maybe she'd understand. She seemed like someone who would.

Tonight, just dinner.

He opened the refrigerator and pulled out eggs.

***

Chapter Seven

TOMORROW

The following week Jacob drove the familiar route to the Grief Recovery Center.

The decision had been building for weeks, crystallizing in moments Jacob hadn't expected. During Sunday service at St. Catherine's, watching Father Alcoa struggle to comfort the Walsh family after their teenager's overdose. At the grocery store, overhearing a mother explain to her five-year-old why Grandpa wouldn't be coming for Christmas anymore. In the courthouse hallway, seeing a young father weep after losing custody of his children.

Grief was everywhere, wearing a thousand different faces, and Jacob had developed the ability to recognize it even when others tried to hide it. His own loss had become a kind of radar for detecting the specific exhaustion that came from loving someone who was no longer present. But recognition was different from response, and Jacob wasn't sure what he was supposed to do with this newfound sensitivity to other people's heartbreak.

The invitation had come through an unexpected source. Dr. Elena Rodriguez, director of the Grief Recovery Center, had been a colleague of Dr. Thornton's. She'd heard about Jacob's months abroad, his return with what she called "hard-won wisdom about living with loss."

"We're starting a new support group for parents who've lost children," she'd explained during their phone call. "Not therapy, exactly, but facilitated conversation between people who understand what others can't. Would you consider co-facilitating?"

Jacob's first instinct had been refusal. He wasn't a trained counselor, wasn't even sure he'd successfully processed his own grief, much less prepared to guide others through theirs. But something in Dr. Rodriguez's voice had given him pause.

"Why me? There are professional grief counselors with decades of experience."

"Because professional grief counselors haven't necessarily buried their own children. Because your legal training means you can listen without trying to fix everything. And because someone who spent six months investigating whether love survives death might have insights that purely clinical approaches can't provide."

That afternoon, Jacob had walked through his neighborhood with different eyes. The Henderson's house, where Mr. Henderson was slowly dying of cancer while his wife maintained cheerful normalcy for their teenage daughters. The Rodriguez family, still struggling two years after their son's death in Afghanistan. The elderly couple down the street, married sixty years, now watching one of them slip away to Alzheimer's while the other held vigil with the determined optimism of someone who refused to surrender.

Every house contained someone learning to live with loss. Every family was either currently grieving, recently bereaved, or about to face the death of someone essential to their understanding of how the world worked. The universality of it struck Jacob with fresh force. His search for Jessica had been fundamentally selfish, focused on his own need for reunion, his own demand for cosmic justice. But grief was communal, shared, an experience that connected rather than isolated when people had the courage to acknowledge their common vulnerability.

That night, he'd reread portions of his travel journal, looking for insights that might serve others rather than just himself. Rabbi Golden's acknowledgment that some questions had no answers. Sarah Rosen's choice to act as if human dignity mattered despite overwhelming evidence to the contrary. Dr. Hassan's integration of intellectual honesty with practical service. Brother Thomas's recognition that faith was less about knowledge and more about orientation toward love.

None of them had provided the proof Jacob had originally sought, but all of them had demonstrated ways of living meaningfully within uncertainty. Perhaps that was exactly what other grieving parents needed, not theological certainties they couldn't honestly believe, but practical wisdom about how to continue loving when the object of love was no longer present.

First thing the next day, Jacob had called Dr. Rodriguez back.

"I'm not qualified to be anyone's counselor," he'd said. "But I'm willing to share what I learned about living with questions that don't have answers."

"That's exactly what qualification looks like in this context," she replied. "Clinical training teaches techniques for managing grief. Lived experience teaches wisdom about transforming it."

The decision had felt like stepping off a cliff into unknown territory, but also like coming home to something he'd been avoiding. His months abroad had shown him that meaning emerged not from solving life's deepest mysteries but from serving people who needed practical help with immediate problems. Grieving parents didn't need cosmic explanations for why children died. They needed companions who could sit with them in the darkness without demanding that it resolve into light.

Jacob had spent his career using analytical skills to solve other people's problems. Now he would use those same skills differently, not to provide solutions but to help people discover their own capacity for resilience, not to eliminate suffering but to find ways of carrying it without being destroyed by its weight.

The first session would meet next Tuesday. Eight parents who had lost children to illness, accidents, violence, suicide, different circumstances leading to the same devastating recognition that love persisted beyond the physical presence of its object. Jacob would share his own search for Jessica, his failure to find proof of her survival, and his gradual understanding that love's reality didn't depend on metaphysical guarantees.

Whether or not Jessica existed in some form beyond death, her influence continued through his willingness to serve others who faced similar loss. Whether or not God existed, acting as if love mattered eternally created meaning that transcended individual mortality. Whether or not there is an afterlife, the choice to honor deceased children through care for living families was itself a form of resurrection, imperfect, incomplete, but authentically human.

Jacob looked around his house one more time, seeing it with the eyes of someone about to begin a different kind of life. Not the desperate quest for cosmic certainty that had driven him across continents, but the quiet practice of showing up for people who needed proof that love persisted despite evidence that it could be lost without warning.

Tomorrow he would start learning how to transform his own grief into a gift for others who were just beginning to understand that some forms of love were stronger than death, not because they survived in heaven but because they continued creating meaning in the choices of those left behind.

***

Chapter Eight

EPILOGUE

Jacob's letter arrived on a Tuesday, tucked between bills and parish newsletters. Father Doyle recognized the handwriting immediately and felt his chest tighten.

He carried it to his study, unopened, and set it on his desk. For ten minutes he simply stared at the envelope, knowing somehow that whatever it contained would change something between them.

When he finally opened it, he read it twice. Then a third time.

By the fourth reading, his hands were shaky.

***

For three days, Father Doyle carried Jacob's letter in his pocket. He pulled it out during quiet moments, waiting for coffee to brew, sitting in his car before hospital visits, kneeling alone in the empty church at dawn.

I can't be Catholic anymore, Father. I can't be Christian. I can't be religious at all.

The words cut deeper each time he read them. Not because they challenged his faith, but because they came from someone he loved. Someone whose suffering he'd witnessed. Someone whose questions he couldn't answer.

Doyle had known grief counselors who lost their faith after too many funerals. Priests who walked away after seeing too much pain. He'd always wondered if they'd been weak, if their faith hadn't been tested properly in seminary, if they'd given up too easily.

Now he understood. Jacob hadn't given up. Jacob had searched harder than anyone he knew. Six months across three continents, asking everyone, demanding honesty.

And found nothing he could verify.

Doyle wanted to write back immediately with arguments. Scripture passages. Theological proofs. The testimony of saints and martyrs. Everything he'd learned in forty years of priesthood.

But he remembered Jacob's words: *Everyone's guessing and calling it certainty.*

Was he?

Thursday evening, Doyle was called to the hospital. Mrs. Chen, eighty-three, lung cancer, hours left. Her family filled the small room, three generations pressed close, holding hands, whispering prayers in Mandarin and English.

Father Doyle administered last rites. Anointed her forehead with oil. Spoke the ancient words about commending her soul to God's mercy.

Mrs. Chen opened her eyes briefly and smiled. "I see Him," she whispered. "Jesus is here."

Her daughter squeezed her hand. "Mama's going home."

Ten minutes later, she was gone. The family wept and prayed and thanked Father Doyle for being there.

Driving home, he thought about what he'd witnessed. Mrs. Chen's peace had been real. Her family's faith had given them a way to love her through death, to believe her suffering had meaning, that she continued somewhere beautiful.

Had she really seen Jesus? Or had her dying brain created comfort in her last moments?

Doyle realized he couldn't know. Would never know empirically.

But he also realized it didn't matter to his answer to Jacob.

Whether Mrs. Chen saw Jesus or her neurons fired their last comforting images, he had been there. He had offered presence, ritual, a framework for grieving. He had helped them bear what felt unbearable.

That was real. That mattered.

Whether it pointed to something beyond or was simply human beings helping each other through darkness, he couldn't prove either way.

But he believed. He chose to have faith. And that faith had shaped him into someone who showed up at deathbeds at midnight, who sat with the grieving, who tried to embody love he couldn't prove was eternal.

Jacob had chosen differently. Jacob had decided he couldn't believe without proof.

Neither of them knew. Both of them served.

***

Friday night, Father Doyle sat at his desk and began to write.

My dearest Jacob,

I've read your letter a dozen times. Each reading breaks my heart a little more.

Not because you've lost your faith, though I grieve that loss, both for you and for the Church. But because I hear in your words the weight of six months searching, the pain of finding nothing you could verify, the courage it took to write honestly about where that search led you.

You asked if our friendship could survive this. You were afraid I'd have to let you go.

Jacob, I'm not letting you go.

I believe in God. I believe Jesus rose from death. I believe your daughter continues in a place where there's no more pain, no more tears, where love is finally unbroken.

I believe these things not because I can prove them, but because I choose to. Because this faith has shaped me into someone I can live with. Because it gives me a framework for making sense of suffering, I'd otherwise find unbearable.

You can't make that choice. You've looked at the same evidence, scriptures shaped by human hands, competing claims, centuries of tradition, and concluded nobody knows. That claiming to know is dishonesty.

I respect that. I understand it. And it doesn't change my love for you.

Here's what I know for certain: You spent six months trying to find your daughter. You destroyed your career, your partnership, your financial security. You asked every question honestly. You refused to accept comfortable lies.

That kind of love, desperate, relentless, willing to risk everything, is sacred whether God exists or not.

The Jessica I knew would be proud of you. Not because you found answers, but because you refused to pretend knowledge you didn't have.

Because you chose honesty over comfort.

I've been thinking about what you said that the Beatitudes are true whether God spoke to them or humans discovered them. You're right. Blessed are those who mourn. Blessed are those who hunger for justice. These things do not become false if it turns out no divine voice spoke to them at Sinai or from a mountaintop in Galilee.

Maybe that's where we meet, Jacob. Not in agreement about ultimate reality, but in commitment to living as if love, justice, and mercy matter eternally.

I'll keep believing they matter because God is real and commands them.

You'll keep living them because they're right whether anyone commands them or not.

Different foundations. Same house.

Last night I gave last rites to a woman who said she saw Jesus in her last moments. Her peace was real. Her family's faith gave them a way to love her through death.

Did she really see Jesus? Or did her brain create comfort as it shut down? I choose to believe the first. You'd say we can't know.

But we both showed up. That's what matters.

You asked if I'd sit with you in the uncertainty. Jacob, I'll sit with you anywhere. In darkness, in doubt, in grief that has no answers. That's what friends do. That's what love requires.

I won't try to argue you back to faith. You've heard every argument. You've thought harder about these questions than most believers ever do. You've earned your uncertainty.

But I will pray for you. Not that you'll believe what I believe, you've made your choice honestly. I'll pray that you'll find peace in your work, meaning in your service, moments of joy that make life bearable despite the questions that have no answers.

And if I'm right, if there is a God who sees your heart, I believe He'll honor your honesty more than He'd honor pretended certainty.

Call me when you're ready. Come to dinner. Tell me about the grief counseling work, about Jessica's foundation. I want to hear how you're honoring her memory.

We'll figure out how to be friends across this divide. It won't always be easy. There will be moments of tension, holidays that feel different, conversations we'll have to navigate carefully.

But you've been my friend since you were twelve years old and terrified after your father's funeral. I'm not walking away now.

I believe in God's love. You don't know if God exists.

But we both know friendship is real. We both know showing up matters. We both know love, even without cosmic guarantees, is worth choosing.

That's enough to build on.

Write back. Call. Show up at the rectory with terrible coffee like you used to. We'll sit together and figure out what it means to love each other despite believing different things about ultimate reality.

I'm not giving up on you, Jacob. I never will.

With love and respect for your courage,

Father Alfred Doyle

P.S. *Even though you may never return to religion, I want to remind you, I have never worried about where you will wind up. If you recall, Pope John Paul II taught that anyone who lives by the Beatitudes, the way Jesus showed us to love, to show mercy, to seek justice, will be welcomed into God's kingdom.*

Son, that's who you are. That's how you've always lived.

You're already halfway home.

Your friend always,

Father Doyle

Father Doyle sealed the letter and walked to the mailbox at the corner. The metal door creaked as it always had. The letter dropped inside with a soft thud.

He stood for a moment under the streetlight, wondering if he'd said the right things. Wondering if Jacob would write back. Wondering if friendship could really survive such different choices about ultimate questions.

He didn't know. But he'd chosen to pray anyway.

***

Three days later, Jacob called. "I got your letter," he said.

"I'm glad you did, Jacob," Doyle replied.

A pause. Not uncomfortable. Just two men who'd learned to sit with uncertainty together. "Dinner next week?" Jacob asked. "I want to tell you about the foundation. The grief counseling work."

"I'd like that very much."

"Your place. But I'm bringing real coffee. That rectory swill is an abomination." Doyle laughed, warm, genuine. "Deal."

After they hung up, Jacob set the letter beside Jessica's photograph. The two things that mattered most right now: his daughter's memory, and the reminder that he wasn't walking this path alone.

He still didn't have answers.

He never would.

But he'd asked the questions honestly. He'd lived with integrity. He'd loved his daughter with everything he had. And if Father Doyle was right, if there was grace in waiting, if good people found their way home, then perhaps his ethics had been enough all along.

And if Doyle was wrong? If there was only this one life, this brief chance to love and show mercy and seek justice? Well. He'd still done that. And in the end, that had to be worth something.

It had to be enough.

Chapter Nine

ABOUT THE AUTHOR

A W Schade served as a Marine Corps sergeant in Vietnam before building a three-decade career at IBM in executive marketing and business development. Early retirement due to PTSD led him back to writing, where his work "The Demons of War Are Persistent" was featured by Nobel Prize-winning journalist Eric Newhouse on PsychologyToday.com and included in prestigious military literature collections.

His three-year spiritual exploration resulted in "The Shattered Mosaic." Other works include the anthology "PERCEPTION" and various pieces exploring faith, doubt, PTSD, and human resilience. He lives in Florida with his wife of 55+ years.

AUTHOR'S NOTE:

This novel emerged from witnessing how profound loss forces people to confront life's most fundamental questions. Jacob's journey through different religious traditions reflects the honest searching many undertake when tragedy shatters comfortable assumptions about meaning and mortality.

While I've endeavored to represent each faith tradition with accuracy and respect, the demands of narrative necessarily required simplifying complex theological concepts. These portrayals should not be considered comprehensive theological expositions but rather glimpses into how different traditions approach ultimate questions about death, meaning, and divine reality.

No single book can adequately capture the depth and nuance of humanity's diverse spiritual wisdom. Readers seeking deeper understanding are encouraged to explore primary sources and engage with knowledgeable practitioners from these traditions. Each faith contains centuries of sophisticated thought that far exceeds what any novel can contain.

This story is written for anyone who has grappled with questions that have no easy answers, those who have demanded evidence from a universe that often responds with silence, who have sought meaning in the face of apparent meaninglessness, who have chosen to love despite uncertainty about whether love transcends mortality. Whether you approach these questions from faith, doubt, or the vast territory between, the search itself reveals something essential about what makes us human.

The novel suggests that perhaps our highest calling is not to solve life's deepest mysteries, but to live with courage and compassion while carrying questions that may forever exceed our capacity to answer definitively.

Chapter Ten

Reading Group Guide

THE SHATTERED MOSAIC

by AW Schade

About This Guide

The Shattered Mosaic follows Jacob Hinsen's spiritual journey after losing his nine-year-old daughter Jessica in a senseless traffic accident. Driven by grief and the promise he made to find her again, Jacob embarks on a global investigation seeking answers to two inseparable questions: Does God exist? Is Jessica still alive somewhere, with God in heaven?

His six-month quest takes him through major religious traditions: Catholic, Protestant, and Orthodox Christianity; Sunni and Shia Islam; Reform and Orthodox Judaism, as well as encounters with secular philosophers and scientists. He discovers a consistent pattern: every position, whether religious or atheistic, makes claims about ultimate reality that cannot be verified.

This guide is designed to facilitate meaningful discussions about faith, doubt, and the human search for meaning when definitive answers may not exist.

Discussion Questions

1. The Nature of Faith and Evidence

Jacob demands "evidence that would satisfy the same analytical standards he'd apply to any major life decision." Is this a reasonable approach to questions about God's existence and whether his daughter is still alive somewhere? Can faith coexist with intellectual skepticism, or are they fundamentally incompatible? How do you personally balance the desire for certainty with the recognition that ultimate questions may exceed human capacity to answer definitively?

2. Childhood Innocence and Tragedy

Jessica is portrayed as an almost idealized child: kind, curious, morally intuitive. How does her characterization affect our emotional response to her death? Does the "innocence" of victims make tragedies more difficult to accept? What does Jessica represent beyond her role as Jacob's daughter?

3. Religious Authority and Individual Seeking

Throughout his journey, Jacob encounters religious authorities who claim exclusive access to divine truth. Yet he also discovers that every tradition fractures internally over interpretation: Catholics vs. Protestants vs. Orthodox Christians; Sunnis vs. Shias; Reform vs. Orthodox Jews. How do you evaluate competing claims from different traditions when they all fracture over the same texts? What role should institutional authority play in personal spiritual development? When, if ever, is it appropriate to reject religious authority in favor of individual conscience?

4. The Problem of Suffering

Each religious tradition Jacob encounters offers different explanations for why innocent people suffer. Which explanations, if any, do you find compelling? How do you personally reconcile belief in a loving God with the existence of seemingly meaningless suffering? Jacob also encounters atheists who argue suffering proves God doesn't exist. Is that conclusion more logical? Is the question itself flawed?

5. **Doubt as Spiritual Journey**

Father Doyle maintains his faith while acknowledging he cannot prove his beliefs, writing: "I believe in God. I believe Jesus rose from death. I believe your daughter continues in a place where there's no more pain." How does the relationship between Jacob and Father Doyle demonstrate different approaches to handling religious doubt? Can doubt strengthen faith, or does it inevitably lead away from it? What is the difference between honest questioning and spiritual rebellion?

6. **The Consolation of Platitudes**

Jacob rejects well-meaning but inadequate religious comfort ("She's in a better place," "God needed another angel"). When do religious platitudes help, and when do they harm? How should communities respond to profound grief without offering false comfort? What is the difference between hope and denial?

7. **The Pattern Across Traditions: Unverifiable Claims and Human Influence**

Jacob discovers that every religious tradition he investigates, Christianity, Islam, Judaism, follows the same pattern:

- Makes unverifiable claims about God's existence and the afterlife (heaven, paradise, the world to come)

- Fractures internally over interpretation and authority

- Has scriptures that were shaped by human hands: oral traditions changing over generations, scribes making copies with errors, councils voting on what's divine, kings and clerics editing texts

- Eventually justifies violence against dissenters despite scriptures inaccuracy

Does this pattern suggest that all religions are human constructions responding to universal human needs rather than divine revelations? Or does it suggest that divine truth exists but exceeds human capacity to capture accurately? How do you evaluate competing claims when none can be verified, and all show obvious signs of human influence?

8. Heaven, Paradise, and the Afterlife

A central question driving Jacob's quest is whether Jessica is still alive somewhere, whether she continues to exist as herself, with her memories and personality intact, in heaven or paradise or some form of afterlife. Jacob finds that:

- Every religious tradition promises Jessica is with God but cannot prove it

- Atheists and scientists claim death is final but cannot prove that either

- Science cannot tell us what came before the Big Bang or what it's expanding into

- Both religious claims and scientific materialism rest on assertions that cannot be verified

How do you understand the relationship between death and what comes after? Can love create meaning even if death is final? What would constitute adequate evidence that people continue after death? Is the question itself beyond human capacity to answer?

9. The Symmetry of Unverifiable Claims

Jacob discovers that religious believers, atheists, and scientists all make claims about ultimate reality they cannot verify:

Believers claim: God exists, Jessica is in heaven/paradise, the dead are reunited with God

Atheists claim: God doesn't exist, death is final, Jessica is simply gone

Scientists claim: The universe began with the Big Bang (but can't explain what came before or what caused it), death ends all existence (but can't prove what happens after death)

Does this symmetry suggest that both theistic and atheistic positions require "faith" in claims that cannot be proven? How should individuals navigate life's biggest questions when all positions involve uncertainty? Is agnosticism the only intellectually honest position, or does it avoid necessary commitments?

10. The Role of Mystery

Several religious figures tell Jacob that some realities must be accepted on faith rather than understood through reason. But Jacob also encounters Sarah Rosen, a Holocaust survivor who maintains Jewish practice while admitting she doesn't know if God exists or if the dead are reunited with Him. Is intellectual humility about ultimate questions a virtue or an evasion? How do you distinguish between appropriate mystery and intellectual avoidance? Where should humans draw the line between seeking answers and accepting uncertainty?

11. Faith Over Despair Without Certainty

Jacob's final position involves choosing "faith over despair": acting as if love, justice, and service matter eternally whether or not God exists and whether or not he'll see Jessica again. This is different from both:

Religious certainty: "I know God exists and will see my daughter again in heaven"

Secular humanism: "I create meaning because it's useful, not because it's cosmically real"

Jacob chooses to live as if meaning is real despite inability to prove it. Is this position coherent? Can this kind of faith, faith in the face of acknowledged uncertainty, sustain ethical behavior long-term? What motivates moral action when metaphysical foundations cannot be verified?

12. Service Without Guarantees

By the novel's end, Jacob commits to grief counseling, establishing a foundation in Jessica's name, and serving others in crisis—not because he's proven God exists or that he'll see Jessica again, but because this work honors who she was and makes his life bearable. He serves others without knowing whether such service has cosmic significance. Is this sufficient motivation for ethical behavior? Can someone live ethically while genuinely not knowing whether God exists, whether there's an afterlife, or whether their actions have cosmic meaning? Does ethical action require metaphysical certainty, or can it stand on its own?

13. The Journey vs. the Destination

Jacob doesn't find definitive proof of God's existence or evidence that Jessica is still alive somewhere, but he achieves a form of peace through accepting uncertainty and choosing how to live despite it. He writes to Father Doyle: "I'm not lost anymore. I've stopped searching for answers nobody has." Is this a successful resolution? Does stopping the search represent wisdom or defeat? How do you evaluate the "success" of Jacob's journey when he returns without the proof he sought?

14. Grief and Growth

Jacob's investigation is driven by grief, but it leads to genuine intellectual and spiritual development. His search also costs him his law practice, his partnership with Tom, and the welfare of people who depended on him. How does suffering function as a catalyst for growth? What is the relationship between personal tragedy and philosophical questioning? Can meaningful growth occur without significant loss? When does grief-driven searching become destructive rather than redemptive?

Themes for Extended Discussion

Religious Pluralism in a Scientific Age

How should diverse religious communities and secular/scientific communities interact in pluralistic societies? Jacob discovers that both religious authorities and scientific materialists claim certainty about assertions they cannot verify. What are the benefits and dangers of dialogue between these worldviews? Can tolerance coexist with strong personal convictions about ultimate truth? How do we navigate disagreement when no position can definitively prove its claims?

The Limits of Human Knowledge

The novel repeatedly confronts characters with questions that may exceed human capacity to answer definitively:

- Does God exist?

- Are the dead still alive somewhere?

- What came before the Big Bang?

- Why does the universe exist rather than nothing?

How should individuals and communities respond to these limits? Is uncertainty about ultimate questions a permanent human condition, or might future knowledge resolve these mysteries? What is the appropriate response to questions that may have no accessible answers?

Science, Religion, and the Afterlife

Jacob encounters both scientific materialism (Arnold the atheist philosopher claiming death is final) and religious faith claims (various authorities claiming Jessica is with God in heaven or paradise). He discovers both make assertions about what happens after death that cannot be verified. How do you understand the relationship between scientific and religious ways of knowing? Can they be complementary, or are they necessarily in conflict? Does science's inability to answer questions about God and the afterlife leave room for religious meaning-making, or does methodological naturalism effectively exclude religious claims?

Parental Love and Protection

Jacob's journey is motivated by his promise to always protect Jessica and be together with her. How do parents navigate the reality that they cannot ultimately protect their children from all harm, including death? What does it mean to love someone when complete protection is impossible? When does love become a destructive obsession?

Scripture as Human Document

Jacob discovers that all religious scriptures, Bible, Quran, Torah, were shaped by human processes:

- Oral traditions passed down for generations, changing with each telling

- Scribes making copies with errors and "corrections"

- Councils voting on which texts were divine and which weren't

- Kings and clerics editing passages for political purposes

- Competing versions destroyed to create standardized texts

How does this historical reality affect religious authority claims about heaven, the afterlife, and reunion with the dead? Can scripture be both divinely inspired and humanly mediated? Does recognizing human influence on sacred texts undermine their spiritual value, or is that influence itself part of how divine truth is transmitted?

Questions for Personal Reflection

- If you faced a tragedy similar to Jacob's, how do you think you would respond? What resources, spiritual, intellectual, community-based, would you draw upon?

- Which character's approach to ultimate questions most closely resembles your own? Which character challenged your assumptions most effectively?

- How has your own understanding of faith, doubt, and what happens after death evolved throughout your life? What experiences have been most formative in shaping your worldview?

- What would constitute adequate "evidence" for God's existence from your perspective? What would constitute adequate evidence that people continue after death in heaven or paradise? What would constitute adequate evidence against these propositions?

- Jacob realizes that both believers and atheists claim certainty they cannot prove about God and the afterlife. Where do you find yourself on this spectrum? Do you claim certainty, embrace uncertainty, or hold provisional beliefs while acknowledging they cannot be verified?

Author's Perspective

The Shattered Mosaic emerges from the recognition that honest spiritual seeking often leads through darkness rather than around it. The novel attempts to treat religious faith, scientific materialism, and agnosticism with equal seriousness, acknowledging the genuine insights and limitations of all perspectives.

Jacob's investigation reveals a consistent pattern across religious traditions: claims about God's existence and the afterlife that cannot be verified, internal fractures over interpretation and authority, scriptures shaped by human hands and political processes, and tragic histories of violence committed by those claiming divine warrant. Yet he also witnesses how these same traditions help people live with dignity, create meaning in suffering, and choose service over despair.

Similarly, Jacob encounters scientific materialism's claims—that death is final, that the universe is meaningless, that Jessica is simply gone—and discovers these assertions are equally unverifiable. Science cannot tell us what came before the Big Bang, what it's expanding into, or definitively prove what happens after death.

The story is written for readers who have wrestled with ultimate questions, whether from positions of faith, doubt, or somewhere in between, and who believe that such wrestling is itself meaningful, regardless of where it leads.

The novel suggests that perhaps the most authentic response to an uncertain universe is choosing faith over despair: acting as if love, justice, and human dignity matter eternally, not because we can prove they do (religiously or scientifically), but because living as if they don't would make us less human. This is neither comfortable religious certainty nor confident atheistic materialism, but the daily practice of choosing meaning despite uncertainty about its cosmic foundation.

Jacob doesn't find God. He doesn't find Jessica. He doesn't find scientific proof that death is final or religious proof that she's in heaven. He finds the courage to live well with questions that may have no accessible answers. Perhaps that courage—that choice of faith over despair—is itself a form of faith worth practicing.

This guide is designed to facilitate respectful dialogue among readers with diverse backgrounds and beliefs: religious, secular, scientific, agnostic. The questions are meant to deepen understanding and encourage honest examination of our own assumptions rather than promote any particular position. The novel honors the intellectual and emotional integrity of multiple perspectives while refusing to pretend that certainty exists where it doesn't.